Love
BY
Knight

Love BY Knight

A PAST LIVES SERIES NOVEL

AC Chenier

North Loop Books
Minneapolis, MN

NORTHLOOP
BOOKS

North Loop Books
2301 Lucien Way #415
Maitland, FL 32751
866.381.2665
www.NorthLoopBooks.com

ISBN-13: 978-1-63505-204-6
LCCN: 2016953424

Distributed by Itasca Books

Typeset by R. Harmon

Printed in the United States of America

By AC CHENIER

Loves of Our Lives

Katie Benjamin is leading a good life; happily married, a great new career, and wonderful friends and family. The only thing marring her quiet life is the terminal cancer diagnosis of her best friend Maria Halford. Maria introduces Katie to the theory of past lives; the notion that our bodies are only a temporary housing for our souls. The soul continues on after the expiration of the current body, and has lived in other bodies many times in the past. Both women embark on past life regression therapy and discover new meaning and connections while exploring their past lives.

Read about Katie's experiences as she meets Elinor Davenport and Catherine Buchanan; two women from long ago who share the same soul. Life in 1700's England and 1800's America is very different from her current life, yet she recognizes the same feeling of being incomplete. She discovers important truths about soul mates, both friends and lovers, and how we reunite with them over and over again.

For Excerpts from this and future books
please see my website at:
www.acchenier.com.

Follow me on Twitter and Facebook.

PART 1

I

Circa 1300, the Village of Eykel

"My lord, look what I found trying to escape from the village."

"Let me see."

Gerard looked with trepidation at the tall man whom his captor was addressing. He could barely make out the dark eyes peeking out from the cloth covering his face and head. The man pulled the protective cloth away to reveal a callous smile that eerily matched the empty and soulless eyes.

"Let me see; a servant; perhaps a stable boy by the looks and smell of him? But who's? Find out!"

They roughly searched him for anything of value. After forcefully examining all his clothes, they found the small token he had taken with him at the behest of his commander.

"Would you look at this? Archangel Michael. Only those sealed to the Knights are given this particular badge. And if I'm not mistaken, this is Godfrey's personal device." The savage man turned back to Gerard, and grabbed his chin to force his eyes up. "So, this little imp must be his servant and perhaps a lover as well? Shall we see if the Commander is more forthcoming about the location of the treasure if we threaten his little one?" He slowly raised his other hand and let a finger trace the line of

Gerard's cheek. "Such a delicate young man; he'll bring great interest at the slave auction. Be a pity should we have to harm him, but the treasure is far more important." The man studied Gerard intensely, and using the hand on his chin, forced his eyes up to look directly at his captor. He whispered directly at Gerard, "Yes a pity to harm him." Gerard trembled in fascination as the man's face drew closer to him all but touching his lips. After a brief staring contest the man dropped his hand, moved away and roughly ordered his men, "Bring him along."

Gerard shuddered in revulsion at the thought of the slave auction, and the look in his captor's eyes that said he would be worth more unharmed. He knew what that look meant. Hauled to his feet and pushed along roughly toward the middle of the camp, he was dragged into the center of the clearing, and saw a number of knights tied, gagged and beaten. He glanced around, his eyes encountering those of Godfrey, his commander.

"No!" The word was torn from his mouth before he could stop it. He knew the reputation of the men who held him. No one would survive their torture.

"So, this imp does recognize his commander. Let's see which one will break first and reveal the location of the treasures. Let's start with this little one. Perhaps the commander has a soft spot for him." His men turned malevolent smiles on Gerard and a few chuckled evilly.

Gerard looked again at Godfrey. Knowing they would both die this day, their eyes locked. Soul to soul they communicated to each other; love, sorrow and a deep knowledge that they would find each other again.

Gerard heard the whistle of a whip as it was made ready to land on his back. He was forced to his knees, but he never let his eyes leave those of his commander. Silently their souls connected as they always did, sharing knowledge, compassion and most importantly love. Both knew the treasures would be safe, left undiscovered until their souls were together again. The whip whistled again.

Present Day, North Sinai

Kelly jerked awake, the last vestiges of the nightmare receding from her mind. Her chest was heaving as she struggled to catch her breath. She could feel her entire body trembling with the aftermath of sound of the whip descending to hit the unfortunate soul in her nightmare. Disoriented, she looked around her unfamiliar surroundings. Where am I, she thought. It took a minute to become oriented, and then she remembered; she was in Egypt just outside of Cairo, and not her own comfortable home. What a nightmare! She could still feel the fear and revulsion that the young man had felt. Where had that come from? It was a hell of a way to wake up. She wondered why she had dreamed it. One thing she knew. It would take a long time for her to forget the merciless eyes of the captor, nor the feeling of peace in the deep connection to the commander. They would both haunt her for days.

She glanced at the clock at her bedside. It was just six am. She wasn't due at the visitors' center until nine, but she figured she wouldn't get back to sleep so decided to get up, and do more research into the village she planned to visit today. It was called Eykel, and was purported to be a Templar village. It had been covered in sand sometime in the mid 1400-1500's and had laid undiscovered until a few years ago, when a wind storm had uncovered part of the church spires. The Carter Family and its Foundation were instrumental in excavating the site, and were now opening it to visitors for exploration. The Carters were from England with supposed roots in the medieval times. She wondered if some of the old tales about Templars escaping the arrests in 1307 were true, and if the Carters were their descendants. The family was considered one of the richest in the world, having created a myriad of businesses over the past couple of hundred years. They had also created the Carter Family Foundation which did extensive charitable work, and was also involved in supporting archaeology around the world, especially the discovery and restoration of Templar holdings.

The village sat astride the old trade routes between what was now Egypt and the Holy Land in Jerusalem. Based on what she had read on the website, it had been abandoned sometime around the time the Templars were disbanded. Then it was covered by a sandstorm and forgotten for five hundred years. She was really excited about this trip. Her studies in the past couple of years about the Templars had been far reaching. She was now convinced that much of the old history of the Templars was inaccurate at best, and downright false in places; probably because it was written by those who had been instrumental in their downfall. She was in the process of writing some articles about her research, and she hoped that this trip would result in a few freelance articles on travel and maybe other aspects of the Templar experience she was going to encounter.

II

Later that morning Kelly pulled into the parking lot next to the building that was the main entrance to the Templar village. She had been in Egypt for the past five days of her summer vacation. This was her first real vacation in four years and now was on the final leg of her extended three week trip to England and Egypt. She had been in England for ten days based in London and taking tours around the town and to nearby areas, including an incredible tour of Stonehenge. That had been breathtaking, something she had always wanted to see, and now she could check it off her bucket list. She had also spent a few days in a rented car touring some of the shires just north of London, like Hertfordshire, Oxfordshire, and Warwickshire. She had wanted to see some of the castles that were attributed to the Knights Templar. She could remember when she first learned about the crusades in history class, she had wanted to learn everything she could about them. She didn't understand her fascination, but it was very concrete. She had been surprised how comfortable she felt in the country north of London. It was almost familiar to her, and she had a number of déjà vu experiences that she couldn't understand. Once when standing in one of the great houses of Warwickshire, she had an uncanny feeling that she knew the place intimately- like she had lived in it at some point. She had shrugged it off as wishful thinking.

While in London she had visited a number of the cathedrals and churches that had been built by the Templars, including Temple Church. Again the déjà vu had been strong in many of those places, especially Temple Church. She could almost hear the organ echoing in the church and a faint ringing of a choir as if the years of music and song had been absorbed by the walls of the church. She still shuddered at the memories. They had been so strong.

Slowly she got out of the car and admired the building in front of her. How it reminded her of many of the English Templar sites she had visited. It was clearly a modern building, but the details on the entrance were as ornate as any she had seen at the churches she had visited in England. It had obviously been built as homage to the past. As Kelly approached the entrance to the building, a middle-age guy was approaching from the opposite way.

"Allow me," he said, and held the door open for her.

"Thank you," she said and preceded him into the office lobby. It was a well-appointed foyer with a nice sitting area. There were security-scan entrances for each of the doors off the lobby, but no security personnel in sight. *At least Kyle gave me his number. I'd have no other way to reach him*, she thought.

*****

The man paused for a moment after he held the door for her, giving her a long look. What an attractive woman, he thought. Shoulder length hair, dark brown with just a touch of soft blonde highlights; fairly tall, but short next to his own 6'1" frame, just the right height. *Right height for what?* He shook his head and moved toward the door on the left. He was running a bit late for his meeting and needed to get into the office. He noticed that the woman was pulling a cell phone out and, he assumed, calling one of his colleagues for whatever meeting she was here for. I'm going to find out who she is, and who she's meeting. She intrigued him, yet he wasn't sure why. She wasn't the type that he typically found beautiful, the tall leggy blonde, but there was something about her, that just attracted him. He took one last long look at her, gave a mental shrug and walked through the door into his offices.

****

Kelly called the number that Kyle had given her. He was the one of the senior tour guides. When she had called earlier in the week, she had been disappointed to find that the tours were not running yet, but due to start in a couple of weeks. There had apparently been a couple of delays with security provisions that had slowed the granting of the necessary approvals. However, when she had explained that she was only in town for a few days, Kyle had offered to provide her an abbreviated tour today. The phone rang and rang, eventually going to voice mail. "Hi, you have reached Kyle"….she hung up. She would try again in a couple of minutes; she was a few minutes early, so he was probably not expecting her call quite yet.

Kelly sat on the comfortable couch in the lobby and waited. She kept trying every few minutes, all to no avail. She was starting to get a bit concerned that Kyle had forgotten her appointment, but she had confirmed with him yesterday morning.

As she sat contemplating her next move, the door behind her opened and the guy who had been so gallant earlier, emerged with another woman. He glanced at her, surprised to see her still waiting.

"You are still waiting? May I ask who you are meeting with?"

"Yes, I'm supposed to meet with Kyle Anderson today. I've tried his phone a few times, but he hasn't answered."

"Oh, that's not good. Tara, can you go see what's keeping Kyle?"

"Sure thing, Neil."

The man walked toward Kelly, extending his hand. "I'm Neil Adams."

"Kelly Taylor, nice to meet you."

They shook hands. Kelly was fascinated by the man's good looks. She felt a tremor go through her body as her hand was held by his. *What was that about?* She glanced at his eyes and was pulled into the electricity she felt emanating from them.

"I'm very sorry but Kyle has called in sick today," Tara said as she re-emerged from the side door.

Startled by Tara's return, Kelly dragged her gaze away from Neil. It took a minute for the comment to register; then feeling a sinking disappointment she exclaimed, "What? Oh, no. He was going to give me a tour today. I'm only in the area from Canada for a few days. Any idea when he might be back?"

"I'm sorry, I don't know."

Neil jumped in. "Ms. Taylor, let me see what we can do about getting a tour set up for you in Kyle's absence. Just give me a few minutes and I'll have someone else show you around."

"Oh, okay that would be great, thanks."

Neil turned and beckoned Tara to follow him back through the door she had just exited. He knew that he had been given a gift here. This was a woman he wanted to get to know. His attraction to her was unlike anything he had felt before. He had been drawn to her good looks, and when they had joined hands he had been attuned to the electricity that went coursing through his system. He wanted to be the one to show her around Eykel, be with her when she discovered the village. But he was unavailable for the next two days. How could he get her to come back in two days? *Thursday?* He wondered, *could she come back on Thursday?* That would be perfect, and he thought he might have just the ideal way to convince her to come back.

"Tara, I need you to postpone the meeting for thirty minutes." He then went on to instruct Tara on the rest of his plan. Kelly Taylor wouldn't be able to resist, at least he hoped not.

****

Kelly watched Neil and Tara exit through the lobby door. *What a nice man, first opening the door for me, and now trying to find an alternative to Kyle for my tour.* She had been quite struck by his good looks when she first saw him; tall, just over six feet, just enough taller than her own five foot six inch frame. He had maple brown hair, with a few flecks of grey. The hair was curly and longish with an unkempt look that made her long to run her hands through it. His face was almost rectangular with a strong jaw and a slightly off-center nose, probably the result of a break at some point in his youth. His eyes had been piercing and knowing when they looked at her; *a wise old soul* she thought;

all in all a mysterious, strong and very attractive man. And then there was that sexy English accent he had. She had always been attracted to the polished language of the English as the cadence and flow spoke deeply to her own soul; probably a legacy of her own English roots. She shook herself. What was she doing? She had sworn off men after all. She surely didn't need to be attracted to this man, an obvious English aristocrat.

Kelly sat back down to await the arrival of her new tour guide. Ten minutes later she was surprised to see Neil walk back into the lobby.

"Ms. Taylor, I'm sorry that took so long."

"No problem, and please, my name is Kelly."

"Kelly, unfortunately I've not been able to find anyone to provide you with a tour today. However, if you could come back in two days' time, we can provide you with a complete tour of the entire complex. What I can offer today is about a half hour of my time to show you some of the highlights, and then a complete tour on Thursday."

Kelly thought about her plans for the week. There was nothing keeping her from being here later in the week. "Yes I can come back in two days. But Kyle said he was out of town on business the rest of the week."

"It won't be Kyle providing the tour, but his boss. I trust that's ok?"

"Wow, I do appreciate this. I'm grateful for your assistance."

"No problem, now if you'd care to come this way, I can show you the welcome center. Regrettably, I have a meeting at eleven that I must attend, so I can only show you a small portion of the complex."

He steered Kelly toward the double doors that were at the back of the lobby, directly opposite the entrance. She hadn't paid much attention to them earlier, and as she approached was surprised at how magnificent the doors were. They were a deep red mahogany color and had ornate carvings in the face. She recognized the seals for the four Archangels, Gabriel, Michael, Uriel and Raphael. Fascinated, she made a note to ask someone about the reason for the seals. Above the door she could see the crest of the Carter family. She wondered what was in the room behind that warranted such strong protection.

"This room is our welcome center. We have created a scale model of the town showing areas that are under restoration and what are still being excavated." Neil opened the doors with a flourish and stepped back to allow Kelly to enter.

As Kelly wandered into the room she caught sight of the model in the middle. It immediately gave her a look at the size and complexity of the initiative underway in this small corner of the world. From what she had read, this Templar village was remarkably intact, having been buried under sand for the past five hundred or more years. The Carter family Foundation had made it clear they wanted to completely unearth the town, and bring it back to life as a reminder of the good things the Templars represented to the history of man. The village was going to be complete with the churches, banks and scholas that had been part of the life at the time.

"This is stunning, the scope of what you're trying to accomplish here, I mean. I could spend hours looking at this vision. Kyle tried to explain it to me on the phone, but words are inadequate."

"Yes, it's been a many-generation passion for the owners of The Foundation to unearth such a find, and help restore the reputation of the Knights Templar. To have it happen now, and to see our dreams finally come to fruition is exciting for all of us associated with the company."

Kelly smiled to herself. Of course she had recognized Neil Adams' name. He was the current chief operating officer of The Foundation and a many-times great grandson of the founders, a member of the prominent Carter family. It was widely expected that Neil would be the next CEO when his grandfather stepped down. Kelly had heard that the Carters were not an easy group of people to be around, but so far, Neil was the opposite of all that she had heard.

Kelly started to move closer to examine the model. At the same time Neil had moved, and they bumped into each other. Kelly was shocked once again by the feeling of '*knowing*' that went through her at even such an inadvertent touch. She had been thinking that she had imagined the electric pulse she had felt when they had shaken hands earlier, but there was no mistaking the feeling this time. She had a sense that she knew this man; *how?* She wasn't sure, but knew him she did.

Neil stepped back and gestured for Kelly to precede him. Kelly approached the long wooden table that dominated the room and looked down at the model laid out before her. It was easy to identify the main building she was standing in, plus each of the main structures in the village: the church, the schola, and the abbey. There was also an area marked as the treasure house/ banking center; so this is where the Templars conducted business those many years ago, or rather one of the many such villages and weigh stations that existed when the Templars were in their glory. Kelly was fascinated by the details.

Neil had moved to the back side of the room while she was looking at the model.

"This here is what I'm most proud of. Let me show you Eykel."

He pushed a switch and the back wall of the room started to move, sliding open. As the wall parted in the middle it revealed a huge picture window that looked down from the center, down into the excavation site. Kelly stared out the window in awe. The view was breathtaking. She could see right into the village and compare it to the scale model behind her.

"This window became necessary when we decided to open up the complex to tourists, rather than just scholars and archaeologists. There will be days when the weather is too inclement to tour the ruins. But from here you can get a sense of what we're looking at in the model. Imagine all of this, covered by sand for so many years, long after the Templars had left of course, but still, the scope of the find here is truly amazing." After a brief pause he added in a hushed voice, "and beautiful."

Kelly had walked nearer to the window to admire the view close up. She turned to Neil as he finished speaking and found that he was gazing at her, and not out the window. She nervously licked her lips, not entirely sure what he had meant by the last.

"I recognize that look in your eyes right now. It's the same one I'm told I had the first time I saw this place. It's quite a sight. I'm glad I was here with you the first time you saw it. It's such a special place."

"I had no idea it would be this amazing. I'm at a loss for words, except *wow*. Of course I had heard all the gossip and the negative reviews. Sacrilege is the nicest term that's bandied about."

"I know. I've heard all the naysayers; how we are exploiting a holy place, or how can we deal with these "heathens" depending on your views of the Templars. And we have certainly had our fair share of bad press about the expansion to the old town to accommodate tourists. I've heard so many times about the horror of a Starbucks being ensconced in a sacred Templar village. It's part of the territory, so we're used to it."

"Excuse me, Neil, but the rest of the staff are gathered for the meeting," said Tara, who had come into the room.

"Thanks, Tara. I'm sorry, Kelly, but I must head out. I have an 'all hands on deck' meeting to attend now. Let me escort you back to the lobby."

"I appreciate your showing me this part already. I can't wait to come back in a couple of days to explore more."

"Here is my business card. Can you be here at eleven thirty on Thursday?"

"After what you have shown me so far, I will move heaven and earth to be here on Thursday."

"Okay call me at this extension when you get here. I'll arrange to have your tour set up for that time. It was a pleasure to meet you, Kelly. I look forward to seeing you again on Thursday."

"Likewise. I really appreciate your accommodating my request. Everyone here at the village has been most helpful."

They shook hands again and looked into each other's eyes as they parted. Kelly quickly looked away, spooked. She felt a deep recognition for this man from half way around the world and from a completely different background. And yet here she was, having fanciful feelings that this was someone she already knew very well after spending less than thirty minutes with him. This was impossible. Shaking, she turned to exit the main building and went to her car for the short drive back to her own hotel.

III

Kelly reached the site again just before eleven thirty on Thursday. She had gone back to Cairo on Tuesday evening to spend some more time at the pyramids, and arrived back at the village late yesterday. She was looking forward to the tour, but didn't want to examine too closely if the cause of the excitement was Neil or the Templar village. Kelly parked the car, noting that there were more cars in the lot than there had been a few days ago. She wondered what was going on.

She grabbed her camera and satchel filled with paper and walked to the front entrance. Inside the lobby there had been a few changes. The door on the right was wide open, and she saw Tara sitting at a table as if she were getting ready to greet people.

Tara saw Kelly and said, "Ms. Taylor, how nice to see you again. Neil asked me to buzz him as soon as you got here. He's in the auditorium putting the final touches on today's presentation. Please have a seat and I'll let him know you're here."

Kelly wondered what presentation was going on today. Neil hadn't mentioned anything. She took a seat in the lobby and waited for Neil. Five minutes later he emerged from the door on the right. She took a long steadying breath. Yup, he was just as striking as her memory had led her to believe. A commanding figure and very well dressed today. He had a fine-looking dark charcoal turtleneck on, with an elegant camel colored sports coat. The color of the coat complemented his natural dark tan and bright intelligent eyes. His long curly hair had been tamed a bit from the last time, but she still itched to run her hands through it. She felt her heart skip a beat. *Not again,* she thought. *I need to keep my cool around him. But he is so good looking and I feel like I know this man.*

"Hello, Neil. I'm really excited to get out into the ruins to see what's out there."

"In time, first I have a surprise for you. Today is the private opening of the complex. We've invited a number of special guests and VIPs to attend a presentation in the auditorium, and then go peruse the model and finally out into the ruins. We're running a number of smaller groups so tour staff can get a chance to trial run their skills in the field. I hope you don't mind, but I thought this would be a great day for you to come and see the place."

"You don't even know me. I'm honored to be included."

"Least we can do, since Kyle ended up being sick the other day. By the way, he's still out with the flu. He was most apologetic when he remembered later in the day that he was supposed to meet with you. I guess he called Tara in a bit of a panic. He was pleased we were able to convince you to come today. Let's get your name card from Tara. Then I'm afraid I'll have to leave you to your own devices with the model. I've got a few more details to take care of. I had hoped to be free by now and enjoy a cup of coffee with you, but that'll have to wait until later this afternoon.

"Tara, do you have Kelly's name tag there? I believe I have her slotted into Kendra's group."

"Here it is, Neil. And welcome, Kelly. I hope you enjoy the afternoon."

"I'm sure I will."

"I'm going to let her into the welcome center, so she can wander around for a while. Would you bring her to the auditorium just before noon?"

"No problem."

"This way, Kelly, I'll let you in."

"I appreciate all of this. This is way beyond anything I expected."

"My pleasure. I do admit; I have another agenda. I hope to have some time to chat with you later as well, get to know you, and maybe convince you to have dinner with me? You're a beautiful woman and seemingly a scholar if you know something of this place and the Templar legends."

Kelly felt herself blush to the roots of her hair. Always a problem for her with her fair skin; blushes always stood out like a neon sign. "Thank you; I'm no model or starlet for sure. But I do know something of the Templar legends. It's been a fascination of mine for as long as I can remember. And when my husband passed away four years ago, it became a deeper passion to learn all I could of the Templars. I have no idea why they intrigue me so much, but I love the research."

Kelly stood staring at Neil wondering what thoughts were running through his mind. He was looking at her so intently. The seconds dragged out for what seemed like minutes. She started to fidget; his gaze was just too intense to handle for long. Neil quickly reached out and grabbed her hand.

"Sorry, Kelly, just wool gathering. It's nice to meet someone who is as passionate about the Templars as I am. That's why I was silent. It's just one more thing about you that I find fascinating."

Kelly looked at her hand covered by Neil's. It felt so right to have it held by him. The tingles that were going up her arm were incredible. She had never ever encountered anything like it in her life. And she had been married to a man she loved to distraction for fifteen years. She had never felt this awareness with him. It startled her again, as it had on Tuesday. She was surprised to find that the memories she had from Tuesday of a deep connection to Neil had not been faulty. If anything her recall wasn't vivid enough.

"Hey, Tara, where's Neil? We've got to finalize the last bits of the presentation and I need his input."

Kelly watched as Neil dropped her hand and looked back out the door to the center, calling out, "I'm here, Kendra, be with you in a minute." Turning back to Kelly, he said, "I'm sorry, but I have to go help the staff finish getting ready. Please enjoy some time in here. Tara will come get you in time for the presentation."

"Okay and thanks. I've kept you from your work long enough. I'll stroll around here until the presentation."

"Great. And I intend to convince you to have dinner with me. Keep a night free."

Neil left the room leaving Kelly dazed and unbelieving. Had she just heard him right? He wanted to have dinner with her? Was fascinated by her? She shook her head. This couldn't be happening to her. She must be in a dream. Handsome, vibrant and sexy men were not fascinated by her. And then there was the connection she felt to him. The sparks that flew whenever they touched were positively explosive. She would have to think long and hard about this. In the meantime, she had about twenty minutes to explore the model before Tara came for her. She intended to make the best use of that time.

****

Neil left the room, with one last backward glance at Kelly. *She's a widow? And so young.* He had understood the subtle dig at him in the 'model and starlet' comment she had made. Now that his divorce was final, he knew that he was considered one of the most eligible bachelors. He had plainly been photographed enough times with models and stars on his arm, to give the world the impression that he was a playboy and enjoying the dating scene after his divorce. The truth was quite a different story, but the press always wanted the dirty scoop. He wasn't surprised that she was intrigued by the Templars. He suspected given her comments, that she likely had a past life as a Templar. He knew that not everyone believed in the theory of past lives and reincarnation but, in this experience, an unexplained fascination with them was a good sign that she was tapping into past memories and actions. His family held a strong belief in reincarnation and had for generations. He knew from his own training that he had been a Templar; one of the many in his extended family. It was part of the reason the foundation had been set up. His many time great grandfather had been one of the last surviving masters of the order. When the order was disbanded his ultimate grandfather had married and had children. He was a direct descendant of that man. The legends of this particular Templar village had been ingrained in him since he was a young boy. And the true test of the lineage was always to determine if the current heir was in fact a reincarnated Templar. That was why he was the current COO and not his older brother or any of his cousins. His soul was an old Templar soul. The others did not have as deep a Templar connection as he did. So his grandfather, the current CEO was grooming him to take over the foundation, and all the family secrets. Neil shook himself out of his reverie; *I better concentrate on the presentation. I have more than enough time to figure out the enigma that is Kelly Taylor.* "All right Kendra, let's finish up with the preparation, so we can get these tours underway. What's the latest problem?"

***

For Kelly the next twenty minutes just flew by. She spent the entire time at the model, first taking a picture, at least as best she could, given the size of it. Then she set out to draw the model in her sketchbook. She started with the core of the village, the church, the schola and the abbey. She was just putting finishing touches on this section when the door opened, and Tara beckoned her out to go to the auditorium.

"I hope you enjoyed your time here. It's been a favorite place for the staff who aren't on the dig site. Every few months a new building is discovered and added to the model. The latest was the stable area that we found on the outskirts of the village. Being a Templar site, we had expected to unearth a stable early on. The horses, especially the war trained ones, were so integral to the life of a knight that we'd been disappointed not to find the stable close to the knights' living quarters. But it's been revealed now, and we are in the process of digging it out."

"I admit I haven't looked at the entire model yet. I've only gotten as far as the center cluster of the church, schola and abbey. Those buildings are fascinating."

"They are. The central court was the lifeblood of the village, along with the banking center. The church is in relatively good shape. The abbey sadly was pretty much reduced to ruins before the sand storm covered the village. We can only speculate, but the feeling is that local tribes took the stones from the abbey but left the church as it was a sanctified site. However, we may never know for sure."

"The true history of the Templars is so covered by the tracks of the European nobility and the church that it's hard to distinguish fact from fiction anymore."

"That's true. It's one of the reasons the foundation exists at all. It's our goal to uncover the truth and bring it to light. The Templars are not the maligned heretics that so many show them to be, nor are they the avaricious bankers that the Kings of France would have us believe. The truth is out there. The story is waiting to be told."

"Yes, and I'm sure the foundation will be at the forefront of that story."

"Perhaps. Here is the auditorium. Please take a seat anywhere. The presentation will start shortly."

Kelly entered the auditorium and found a seat toward the back. She glanced around in interest to see who else was in attendance. The room was half full. There was a diverse group of men, women and children in the room. Some were dressed to go on a dig site and others were dressed in formal business attire. She wondered what the connections were amongst the people here and how they came to be on the Foundation's special guest list.

The lights in the auditorium dimmed, and a presentation was displayed on the front screen. It said:

WELCOME ALL SPECIAL GUESTS

Then Neil came out onto the stage escorting an older man and a woman to the front where the microphone was set. Kelly saw the woman urge the older man to sit on the chair provided, but he refused and walked up to the microphone and began.

"I would like to welcome you all to the historic Templar village of Eykel."

There was resounding applause to that statement.

"The Carter Family is very pleased, at long last, to have this private opening to the Templar village. The public Grand Opening is scheduled for a few weeks from now and will coincide with the readiness of the hotel and other amenities in the neighboring town. I am pleased now to turn this over to my grandson Neil Adams, the second son of my daughter Katrine and her husband Christopher Adams." He had nodded in the direction of the woman on stage, so Kelly assumed that she must be Neil's mother. She could now see the family resemblance amongst all three of them.

Neil took the microphone from his grandfather and urged him to sit down. His grandfather and mother both moved to the seats and sat down.

Neil looked around the room and started his speech. "Family, friends and special guests, it is the Foundation's great pleasure to welcome you to this private opening of the Templar village. Each of you here is a special friend to the foundation; whether you are spouses and children of our many staff members, or donors, or scholars whom we have worked with. Each of you has been a special part of the work here for the past five years. And in fact for even longer, as the Carter Family has striven to fulfill the vision of our many-times great grandfather who was the first to envisage the complex you are about to tour. We could not have gotten to this point in time without your support. This is a small 'Thank You' from the Board of the Foundation to you all."

Applause greeted this statement.

"For many of you, this will be the first opportunity to set foot into the village itself. To ensure your safety and to give our staff some more training, we are going to send you out in tour groups. We are keeping the groups small today, so as to not intimidate our newer guides. Please feel free to ask them any questions you may have. Only through your active participation can we fill any gaps that we have in their training." The audience gave a small chuckle at the notion that they would provide final training to the experts at the foundation.

"Please enjoy your afternoon in the village. The weather has cooperated with us today, as we have beautiful sunshine but it's not too hot. Each of you has a name tag that is color coded. I will now put up the color matches for each group. Our guides are spread throughout the auditorium and into the side conference rooms. Please find the room or guide that matches your name tag. In order to provide the best experience for all, we will start most of the tours in the welcome center back out through the lobby. Please follow your guides as they take you to the appropriate areas. We want to give you all the best tour possible, but there are some logistics to get everyone through. As I said, enjoy your day in the village."

Neil finished up and led his grandfather back off the stage. Kelly looked at her yellow name tag and looked around for the yellow banner. She noticed on the screen that the yellow tabs were to proceed to the Acre room. She rose from her seat and followed the crowd out of the auditorium. The signs on the wall pointed left to the Acre room; she followed the corridor until she found it. She slipped inside and noted Tara speaking to a woman at the front. She assumed the other woman was Kendra, whom Neil had said would be her guide today. She looked around the room and noticed the others filing into the room with yellow tags, she realized that all of them were dressed as if they were on an archaeological dig. So, she must be with a group of scholars. This made her slightly uncomfortable, as she was well aware that she had nowhere near the experience of these people. Tara caught her eye from the front and waved her forward.

"Kelly, let me introduce you to Kendra. Kendra is the head of the public relations department, and an accomplished Templar historian. Kendra this is Kelly Taylor who was supposed to meet with Kyle on Tuesday."

"Kelly, my pleasure to meet you. Neil explained the circumstances that led him to invite you today. I'm pleased you could join us."

"My thanks as well. I hope that I'm not going to slow this group down. They all look like dedicated historians and archaeologists. I'm an amateur and only really embarking on my studies."

"No worries, this group will be welcoming. From what Neil has said, you have already spent some time at the model. This group is going directly out to the site, as they have little to no interest in the center itself. Neil felt you would also want to get right out to the site, having already seen the view from the center."

"Oh, for sure. The center is wonderful, and I'll want to spend more time in it. But I absolutely want to get out to the site."

"We have time enough to chat later, why don't I get this group rounded up, and we'll get started."

Kendra moved to the front of the room, went through a few papers and then motioned for everyone to pay attention.

"Can I have everyone's attention please? I would like to echo Neil's welcome of a few minutes ago. We here at the Foundation are pleased to have you all with us today. And we look forward to welcoming you all back many times over the next few years, both as you complete your own research, and to help us uncover more of the secrets of this beautifully preserved village."

There were murmurs of agreement to this statement.

"As you are all noted scholars and archaeologists, we have decided to have this group forgo the welcome center in the lobby. We thought you would all be eager to get out to the site, or for some of you, to get back to the site. So, please follow me as we take you to the village. And please, I shouldn't have to remind you, but these ruins are delicate. Please do not attempt to take anything with you."

Kendra then led the way out the door of the room, turned right, and headed down a hall to a back door to exit the main building. Kelly caught a brief site of Neil as she followed the group. He was in a deep conversation with a well-dressed gentleman who was plainly one of the donors to the foundation. Neil looked up as she passed the room he was in. He smiled and waved to her as she followed the rest of the group. She wondered how he had been aware she was nearby. She knew before she got to the open door that he was inside. She just knew he was near. And there he had been. A chill went down her spine.

IV

The time flew by for Kelly as they wandered through the grounds of Eykel. Kendra had proven to be every bit the scholar Tara had indicated. She realized that she learned a lot just by listening to the various theories that were thrown around by all the experts in her group. They had visited the abbey ruins, the schola and were now in the church. Other groups had come and gone through each of the sites, while their group had lingered. It was the in-depth conversations and debates that had slowed their group down at each location. But Kelly was truly enjoying herself. She loved the feel of each building and could almost picture herself being there. The church in particular had been a marvel to her. She could stay in it for hours, just studying all of the small details in the construction. Whatever else the Templars would prove to be, one thing was for sure, they were master builders. These buildings although small in size were every bit as majestic as the other structures scattered across Europe that were credited to them.

Kendra was trying to gather up the group to leave the church when Kelly noticed that Neil had just entered. Or rather, Kelly *felt* Neil's presence, turned around only to discover that he had just entered the open front where the doors used to hang. She again shivered. Her awareness of Neil was truly uncanny.

Neil waved to her. He stopped to greet the other guests who Kendra finally had gathered up. He spoke briefly to her. She looked in Kelly's direction, nodded, and then led the group out. Kelly went to follow the group, but Neil waylaid her before she left.

"Stay behind. I let Kendra know that I'd take you around the rest of the complex. You're welcome to stay here as long as you like. The rest of the tours have already wrapped up. Kendra's group is taking the longest, as we expected. I hope they didn't bore you with their long-winded theories."

"Not at all, in fact I was mesmerized listening to them. I know there is so much speculation as to who and what the Templars were, and all the other legends surrounding them. Some of what I heard today was new to me, so I am incredibly grateful to you for including me in that group. Heck, I'm grateful that you invited me to attend today at all. It was obviously meant for those who had contributed to the project along the way. I'm certainly not that."

"No, but as I said, from first meeting you, I'm fascinated by you. And I want to learn more about you. This seemed like a great opportunity to spend time together. Now come, I want to show you something that we don't take the tours to. It's a special place for me and my grandfather."

Neil turned and walked back down the main aisle. As they progressed, Kelly was drawn by the perfect symmetry of the building. She had visited Notre Dame Cathedral in Paris on her honeymoon years ago. This building could have easily been made from the same blueprints as that famous cathedral, albeit on a much smaller and far less grand scale. The columns marched down both sides of the aisle in perfect order. The dais at the end was slightly raised. The benches, or what was left of them, were in stately order down the center. Narrow walkways went down the outside of the columns.

Neil moved past the altar and paused at the back of the church to look down the aisle they had just traversed. "It has such beautiful symmetry in here. The place is stunning in the simplicity of its proportions."

"I know, I was just going over my memories of Notre Dame Cathedral. To my untrained eye it has many of the same features and lines."

"Your eye isn't mistaken. They are much the same creation. Is it any wonder that there is strong speculation about the builders of Notre Dame, and their connection to the Templars? Notre Dame was definitely built during the years that the Templars were most active in France and abroad."

"I had never put those two together. But of course, Notre Dame was built in the 1100's wasn't it?"

"Yes, it was started around 1160 and took about two hundred years to complete. The Templars were first founded around 1119 and were disbanded in 1312 by Pope Clement. So, the building of Notre Dame was right in at the height of the Templar power. We currently believe that this village was built around the 1180's and housed Templars for at least 100 years, if not right up until they lost Arwad Island in the early 1300's."

"The history of the period is so fascinating. But I am sure life was hard. I can only imagine the extremes of fanaticism from religious differences. It's something I can only speculate about."

"Very true, it was a hard time. But come, what I want to show you is up these stairs."

Neil led Kelly up a long stone stairway that was seemed to be going to the remaining tower on the church. The stairs were uneven and slippery with sand. Neil had brought a light with him, and was using it to help her find her way. He held out his hand to her a number of times to help her negotiate areas where the stairs were crumbling.

"As you can tell, this is an area that will be off limits to most tourists. It's an accident waiting to happen. At least until we can get some expert stone masons in here to rebuild the steps."

"It has been a challenge to get up here. I can't wait to see what is at the top."

"Patience my darling, you'll see soon enough."

Kelly was startled at the 'darling'; she wondered if he was even aware he had said it.

Another few minutes and Kelly could perceive a lightening in the gloom around her. She knew they must be getting to the top. She suspected they were climbing the tower that would have held the bells when the church was active with Templar worship. And she was right. They got to the top and she looked up to see an unmistakable opening where those bells would have hung.

Neil urged her to the opening on the side of the tower, and said, "Here, this is what I wanted to show you. Take a look at the most beautiful view you can imagine."

Kelly looked out and gasped. He was right. The view was astounding. To the north she could just make out a shimmering of water. *Is that the Mediterranean?* She could also see miles and miles of desert around all of the other sides. To the west she fancied that she could see a city low on the horizon, probably Cairo. The breeze coming into the opening of the tower was cool and refreshing. As Kelly turned her eye back to the shimmer of water, she could also see the remains of the abbey just below her. She had a feeling of déjà vu. This place was so familiar. She could almost hear the bells in the tower chiming away, an echo of the past. The sense of belonging was so strong it almost made her light-headed. She closed her eyes briefly to clear her senses. *I must be too hungry*, she thought, it was way past lunch time. She opened her eyes and looked at Neil. She could see by the twinkle in his eyes that he knew exactly what she was feeling. The marvelous view, along with the peace and tranquility was astounding - and this man at her side, sending shivers through her at the mere touch of his hand. It was almost too much to take in.

In a subdued voice Neil said, "I know what you're feeling. It's the same thing I felt the first time I came up here. It's incredible. And it's not only the view; it's the feeling of being on the edge of the world. And I can only describe it as a holy experience. I feel closer to our creator here than I do anywhere else in the world. It's a magical place for me, peaceful and tranquil."

"Yeah. Funny you should say peaceful and tranquil. Those were the first two words that sprang to my mind. It is incredible, that's the best word for it. I wonder how often the bell ringer came up here and forgot his duty because he was so caught up in the perfection of the view from here; the sea, the village, and the desert. It's breathtaking. Thank you for sharing this with me. I'm honored."

"Kelly, I knew you would find this place spectacular. Don't ask me how I knew that. I just seem to know you. I can't believe we only met for the first time on Tuesday. I feel like I've known you forever."

They stood in complete silence absorbing the view. Time flew like it was standing still. Occasionally their hands would inadvertently touch as they both swayed slightly in the breezes coming into the tower. At each touch of their hands, Kelly experienced feelings of déjà vu. There was something about being here with Neil that was touching a cord deep inside her. She again started to feel a little light headed, and then her stomach gave out a loud and angry growl. She and Neil looked at each other and laughed.

"Guess I'm getting hungry."

"Yes, it seems so," agreed Neil. Looking at his watch he added, "Based on the time, I think we should head back to the center."

After walking down the stairs, they stopped for a brief moment and in unspoken agreement sat down on one of the stone pews that had been restored. It just felt so natural to sit and enjoy the quiet of the empty church, like it was awaiting the Templar inhabitants of Eykel to come back for another service. Kelly took a deep breath, closed her eyes, and settled into a deep silence. She felt the echo of the long-ago services held in this exact spot. At the edge of her perception she could hear words being mumbled around her. As she focused on it, she thought she could make out, *Sancti spiritus adsit nobis gratia.* Startled she opened her eyes, half expecting to see ghosts around her. She didn't know where those words had come from as she didn't know any Latin. She took a deep breath to calm herself down. Letting out a sigh, she could still feel the sanctity of the place as it reverberated all around her in the stone, helping her to relax and find her balance again. There was such peace and silence, but on the other hand, she could feel the heat from Neil where he sat beside her.

"Neil, there you are. Your grandfather is looking for you as he wants to head home," said Tara entering the church.

Kelly and Neil both swiveled their heads around at Tara's first word.

"Hello, Kelly. I see Neil has been showing you the deep history of the church."

"Yes, he's been giving me the guided tour. It's such a beautiful place, and amazingly well preserved. And I've noted the places where restoration is ongoing, like these pews. You can almost imagine the Templar Knights and their servants attending Mass here almost a thousand years ago. It's enough to give you chills." Kelly privately thought the chills she was feeling were directly caused by the man beside her and not so much by the church.

"Tara, let my grandfather know that I'll be back to see him shortly. I just want to show our guest a couple of more things."

"No problem, boss, I'll let him know." Tara turned and left.

"Kelly, if you don't mind, I must see my grandfather before he heads off home. Do you want to stay here or come back to the center?"

"I'll come back with you. I'm actually getting quite thirsty, so probably should head out to my hotel soon. I have my own packing to do over the next couple of days, as I head home on Saturday."

"Saturday? Oh."

Kelly looked at Neil as she registered his surprise at her statement. Their eyes locked together yet again, and she found herself lost in them. They were a startling shade of blue, clear and intense. She felt the world fade away as she looked into their depths.

"Darling," Neil breathed out in a slight whisper.

Kelly looked quickly away. The naked need and longing she saw in his eyes scared her. She wasn't ready to admit that she was attracted to him to the depth of her soul. It was too much, too fast. She needed to get away.

"Come; let me take you back to the center. I want to have dinner with you tonight, but I fear that my mother and grandfather already have dinner plans with me. Can I convince you to have dinner with me tomorrow?"

Kelly thought about dinner with him. She was scared to go, for fear of the attraction she felt. She had sworn off men after her husband's death. Love hurt too much. No, dinner wouldn't be a good idea. She was completely startled when she heard the words 'yes I'll have dinner with you' emerge from her mouth. *What made her say that?*

"Great, I look forward to seeing you again tomorrow."

They walked in silence the rest of the way. Kelly noted how much of the village she had yet to see. She knew she would be making a return trip to this land so she could see more of this fabulous Templar site.

"I hope you had a great day today. You know, selfishly I'm happy Kyle was sick the other day. It meant I was with you when you saw the village for the first time and I was able to show you the bell tower today. I cannot wait to have dinner with you tomorrow. I want to know more about who you are. What makes Kelly, the wonderful woman I see before me?"

Kelly felt herself blushing again and dropped her head down a bit to try to hide the color of her cheeks. "Thanks," she murmured, "this has been an amazing couple of days. Far out-stripping my imagination for what I would find. I'm grateful you showed me all that you have. I'm already trying to figure out how and when I can get back here to explore more."

"Good. I want you to come back."

"And as to dinner, I'm looking forward to it. Should I meet you at the restaurant in town?"

"No, I'll pick you up at the hotel. Can you be ready at five-thirty?"

"Yes, I'll be ready and waiting."

They had made their way to Kelly's car while they talk-ed. Kelly fumbled for her keys in her pocket and got the car door open.

"Until tomorrow, Kelly." And Neil leaned in to give her a kiss on the cheek. He gave her one last long look, then turned and walked back into the main building.

Kelly could feel the imprint of his lips on her cheek. She was filled with longing for this man. She chided herself. She had only met him on Tuesday; how could she be so smitten with him? She would have to be careful here. She reluctantly climbed into the car. Gripping the steering wheel she took a deep breath, *I'm not a school girl with my first crush!* I will get this under con-trol. With one more deep breath and loud exhale, she inserted the keys into the car and turned over the motor. With care she pulled out of the parking lot and drove back to town..

*****

Neil was standing in the lobby of the welcome center, staring out the front door as Kelly's car slowly made its way out of the parking lot. He could sense his mother coming up behind him.

"Is that her?"

"Yes, Mom, I've finally found her. And she lives on the other side of the world."

"For now, Neil, for now."

"I think I now understand just a bit of what you and Dad, and Grandad have always talked about when you find the other half of yourself. This is the most intense feeling I've ever had. Soul mates. Incredible."

"It is incredibly powerful and life changing. But come, let's get Dad and go back to Cairo. He needs to rest for the night before we get on the plane back home tomorrow."

"Ok, Mom." They walked away, both contemplating the woman who had just left the site.

V

Kelly awoke the next morning feeling disoriented and dazed. She had just woken from a dream that she could just grasp the remaining threads of. She could remember being dressed as a servant, and attending men she could only describe as knights, but that was the extent that she could remember now that she was awake. But she was left feeling alone. At least this one hadn't been a nightmare like the one earlier in the week.

She planned today to wander around the small village where she was staying. It dated back to the 1600's and had beautiful architecture to study. She wanted to visit the church to see what else she could learn about the current inhabitants and any connection to the old Templar village.

She scrambled out of the bed to get ready for her day. An hour later, she was dressed and heading out the door. The new hotel that the foundation was building was a few blocks over and would house a hundred plus rooms and all the amenities that visiting tourists would want, but Kelly preferred the quaint charm and coziness of this small hotel. She hoped that it would remain open after the new one launched. It would give a nice alternative to people looking for more of an authentic feel into the village. Kelly turned towards the old center of town where the church and other historic buildings were located. She wanted to spend time just drinking in the ambience of this place.

Sometime later, Kelly found herself at the edge of town where the new hotel was being constructed. She gazed up at the new structure. It was surprising how much care the Foundation was taking in making sure the building fit into the overall architecture of the village. Suddenly the town tower started chiming the hour. To her shock there were twelve gongs after the flourish. *Noon already? Where had the morning gone?* It seemed like she had just left her hotel room to wander around the town. She had better look for some lunch soon.

She turned to head back towards the town center, when she heard her name called from across the street.

"Kelly!"

She turned and saw Neil standing at the edge of the hotel construction zone. He waved to her to cross the street to see him.

"Kelly, come over, how are you today?"

"I'm fine, thanks, Neil. I've just been exploring the village this morning. I didn't realize I had wandered this far until I saw the hotel."

"I trust you're enjoying yourself?"

"Very much so, it's such a beautiful place. I could spend hours just wandering around the town square. It's so spectacular."

"Yeah, I can't believe it has such remarkable architecture. Between the Templar village and this place, tourists are going to have a great experience when they come to this small corner of the world."

"True, I just hope that all of the new arrivals don't disrupt the rhythm of this place. It's so peaceful and slow just the way it is."

"It's why we're building out here on the outskirts of town. They had proposed that we build in the downtown core. But we didn't want to be responsible for tearing down any of the old structures to make way for the hotel. So, we selected this unused piece of land out here. We're going to offer reliable transport to get people into the core so they can explore the area. Did you go into the church here?"

"Yes, I was carried back in time in there. It was kind of eerie actually. It's an amazing place; so like the old church in the Templar settlement. There is no doubt in my mind that it was modeled after it, even though Eykel was probably mostly buried by the time people built the new one."

"I agree. It has an uncanny resemblance to the old one. But then again, almost all of the Templar churches have a similar architecture. So perhaps the one here was built by a descendant of the original settlers."

"Perhaps." After a brief pause which felt strange and awkward to Kelly, she continued with, "I better let you go. I was just about to head back to the town square to get some lunch."

"Care for some company? I was just about to wrap up here and head out to the office. I can have lunch here with you just as easily as at the café. In fact, here would be preferable. I'd have you for company."

Kelly looked at Neil for a brief second before saying, "Yeah, um sure. I'd enjoy that."

"Just give me a couple of minutes. I'll be right back. I would invite you into the hotel, but we are a construction zone, so I can't let a civilian in."

"No problem, I'll just wander back down the street to that little park and wait for you there."

"Perfect, I'll be about five minutes."

Neil turned back into the partially finished hotel, and Kelly went down the street to the park. She had surprised herself by agreeing to lunch. After all she was having dinner with the man tonight. Was this too much of a good thing? But, she was leaving tomorrow, so why not indulge herself today?

After wandering back down the street at a leisurely pace, Kelly settled onto the bench and watched some neighborhood children on the play set. She looked carefully and realized it looked like new. She hoped the town was getting support from the Foundation to improve some of the amenities for the locals. After all, they were soon going to lose their privacy and anonymous lifestyle. Seemed like a good compensation to upgrade some of the town's parks and schools.

A few minutes later she saw Neil walking down the street. She watched him approach, drawn by his classic look, tall and proud, as only an English aristocrat can look; someone borne to wealth and privilege. She couldn't see his eyes yet, but any woman would love the handsome face and well-formed body, especially since he always seemed to be impeccably dressed. He evidently worked out as it looked like he had little fat on his body. Perhaps all the work in the Templar village kept him fit.

"Sorry that took a few minutes longer than planned."

"No problem, I was enjoying watching the kids play. The playset looks new."

"It is. One of the things the Foundation is doing for the town. We've paid to upgrade all of the parks with new playsets. The ones that were here were very old and in need of major repairs. They were actually unsafe. We insisted that they be replaced."

"That was generous."

"We just wanted to give something back to these people. Their lives will be changed forever when Eykel opens for tourists and further study. It seemed fitting that they benefit from that. Come; let's head to the town square. There's a great little family-run place just off the main road. It's hard to find, but the food is sensational."

They walked in silence, each deeply engrossed in their own thoughts. Neil suddenly made a left hand turn down one of the old side streets. Kelly was pulled from her reverie by the abrupt move, and had to skip a couple of steps to catch up with him.

"Here it is. This is the place I wanted to show you."

Kelly looked up at the small sign on the front. Based on her rather rough language skills, she thought it said the equivalent of Café. She paused at the front as Neil opened the door for her. She walked inside and was engulfed in the cozy and warm interior of the café. It only held seats for about ten guests, a few occupied. There was a short line at the counter to order.

"Do you trust me to order for you? I know most of the dishes, and I can select one if you like."

"Sounds like a plan to me. I wouldn't even know where to start."

"Anything you'd like in particular?"

"How about soup or a vegetarian meal? I know we have dinner plans, so I don't want to overeat."

"I know the perfect dish. It's a hearty soup that will give you lots of energy to continue wandering around the town."

"Sounds good. I'll grab a seat and let you deal with the order." Kelly moved toward a table at the side that would allow her to watch Neil as he ordered lunch.

A few minutes later, Neil came and sat opposite her at the small table. "The lunch will be ready in about fifteen minutes. They keep the soup broth ready to go, but add fresh ingredients for each order."

"Okay. I didn't realize how hungry I was until I came inside. It smells so good."

"Yeah, it is. So, tell me what have you seen so far?"

"I've wandered through the church and the town square. But that's it so far. There is so much to see around this place. I wish I had more time to explore both here and the Templar village. But unfortunately, I'm due back home next week. The school year starts soon, so I have to be back for that."

"Oh, are you a teacher?"

"Yes, elementary, usually grade two or three. This year though I'll have a grade five class. What I've learned on my summer travels will give me some new things to teach them when we study history."

"You've been traveling for the summer?"

"Just the past three weeks. I spent ten days in London, visiting the main tourist attractions. I also spent some time outside London, trying to see some of the supposed Templar sites there. And of course, the highlight was going to Stonehenge."

"I love Stonehenge. I grew up in England, obviously. Our family seat is north of London in Derbyshire. But I spent a great deal of time around Bath, so Stonehenge wasn't that far from me. I've always loved the old history and mystery associated with the site. I can just imagine Merlin in King Arthur's time as the architect of such a place."

"I know what you mean, the place is amazing."

Kelly and Neil continued to talk about her travels through England and the various castles and churches she had seen. He had been to most of them, and they talked at length about her time in London. He added some great insight and lesser known facts to the information she got when there. His stories about the Tower of London in particular were fascinating to her. She pulled out her notebook to jot some down so she could incorporate the information into her history classes at school, and for her freelance articles too. She had a couple of thoughts that were writing themselves in her head while she talked to Neil.

The soup arrived during their discussion and Kelly tasted it.

"You were right about the soup. It's delicious and filling. Thank you for ordering it."

"Yeah, it's my favorite little place here. I'm hoping to convince them to let me have a couple of their recipes for the hotel. That way we can serve some authentic regional dishes; although we'll never be able to duplicate the ambience." Neil looked at his watch. "Kelly, I hate to cut this short, I'm having such a good time, but I've got to get back to the office for a meeting this afternoon."

"Wow, I didn't realize it had gotten so late. Time flies when I'm with you."

"Yes, it does. I've so enjoyed lunch today. And I'm looking forward to dinner tonight. Can I see you back to your hotel?"

"No thanks, I'm going to wander around a bit more, then head back and rest up for tonight. I'm looking forward to it too."

"Okay I'll see you tonight."

Kelly watched Neil walk back toward the hotel. She loved to watch him move. She cautioned herself. *Keep some distance.*

She was too attracted to him by far, and was not up to just a summer fling. However she planned to enjoy their dinner. She, little Kelly Taylor, had a date with international businessman and most eligible bachelor, Neil Adams. That would be something to share when she got home.

VI

Kelly got to the lobby just before five when Neil was due to pick her up. He had asked if she could leave a half hour earlier than originally planned, which was fine with her. After lunch she had finished packing for her trip home. She had an eight p.m. flight to Amsterdam tomorrow with an overnight stay and a final flight home late on Sunday. She was due at the school on Tuesday, for a week of prep before the year started. She knew she would have a bunch of work to do, as this was an entirely new grade for her to teach. The principal had asked her to take it on last spring. The regular teacher was on maternity leave, and they all felt that Kelly was the perfect person to fill in the gap. She was looking forward to teaching something more challenging than grade two mathematics this year.

Kelly looked around the lobby of her hotel. She had come to adore this little place. She sighed a little. She wanted to come back, but had no idea when she would be able to swing this big a trip again. Being single now made it more difficult to save money. Kelly shook off that thought. She would worry about her finances and other things when she got home. For tonight she was going to enjoy herself. She was going out to dinner with an incredibly sexy man, wealthy to boot. She planned to enjoy this last night of her vacation as much as she could.

She turned to the front door. She knew it was Neil, she had felt his presence before the door even opened. She shuddered inwardly. She had never had this sense of awareness about anyone in her life before. She wondered about it. It would be something to consider and examine when she got back home.

"Kelly, there you are, prompt as always. You look wonderful, perfect for a night out on the town."

"Thanks, Neil, I wasn't one hundred percent sure what to wear. You said dressy casual. This is the best I could come up with in the rather limited wardrobe I brought with me." Kelly looked down at her black dress and white sandals. It was the one dress she had brought with her, feeling she'd like something a little dressy for the odd dinner out. It was a simple sheath dress with narrow straps, flowing from her shoulders to just above her knees. A simple gold chain hung from her neck to decorate the front. Over her arms she had a simple burgundy shawl that would protect her in cool air conditioning.

"You look perfect to me. But then I suspect you would look perfect if you had on nothing but a burlap sack. Come, let's go, I left the car running." Neil escorted Kelly from the hotel and down to his car. She paused for a minute to admire the sexy two-seater that was parked out front. She raised an eyebrow at Neil.

"Not a particularly practical vehicle out here is it?"

"Not at all, but I wanted to have it here, just for the odd chance I get to drive it around town and on the one highway out here. It gives me an excuse to go fast."

Kelly slid into the seat and watched Neil proceed to the other side. She wondered what restaurant they would go to out here in the wilderness. *Maybe he'll drive to Cairo?* She settled into the luxurious interior of the little car to enjoy the ride, wherever it was taking her. A few minutes later they pulled into the airport parking lot.

"The airport? We're having dinner here?"

"No, just getting onto the family jet. I wanted to take you up to the Mediterranean for dinner. We're flying from here to Cyprus, where there is the most wonderful waterside restaurant you've ever seen. It's an historic site, so I knew you would love it."

Kelly looked at Neil in astonishment. "You're flying us to Cyprus for dinner?"

"Yup, come on, the pilot called me just before I left to pick you up. The jet is ready to go as soon as we're on board."

Neil escorted Kelly into the small airport terminal and over to the security gate and agent.

"Mr. Adams, good evening. I see you're planning a return later tonight."

"Yes, Wallace, we're just heading to Cyprus for dinner; we'll be back before curfew."

"All right, Mr. Adams, enjoy your flight. Lawrence already cleared the flight itinerary with the control tower. You are cleared to go whenever he has the final go ahead."

"Thanks, we'll head out to the plane now." Neil escorted Kelly into the evening air and to the plane.

Neil climbed the stairs into the jet and turned to greet the pilot and co-pilot who were just finishing instrument checks. "Good evening, Lawrence and Charles. How are you both to-day? Looks like a great weather for flying."

"We're fine, Neil. Glad to have you onboard. We just delivered your Grandfather and Mother to Rome and turned around to come back for this. The land-side crew has refueled us and we're ready to head out as soon as you and your guest are settled."

"Let me introduce my guest. This is Kelly Taylor from Halifax, Nova Scotia. Kelly this is Lawrence and Charles, our company pilots. They take great care of all of us who fly on this jet."

"Nice to meet you both. I've never been on this small a jet before. This could be a truly interesting experience."

"Just get yourself settled into the seats in the back, and we'll finalize the last safety checks and get on our way. The sun should be setting as we get to Cyprus. The site from up there is always spectacular out here in the desert."

Neil led Kelly into the main cabin area which was luxuriously appointed with six captain's chairs, what looked like a fully stocked bar, and a back area that seemed to contain a bed. Kelly gulped a little at the intimacy of the entire interior. Neil offered her a seat in the main cabin. She settled in and reached for the seatbelt as she would on any flight. Neil looked at her with a chuckle.

"Nervous passenger?"

"I actually haven't flown all that much, five times, including the trip here. And this is by far the smallest plane I've ever been on. So, yes, I'm a little nervous."

"Don't worry, I'll sit right here beside you and hold your hand. Lawrence and Charles are the best in the business. That's why we hired them. They know what they're doing. We can even listen in on the cockpit conversation on those earphones; makes for interesting listening sometimes."

"Thanks all the same, but I think I'll pass on that for now."

"Neil and Kelly, we've just finished up our checks. We'll close the front door now, and rig for take-off. Since Kelly is new to this plane, I will point out the emergency exits at the front of the plane. Should an emergency occur you will see the emergency lights glowing. Follow Neil's lead as he has been through the drill with us a number of times. But for now, sit back and relax. We'll have you in Cyprus in a couple of hours." Charles pulled the front door closed and locked it for flight. He returned to the cockpit and shut the door.

Kelly heard the jet engines start and warm up for a short while. Then the plane started to move. "Neil and Kelly, please take your seats and buckle up, we're taking the short taxi to the runway. Be in the air in a few minutes. Neil, the champagne is chilling on ice in the main galley, along with a few snacks that your mother insisted that we bring for you."

Neil chuckled at the last. "Trust my mother to figure that we should have something to eat while we sip on champagne in the air."

Within a short few minutes, the plane taxied to the runway and lifted off the ground. About ten minutes after that, Charles opened the cockpit door and moved out into the cabin.

"Okay we're passed the expected turbulence and you can now release your seatbelts and move about the cabin. Lawrence wanted a pop, as do I. Shall I open the champagne for you?"

"Thanks, Charles that would be great. Probably a couple of waters would be good too?"

"Okay."

Kelly was awed by all this. First to have this incredibly sexy man sitting beside her, then the private jet ride to dinner, and now champagne? It was almost too much to take in at one time.

"Here you are, Kelly, a bottle of water, and for you, Neil. I'll just pop the champagne and leave it out in the galley in the container in case of unexpected turbulence. The food is in the fridge when you're ready for it."

Charles disappeared into the middle section of the plane into the galley. Kelly heard the unmistakable pop of a champagne cork. He came out a few seconds later with two glasses of champagne.

"Here you go. I'll just grab the drinks for Lawrence and myself and leave you two alone. We will let you know about twenty minutes prior to landing."

After watching Charles complete that task, and close the cockpit door behind him, Kelly just stared around the interior, "I don't know if my students will quite believe this adventure if I told them during "What did you do this Summer". It's a long way from what this girl from Nova Scotia has ever encountered before."

Neil chuckled. "I'm sure it will sound like an adventure. I hope we can repeat it many times together." After a brief pause, he continued. "We've a couple of hours until we get to Cyprus. So, suppose you tell me about yourself? I know I'm fascinated by you. But, I know so little about you, other than you're a school teacher, love Templar history, and I believe I heard you mention being a widow? Please, tell me more."

"Well, I'll give you a brief history of myself, in exchange for getting one about you. The real story, not what we read about in the press. I know based on my short acquaintance with you that you're far more than what the press likes to portray."

"Ah yes, the good old press. They have me pegged as a playboy, "Most Eligible Bachelor" and all that other stuff. It's frustrating as hell having all that floating around. It is impossible to have real conversations with people. They keep expecting to hear something stupid or see me pull out drugs or something. I've actually never taken any recreational drugs in my life. I've no idea how the press came up with that one."

"That sure sounds like the press, any angle to sell a paper. I'm trying my hand at a little freelance writing in the summer time. I've had to rewrite pieces a few times for the editors because they wanted it to be more suspenseful or other such nonsense. I refuse to write anything that is a falsehood, so I usually just pull my piece from any magazine that wants a sensational piece. It's why I want to try my hand at travel writing. I think that's where I could excel. That's what this trip was for, to combine my love of Templar history with a potential for a good travel article that I could sell to travel magazines."

"I wondered what brought you to our doorstep. If I can help in anyway in getting the article written or published, I would be happy to help."

"Really? I'd love to do a complete narrative on Eykel and other Templar villages, including some insight into the family and the foundation behind the work here. Would you be willing to help with that?"

"I see no reason why not. But I'll have to let our public relations department read the article prior to release if you're going to quote me or anyone on our staff. It's our policy to not let anything be published unless we approve it first."

"That sounds fair. I'll probably start working on it when I get back to Canada. I'll send you copies of it as I get it into draft and final form."

"Okay. Now I suggest you stop avoiding the question I asked you earlier. Please, I want to get to know you."

Kelly felt herself blushing and reached for the champagne in front of her. Had she been so obvious? *How do I avoid talking about me? I hate that topic. I'd rather talk about him.* She took another sip and contemplated what to tell him.

"So, why don't we start with something straight forward? Why did you want to become a teacher?"

"Oh that's easy. My mother was a teacher, so I grew up with that as a profession before me. My father was a fisherman. He passed away when I was a teenager. He was lost at sea in a big storm."

"Oh honey, I'm sorry for your loss. That must have been hard."

"It wasn't easy for any of us. I've two older brothers, who had both been intending to follow Dad into the fishing business. One was already helping out on the boats, but had caught a bad flu just before Dad went out for the last time. Otherwise we would have lost him too. I suspect he feels some guilt over that. But after the storm my mother put her foot down and sent the boys to school. She got her wish, as neither went into fishing. My eldest brother is an accountant and the other one is an architect. They are both settled in Halifax. My mom moved to Kentville, about an hour from Halifax, a few years ago when she retired from teaching. She is in a retirement community there and still bossing the other residents around or rather, convincing them that her solution is always the best. She's still a going concern even now that she's in her seventies."

"She does sound feisty if she convinced your brothers to give up the sea for desk jobs. That can't have been an easy task.

I know the sea is like an addiction. Once it's in your blood, it's almost impossible to give up."

"Well, they didn't give up the sea entirely, as they both have sailboats that they take out on a regular basis. They just don't sail at all in bad weather, that's their agreement with Mom. It's too hard a memory for any of us."

"Here, let me top up your champagne. Can you give me a hand with some snacks too? I don't think we should drink too much up here in the thin air without some sort of sustenance."

Neil gestured for Kelly to walk with him into the small galley. Kelly glanced to the back and sure enough saw a small bed tucked into the aft section.

Noticing her glance, Neil commented, "We had that put in a few years ago for Granddad. He still wants to travel the world looking in on all the businesses, but he finds it harder as he gets older. Having a nap during the flights helps to keep him going through meetings."

"I wondered what was back here. Looks like a comfortable cabin. Actually, now that I'm up, I could use a washroom break. Where is it?"

"Just keep going to the back. It's right at the back behind the bed."

"Thanks."

Kelly went to the back and located the washroom. She took the time to freshen up and to contemplate what she had told Neil about herself already. Why had she opened with the death of her dad? She didn't tell many people about him. It was still a painful subject to her. She had been so close to him and had been devastated when he didn't come home from that last fishing trip. The loss had diminished over the years, but the wound had been torn back open when her husband Ken had died just four years ago. That one still hurt a lot, although the pain had noticeably dulled in the past year. She looked at herself in the mirror. *Be careful! Don't let Neil in. That would lead to more pain. It is better to be self-sufficient and strong.* She sighed; with all she had suffered her new motto was to never love again. Love equaled pain.

Back in the cabin, she helped Neil put out a few snacks to nibble on. They stood for a while in the galley area alternating between eating, sipping champagne, and talking about her life as a teacher. Neil appeared to be truly fascinated to learn about her classes, the subjects she liked to teach, and some of the interesting and funny anecdotes she had to tell. In turn he told her about his early travels with his grandfather when he had been young.

They soon became absorbed in the light hearted conversation and passed the two hours as genuine and comfortable companions.

"Neil and Kelly, we are about twenty minutes out from Cyprus and will be descending soon. Can you please put away anything that you took out and store it properly for landing? Then take your seats and put on your seatbelts."

"Go ahead and sit, I know where all this stuff goes."

Kelly acknowledged his suggestion and headed to her seat. She glanced out the window beside her and was impressed by the beautiful scene below of the islands of the Mediterranean. The sky was just darkening, and she could see the lights on the island reflecting back off the sea. There was a distinct glow that abruptly stopped at seaside. But the shimmering of the sunset off the water was creating an eerie light. She sighed at the beauty.

She had never expected to be in these islands. It was going to be an interesting evening to say the least.

"Okay, all done. Let's settle in for landing, and then we can set off to the restaurant."

Thirty minutes later they were on the ground and parked at the terminal building. They deplaned, and Neil led Kelly over to a limousine that was parked just outside the tarmac area.

"Mr. Adams? Please allow me to settle you into the car. I understand your destination is the Lighthouse Beach area?"

"Yes please, my thanks for meeting us at the airport."

"My pleasure, sir."

The car quickly left the airport behind and drove toward the waterfront area. Neil pointed out a spectacular church on his side of the car, and Kelly was so busy taking in the views around her, that she scarcely noticed when he slid his arm around her shoulders and pulled her close to him. The feeling of his hand and arm around her shoulder felt so natural that she just snuggled closer to him. His hand tightened on her. She looked at him in the dimly lit interior of the car. She recognized the passion she saw in his eyes, and was pretty sure that it was reflecting the passion in her own eyes.

They stared at each other for a brief moment. Kelly saw his gaze start to drift lower to her lips. She licked them nervously, both wanting and fearing his kiss. He bent his head and gently placed his lips on hers. Kelly let herself drift with the sensations that engulfed her with the tender pressure of his lips. It was unlike anything she had ever felt before. There was softness and yet a harnessed passion that she could feel within him and building within herself. She was struggling with the heat pooling in her body. This was a feeling both sudden and startling in its intensity.

She suddenly realized that the car was no longer moving. Drifting on the passion of the kisses, she could vaguely hear the chauffeur commenting that they had arrived. As he opened his door, the spell she was under was broken. Nervously she pulled away from Neil as the door was opened and they exited the car, moving toward the restaurant.

****

Neil took a deep breath as he helped Kelly out of the car. He paused, thinking about this woman by his side, and the feelings for her that had developed so quickly. It was scary and welcoming all at the same time. He knew she was the other half of him. He intended to make sure that she became his wife at some point. He wasn't going to push or pressure her. But they would be married at some point this time around. He wondered about the "this time around", but knew deep down that this was a true statement. Since he already knew that he had been a Templar in a past life, it was only logical to assume that Kelly had been in his life before; especially given his intense reaction to her presence. He understood now the deep and abiding love that his parents shared. Their bond was much like this. And that kiss they had just shared. Incredible. When he had gently placed his lips on hers, a fire had been ignited in his entire body. The passion flared and he knew that he was going to have to make love to this woman beside him tonight, before she left town. He needed to claim her as his own before she left for Canada.

VII

Kelly awoke the next morning and found herself in strange surroundings yet again. She sat up in the king size bed. *This certainly isn't my little hotel room.* Disoriented, she looked around the massive bedroom suite she was in. It was painted a lovely shade of pale yellow that brightened the room. Based on the light she could see around the shades on the window to her right she could tell the sun was well up already. *What time is it?* She looked at the clock on the bedside table showing eight am. Shaking her head, she glanced at the bed beside her, and could still see the impression of a body in the covers. *Neil. I remember, I'm at his place, in his bed.* But where was he? Glancing once again around the room, she examined it in greater detail, given how little she had seen of it last night. It was actually quite understated for the wealth of the man who lived here. But she did remember the spectacular view from the living room windows. This was the penthouse in the hotel and took up the entire top floor. It had been finished as soon as the hotel had been fully constructed so Neil and his family had a place to stay. They accessed the area from a separate elevator that went directly to this suite. Kelly reclined in the bed and reminisced about the prior night, and how she had come to be in Neil's bed this morning. She knew they had made love a number of times during the night. She could feel the slight soreness in her breasts and private areas. She hadn't been with anyone since Ken had died, so she wasn't surprised to be a bit sore this morning. Kelly closed her eyes and drifted back through the evening, from that first kiss in the limo.

They had gone into the restaurant where Neil had been greeted like an old friend by the owners. They had been shown a table in a quiet, exclusive corner of the restaurant on the second floor. It was a section set aside for the exclusive use of patrons looking for privacy from media and other gawking tourists. She had recognized a couple of celebrities in some of the other dining nooks. Neil had greeted a couple of the other men whom he knew; she suspected from his business dealings.

Neil held her chair for her to sit and had briefly brushed his hand across her cheek and shoulder as he pushed the chair in. There was already a bottle of white wine chilling. Neil sat down, and the maître-d' poured them both a glass.

As he had moved away, Neil held up his glass in a toast. "To us, and a wonderful evening that's just starting."

Kelly clinked her glass with his and took a sip of the wine. It was clearly an expensive bottle, smooth and delicate.

"Oh, this is exceptional. I don't think I've ever tasted one so delicate."

"It's from France, and they carry it here exclusively. You can't get it anywhere else, except at the vineyard."

"That *is* exclusive." Kelly looked around the restaurant. "What is this place? It looks like a standard restaurant downstairs, but up here?"

"It was a brainchild of the owners. There are always lots of celebrities looking for some quiet and escape from the news and media. Benedict the owner decided to open this second floor to cater to them. I've known Benedict since university. I've a standing table, whenever I want it."

"Nice perk."

"I don't take advantage of it often. I've had my mom here a few times for birthdays, same for my sister. My ex didn't like this place much. It wasn't "showy" enough for her. She wanted the limelight when we were out together."

"I knew you were fairly recently divorced. I mean, how could anyone not know, as it was covered in the so called popular press? Even a couple of my grade three students knew of it and used it as part of a project that I had them do on news and media coverage."

"Yes, Patricia and I had actually been separated for a couple of years already. But the media made it sound like a circus show from the get-go. Patricia of course wanted to have way more than was reasonable. She took her "story" to the press to try to sway sympathy toward her. It didn't work that favorably, as she came across as reaching, grabbing, and self-centered; which she was. But I didn't find that out until after we were married. But in my world, a marriage is for life, and something to work on. So even after I found out what she was actually like, I stuck the marriage out for ten years. But I finally had enough last year and started divorce proceedings. It took twelve months to get everything settled, but as I said we hadn't been living together for some time prior to that. Still the experience has been less than positive for me. I'm gun shy now around women. Well, that is except for you. You I find fascinating, and I can't wait to get to know you better."

At that time, their waiter arrived with the first course.

"I took the liberty of ordering for us when I arranged the table. I hope you don't mind. We're having pork tenderloin; it's the house specialty."

"Not at all. After the lunch today, I would trust you to order for me anytime."

They both dug into the salad that had been placed on the table, evidently hungry after the flight to the island.

Kelly came out of her reverie. The dinner had been delicious, one of the best she'd ever had. The pork tenderloin had been delicately flavored and perfectly cooked. She had loved the taste so much, she had asked for the recipe since pork tenderloin was one of her favorites. Benedict had been happy to share it with her, as it had been one of his grandmother's recipes.

She could smell coffee coming from the kitchen. She decided to slip out of the bed, visit the washroom and get a bit cleaned up. She found her suitcases where they had left them last night and pulled out a silk wrapper to cover herself. After cleaning up a bit, she looked at herself in the mirror. Funny she didn't think she looked any different than she remembered from yesterday. But she sure felt different. The connection she felt to Neil was earth shattering. The sex last night had been the best of her life. She couldn't believe that the mind altering time hadn't left a visible mark on her. The coffee smell was even stronger now, so she figured Neil was whipping up some breakfast for them. She wandered out of the bedroom into the living room and kitchen. She was right; Neil was busy in the kitchen, setting out coffee and some fruit.

"Good morning, love. I hope I didn't wake you."

"Morning. No, you didn't."

"Sorry, I don't have much here for breakfast, I wasn't expecting company. Hoping you'd stay, but not counting on it. I have some fruit and bread if you'd like toast."

"Coffee, fruit and toast sounds perfect to me."

"Great, have a seat. But first, come here."

Kelly walked around the counter to face Neil. He pulled her into his arms and gave her a good morning kiss. It was far from a gentle peck. It was filled with passion and need.

"Now that is how I like to say good morning."

Kelly looked at Neil, suddenly feeling shy, but murmured to him "me too", then reached up to give him another kiss. That kiss quickly became very passionate. Neil reached inside the silk wrapper and pulled Kelly's naked body against his chest. Kelly shuddered as she heard him growl and groan against her lips and felt him harden with desire again. He grabbed Kelly's hand and pulled her back to the bedroom then she felt the world tilt as he reached down, picked her up and placed her back on the bed she had just vacated. She watched as he untied the silk wrapper and admired her body yet again. Her breasts were already getting firm as he looked at them and started to caress them.

"Please Neil, make love to me."

*****

A while later Neil rolled onto his side, taking Kelly with him to have her nestle in his arms. It felt so right to have this woman beside him in bed. He wanted her to stay with him forever. He had stopped moving earlier to watch her climax. The look on her face, coupled with the spasms of her body told him all he needed to know. She was his, body and soul. He had started moving inside her again, knowing his own climax was close, but wanted her to feel it once more. He held himself back as best he could, but after a few more thrusts, he knew he was going to climax. He drove deep into her once more, and felt her body react at the same time that he spilled his seed. The release was like nothing he had felt before. He had gradually come to himself and rolled onto his side, taking Kelly with him to cuddle her in his arms.

He could tell that she was drifting off again, as she had last night. He kept his arms wrapped around her and savored the feeling. He was still basking in the wonderful afterglow, remembering how quickly he had complied with her request, to make love to her. He had been as eager as she to be inside her. He felt her contract around him as he entered her body with care and gentleness. The feeling was incredible. How intense it had been.

He let his thoughts drift back over the prior night. The dinner had been as wonderful as it usually was at the island. But this time it had been extra special for him with Kelly across from him. They had talked through dinner about their families. He had learned a lot more about her two brothers and how close they were as a family. He had related his own family story of siblings and cousins. How he had come, over time, to consider the Foundation as his future. It hadn't been his original plan. He had wanted to be an architect, like her brother. But his grandfather had gradually convinced him that the Foundation was his future. And now that he was deep within the Templar village and studying more about the Templars, he was glad he'd made the choice. He could still indulge his love of architecture; he was just doing it on old buildings.

The only thing they hadn't discussed was the one thing he really wanted to talk about, her husband and what had happened to him, and how she was doing now about that loss. It was the one thing he didn't want to ask her; yet it was the one thing he desperately wanted to know about.

After dinner, they'd gone for a stroll along the waterfront. It was a full moon and had been a romantic walk along the pier. He'd held her hand for a while, and then not satisfied with that small point of contact had put his arm around her shoulder when they stopped to stand at the look out and enjoy the full moon shining on the water. While standing and holding her there, he'd looked down at her, and known that he would have to kiss her again. And he had. The kiss had started as a simple "get to know you" kiss and turned passionate and full of need shortly. At that moment his cell phone had gone off with a reminder from Lawrence that they needed to be in the air within forty five minutes in order to get back before curfew. Neil had silently cursed the interruption, but also knew that he would have more time with Kelly alone on the plane. He was determined to ask about her husband.

"Kelly, we have to get going now. That was Lawrence reminding me about the landing curfew back home. We need to get in the air shortly."

"That's okay, I am starting to get a bit tired, and I've got that flight home tomorrow."

Neil summoned the car to the restaurant, and they journeyed back to the airport, boarded the plane, and were shortly on their way. Settled comfortably in the side by side captain's chairs, Neil poured them each cognac to enjoy on the flight home.

"You know, I haven't had this much to drink in a long time. Like since before my husband died. We used to drink a bottle a couple of times a week, but since he passed, I haven't had much."

Neil gently took her hand and looked at her with compassion, "Tell me about him. What happened?"

Kelly sighed. "I don't talk about it much; it was a pretty painful time in my life. And after having lost my dad so young, I found it really hard to cope with Ken's passing."

Kelly paused for a long while. Neil was afraid that she wouldn't open up about that time in her life. But Kelly continued, "Ken and I met in university. We were both studying for a BA. I was going to be a teacher and Ken wanted to be a lawyer. Unfortunately Ken never got the marks he needed to get into law school. So he ended up leaving university to pursue legal assistant in college. We started to date before he changed schools and continued on through the last year of my BA. I then went to teachers college in Ontario. I had wanted to travel a bit and the opportunity to study in Ontario came up, so I took it. Ken wasn't happy about a long distance relationship, but we managed to make it work for the year I needed. When I got back to Nova Scotia I was able to get on as a substitute teacher and gradually worked my way into a full time job. In the meantime Ken had finished his legal assistant courses, and got a job at one of the legal firms in Halifax. Shortly after getting the job, he proposed to me. We were married a year later. We went on happily for the next ten years. We never ended up having children, although we tried. Turned out Ken couldn't have any, something neither of us knew about until later." Kelly paused in her narrative.

"Sounds like you had a good marriage."

"It was a solid marriage. It was comfortable. We had a lot of good times. We travelled a bit, to Paris for our honeymoon, but generally just lived our lives in Halifax. We shared a few hobbies, but mostly went about our lives like we had before we got married. Then about five years ago Ken started to feel poorly. He couldn't catch his breath; he was cold all the time and just not himself. He finally visited the doctor and they diagnosed him with a heart problem. It had probably been around for years, but had gotten substantially worse in the past couple. The doctors tried all sorts of things to help him, but nothing worked. He finally succumbed to a third heart attack. After the second one he was hospitalized. The third one happened in the hospital, and they couldn't save him. I'd been visiting when the attack started. It was such a hard time for me."

"I can only imagine. I'm sorry you've had to deal with such pain and loss in your life at such a young age."

"Yeah, I've had my share of heart break, but I'm getting my life back on track. The first couple of months were so hard. I almost didn't want to keep living myself. The kids at school were the ones that saved me. They gave me a reason to keep going, along with my family and my fellow teachers. They all rallied around me and kept me going. My dog Sandy was also a god-send. She cuddled by my side every night and seemed to know exactly what I needed and when I needed it. Gradually you start to live again. It's a long process, but you move on. Now four years later, I almost feel like myself again. I've found a new purpose in life. This research work into the Templars has excited me like nothing has in a long while. And branching into free-lance writing has been therapeutic. The first few articles I wrote were about being a widow and how we get moving again. I had four published over a two year period, essentially tracking my progress through time. From there I looked into other areas of interest and had two to three articles published each summer. That was enough since I work full time as a teacher."

"Sounds like writing was a hidden talent you hadn't pursued before. Can I refresh your drink?"

"Sure. And yes, you're right about the writing. In a lot of ways that is exactly what it's been. The Templar research was always in my blood so to speak too. I've been fascinated for years by the Templars and all the stories about them. I've read more fiction and non-fiction books than you can imagine about them. But the writing took me by surprise. It started with just a journal I kept after Ken died. It's one of those things they tell you to do when you're grieving- write letters to your loved one, so you can release any feelings. And it took off from there. It's been a new lease on life."

Kelly had gotten up and followed Neil to the galley for her drink refill. He looked deep into her eyes as she came up to him. He could see the haunting pain that she had felt four years ago. It was obviously still just below the surface. He pulled her into his arms and just held her. He funneled all the love and compassion that he was feeling for her into his arms and sent it to her. And love was what he was feeling. A deep and passionate love that far outstretched the length of time they had known each other. It was a love of lifetimes.

VIII

Kelly settled herself on the plane that was to take her miles away from Eykel and Neil Adams. Shortly they would depart for Amsterdam and then home, back to her real life. It had been a long three weeks away, and she was looking forward to getting back to her place and seeing Sandy. Her eldest brother had been looking after her, or rather his kids had been. He had two and they had been sharing the duties of Sandy, along with their own dog, Fred.

Kelly thought of the man she was leaving behind. How hard it had been to leave him at security when her flight was called for boarding. Neil had exacted a promise from her to keep in contact with him. They knew the time difference would be tough, but Neil had been insistent that the connection they had was deep and real. Kelly couldn't argue with him. She knew she had fallen in love with him in the past two days, something she had sworn never to do again. Love was too painful. It was something she had never expected, but it had happened. She was in love with Neil Godfrey Carter-Adams.

As she sat on the plane, she stared out the window and let her mind drift back over the past week. *What a whirlwind it had been.* She allowed her thoughts to replay what had happened after they had landed from Cyprus. They had hopped into Neil's car for the drive back to her hotel. Instead of going there, Kelly found herself at the Foundation Hotel. Neil pulled into the underground garage and parked beside a four wheel drive that was more appropriate to the area.

"Will you please come up to the apartment here? There is something you need to see before we call it a night."

"Okay, but only for a short while, I need to get some sleep tonight as I won't get much over the next two days with my flight connections."

"Sure thing." Neil escorted her to a set of elevators that were apart from the ones that said *Lobby* on them.

"This is a private elevator that allows the family to access the penthouse suite directly from the parking garage. We had the penthouse turned into an apartment so anyone in the family could stay here while we work on the village."

They went up the floors to the top level and exited into a foyer for the apartment. Kelly noted a muted glow from the moonlight that was coming in through the wide open windows in the living room. Neil led her to the window and let her drink her fill of the scene below. The moonlight was shining down on the old Templar village and illuminating the church spire and the edges of the schola. The effect against the old buildings was that they almost glowed from within with an eerie inner light. Kelly gasped in delight at the perspective.

"Neil, it's spectacular. I can't believe the effect of the moonlight on the village. It's fascinating and eerie all at the same time. It's dazzling."

"I knew you'd love it. Can I get you a glass of wine or water?"

"No thanks, I should probably get back to my hotel to get some sleep tonight."

Kelly looked back over her shoulder and spotted what looked like her suitcases sitting in the front entry of the apartment. She walked over to them. "What the hell are my suitcases doing here? How dare you assume that I would stay here tonight!"

Neil went to Kelly and took her hands in plea, "Please Kelly, listen to me. I want to spend every minute that I can with you before you leave tomorrow. The passion and connection I feel for you are so deep and real that I believe we've got to give this a chance, to understand what it is that's drawing us together. You can't tell me that you don't feel the same connection that I do. I saw the look in your eyes in the Templar village and again today when we were wandering around town. I know you feel it too. Please, let's give this a chance to see where it'll go."

Kelly wanted to be angry with him for his high-handedness. But she had to admit that the connection and passion he was talking about had affected her too. She knew that she was falling for this man. *Is it worth the risk? I've loved and lost too many times,* she thought. It frankly scared her, but on the other hand, she wanted to explore where this might take her, this man who seemed to know her so well. *I want to kiss him again. That kiss in the car, I want more of that.* She wanted to know what it would be like to make love to this man. She mulled over the risks of staying with him, *just one night; what scars might it leave?* She felt her body singing with excitement. This man beside her was dazzling her senses. *Surely one night won't scar me for life? Take the risk!* Her mind and body were telling her.

Letting a sigh escape her lips, she said, "All right, Neil, I won't ask that you take me back to my hotel for now. I can't make any promises beyond that."

"Thank you, Kelly. I truly believe that there is something special between us. I want to spend every minute I can with you until you leave tomorrow. If I thought I had any chance of changing your mind, I'd ask you to stay for at least another week." Neil lifted his hands to gently cup her face as he gazed into her eyes.

Kelly looked back at him and knew that her apprehension and confusion was shining in the depths, but she couldn't conceal the small shiver that ran through her at his touch. Nervously she licked her lips, wondering if he would kiss her now. But he only touched his lips to her forehead. As he dropped his hands, he asked, "Will you have a nightcap with me?"

"Yes."

Neil left her to go to the kitchen to grab a couple of glasses and then to the bar to pull out an after-dinner liqueur. He poured two and brought one to Kelly who had gone back to the window to gaze at the ruins. Neil moved close to her and put his arm around her as they looked into the past. They remained silent. Kelly knew that if she stayed for any length of time, that she wouldn't leave at all. She wanted this man beside her, as she had never felt desire before in her life.

After a few minutes, Kelly moved a little in front of Neil so she could lean against him; a silent invitation. Neil put down his glass and wrapped his arms around her. Kelly felt passion blaze at his merest touch. Removing one hand, Neil took her glass, put it down and returned his hands to her arms. She felt the gentle pressure of his hands as they invited her to turn around to face him. He moved his hands from her shoulders to reach out to cup her face. Electricity shot through her and made the smoldering embers burst into flames. Neil reached down to touch her lips with his and gathered her close in his arms. Passion flared. The kiss quickly became full of need and desire. Neil bent down and picked her up. She protested slightly, but he just brought his mouth back on hers and she was lost in the ecstasy again.

He carried Kelly into the master bedroom, where he placed her carefully on the bed. He lay down beside her, reached over and continued to kiss her. Kelly could feel the passion building ever hotter inside. She knew that she was getting wet just from his kisses. She hadn't been with a man since Ken had died, but this intense a feeling felt unreal, and she didn't think it was simply due to time. The passion was due to this man. He was lighting a flame that she didn't even know existed inside her

"Please, I want to hold you and kiss you all over."

"Yes, Neil, please, make love to me."

That was all the encouragement Neil needed, and he started to remove her clothes. He took his time and gently explored each inch of her as her clothes came off. Kelly grew impatient with need. She reached out to him and started to remove his shirt. She needed to run her hands over his chest to feel every inch of him. Within a few minutes they were both naked and engaged in a battle to explore the other. The need to consummate this passion was growing with each kiss and caress. Kelly reached out to hold Neil's erection in her hand. He groaned with desire and allowed her to guide him to her core so that he could enter her. He opened his eyes and looked deep into hers as he slid gently inside her. He could feel their souls connecting at some level of inner awareness. Kelly shivered in need and passion as he entered her; feeling at the same time lost in his eyes and soul like nothing she had ever experienced. It was a perfect blending of the physical connection of the body and the immortal connection of the soul. She quivered and felt herself building to a climax almost immediately. It washed over her quickly.

Kelly sighed in recollection. How incredible that first time had been. She stared out the window of the plane, realizing that they had taken off while she had been absorbed in her memories of last night. That had been the first time they had made love. They'd slept for a couple of hours and woken up to make love again. The second time they had explored each other's bodies more thoroughly, but had soon left that behind to be joined as one yet again. That had continued for most of the night until at about four am they had gotten up and had a bit of ice cream and water. When they had gone back to bed they had simply nestled in each other's arms and fallen asleep. Kelly had woken in the morning to find Neil up already. As she continued to stare out the window she allowed her mind to drift back to her memories of early this morning; how they had made love yet again before they had even tackled breakfast.

After her morning nap, when Neil had left the bed with his cell phone, Kelly had known that the real world was intruding on the little piece of fantasy they had created. It had been time to face reality and get ready for her flight back home and to her real life.

Neil had returned in fifteen minutes commenting that he had cleared his day.

"Neil."

"Did you really think I was going to let you leave without spending every last minute I could with you? You've still got a lot to learn about me if you think I was going to let you out of my sight today."

Kelly had remembered chuckling at that image. Neil had continued.

"Besides I have to convince you to come back here soon so that we can continue this and see where it leads. I know that I've fallen in love with you, and I'm pretty sure that you love me too. That is the only thing that matters, our love for each other. That is what will sustain us through the next few months."

Kelly was surprised at how deep the love they shared was. It was amazing that she had just met him five days ago. But that was how it was. She was in love. And more in love than ever in her life. In love with a playboy. In love with a billionaire. In love with "The Most Eligible Bachelor". She only hoped that he didn't end up breaking her heart.

IX

A few weeks later, Halifax, Nova Scotia

Kelly looked up from her writing when she heard the door to the staff room open. She saw her fellow teacher, and best friend, Sandra, walk into the room.

"There you are Kelly; I wondered where you'd gotten too. Working on that freelance piece again?"

"Yeah, I'm getting close to having it done. The paper wants to run the article in the next few weeks, so I've got to work hard to get it complete. I wasn't expecting those query letters to come back so fast, but it just goes to prove, expect the unexpected."

"True, but given all the interest in Oak Island here, it's hardly surprising that the paper would want to run an article about the Templars. Just makes sense to tie it into all of the other publicity."

"Yes it does, but it's left me in a bit of a bind getting it written at the same time I'm trying to get up to speed on the grade five curriculum. It has made me extra busy."

"Heard from Neil recently?"

"Yes, we talked last night actually. He's in Spain right now, so made it a bit easier. I think it was nine his time."

"I still can't believe that you're in a long distance relationship with Neil Adams, one of the most eligible bachelors in the world. I was shocked when you first mentioned him after you came back."

"I still have trouble believing it myself. And I wouldn't say we're in a relationship; rather we had a whirlwind romance in Egypt. Now, it's getting harder to remember the passion. It's so hard that we can't talk regularly. But we do email every day."

"Does he ever come to the US? New York wouldn't be that hard for you to get to just to see him."

"He hasn't mentioned a US trip to me so far. I'd assume that he comes at times. After all the US still has the largest population of people with enough money to support the work the Foundation does. The Carter Family would almost have to have New York connections."

The door to the staff room opened again and Dan and Tom walked in.

"Good afternoon ladies, how's your day so far?'

"Doing good, thanks, Tom. My class was in the gym for the past forty minutes, so I took advantage to write for a while. But I'm due on lunch duty today. I should get going for that."

"Hey, Kelly, we have tickets to the theatre for Friday night. Want to join Mary and me?" Dan asked

"I'll let you know tomorrow, Dan, if that's ok? I'm supposed to connect with my brother, but he might have to work late. He'll let me know tonight."

"Sure, let me know in the morning when you get in."

Kelly packed up her writing and moved to gather her coat and gloves so she could join the kids outdoors for the lunch break.

Outside it was a beautiful fall day. A bit cool, with a decided nip in the air, but the sun was shining, and if you stayed out of the wind, you could actually be quite warm. Kelly opened her jacket where she was standing. The steps on the side of the school gave her a good view of the yard so she could watch the kids play at lunch time. The other two teachers on yard duty had volunteered to make a complete circuit of the yard for the first while. Kelly would alternate that chore with them.

Kelly relaxed in the sunshine and drifted back to her chat with Neil last night. He had been telling her about some of the new work the Foundation was doing.

****

"Kelly my love, it's so good to see and talk to you."

"You too, Neil. I miss you so much."

"I know, love. I'm hoping to figure out something to get me to New York in a few weeks. Would you meet me there if I can arrange it?"

"I might be able to. Let me know what you can do."

"I will. How is that freelance piece coming along? From the email, it sounded like a great opportunity."

"It's going good so far. I've got another few pages to write. Then it'll be time to edit, edit and edit. I hope to finish it all by next week. Then I can send it to them for a first look."

"Let me know if I can add anything from the Foundation perspective."

"I don't think I'll need that this time. But I'll be looking for quotes from you and Kendra for the travel article I'm writing."

"Anyway I can help, let me know. Speaking of Kendra, I've got to tell you about the stuff they've found in the village. There was a big wind storm again last week. It was very obliging and blew sand away from the area just to the north of the church. We suspected that there was a road of some sort leading away from the church to the north, and now we've found it. The start of it at least. The wind uncovered the front of a building just past where the square currently ends. It's going to take months of excavating to figure out what it all is, but it looks like offices or residences or something. I'll email pictures, once I have them from Kendra. You can imagine how excited she is."

"That's fantastic. I can't believe there is still so much under the sand there. Amazing what it might cover."

"Yeah, for sure. The sand has been blowing around that area for thousands of years. I can only begin to imagine what else is covered all across the desert. There was enough in the Cairo area to keep them busy excavating for hundreds of years. They still find stuff there."

"Yeah, the winds of change for sure."

"Kelly, just a sec, would you?"

Neil turned from the screen to talk to someone else in the room. "Jason, hold on a sec would you? I'm talking to someone; be right with you."

"Sorry, Kelly, that's my cousin Jason. He just got to town for the conference we're attending tomorrow."

"Yeah? Remind me, why are you in Spain?"

"There's a conference held every few years about the Templars. Spain and Portugal were two of the places where they sheltered after the arrests in France. The supposed descendants here like to hold sessions at the university, for like-minded people to study the history of medieval times. Jason is currently finishing up his master's degree and has been invited to speak about the work he's been doing in the Templar world. It's a little outside the traditional view of history, so it will prove a bit controversial to the scholars here. He asked me to come for moral support."

Kelly laughed. "I'm sure it will be interesting. Knowing the Carter Family penchant for what are considered controversial theories, I can only imagine what your cousin has learned."

"It's a combination of a lot of history, rewritten with less bias toward the victor's viewpoint. His basic premise is that the Templars were only destroyed because they threatened to reveal the truth about Jesus and his followers and how inaccurate the bible was in its teachings. Couple that with the fact that most of the kings of the day were in debt to them, and you have a great conspiracy theory that connects the kings of Europe and the Vatican in an effort to maintain their own power and hold over the people. I know Jason wants to work in a major museum. But I think his views might just be a bit too controversial for most to take on. We'll see."

"Sounds like it will be a good couple of days for you."

"Yes, it will. What about you? I think you mentioned Canadian Thanksgiving was coming up soon? Any plans for that?"

"Not yet. I'll talk to my mom in the next week or so and see what she wants to do. Other than that, I might just spend the weekend with Sandy."

"Lucky dog." Neil paused for a few seconds and looked at Kelly. "I miss you so much, Kelly. I can't wait to hold you in my arms again. Is there any chance you could come to England in the next few weeks? Maybe for Christmas?"

"I'd not be able to do anything until at least Christmas at the earliest. I'm just too swamped here between the new curriculum, the freelance work, and family stuff. Sorry, Neil, but I just can't get away, much as I want to see you too."

"Ok. But promise you will think about Christmas? Christmas in Derbyshire?"

"That's sounds intriguing. Let me see what I can do about that."

"I'll send the jet for you, so you don't have to fly coach to get there."

"Neil!"

"Hey, ulterior motive; at least if I send the jet, I know you'll come."

Kelly could hear a voice in the background, "Hey, Neil, we've got to get going to that reception."

"Do you need to get going?"

"Yeah, sorry, Kelly, but there is a reception tonight prior to the conference. Jason wants me to go with him. He needs all the friends he can get amongst these sharks."

"Okay, have a good time"

"I'll try, but you won't be here with me. I'll talk to you soon. I love you, Kelly Taylor. Never forget how much I do."

"Love you too, Neil. Talk to you soon."

****

Kelly looked around the school yard. She wondered if she could figure out a way to get to England for Christmas. It sounded like a wonderful way to see Neil again. She hoped she'd find a way to make it work. Somehow, somewhere, she needed to see Neil again.

PART 2

I

Two Years Later

Kelly unlocked the door to her new home and walked into the front foyer. It was so nice to have the condo completed and be living in it. Sandy greeted her at the door as always.

"Hi, Sandy, I bet you're ready to go for a walk. Let me just change then we can go to the park for a long run."

Sandy wagged her tail like she understood every word Kelly said, and she probably did. At least 'walk' and 'park'. It was an off-leash park, Sandy's favorite place to go, as she could run with all the other dogs. For Kelly it was a great opportunity to meet her new neighbors. Many had proved to be great people to hang out with.

She glanced at the clock on the stove. She would have to be quick tonight. She had agreed to go on a date with Sam, one of the guys she had met at the park. He was there on the weekends with his dog Buster. Buster and Sandy had a great time playing together, since they were about the same size. It was the first time they played that Kelly had met Sam. A good looking guy in his early fifties, he was divorced about ten years ago and had raised a daughter by himself. She had recently left home to go to college in New Brunswick. Sam had found himself alone for the first time and had started going to the park to have some adult conversation outside his day job. Kelly found him easy to talk to and be around. It wasn't the all consuming passion and sparks she had felt with Neil Adams, but it was a nice, enjoyable companionship; and that was perhaps for the best. Grand passion and love just led to heart break. She had enough of that for many lifetimes. A nice safe quiet extended friendship was just what her battered soul needed.

Kelly was startled out of her thoughts by a large paw on the back of her knee. She turned to see Sandy staring at her, with her leash in her mouth.

"All right, Sandy, all right, I'm coming. We'll get to the park."

Chuckling Kelly moved upstairs to her bedroom to change into blue jeans and a t-shirt for the jaunt to the park. A few minutes later, she and Sandy were wandering down the street. Sandy whined quietly as she saw the other three dogs playing. She wanted to join them.

"Okay, Sandy, there you go…have fun with Rusty and Pepper."

Kelly waved at the dog's owners and then settled onto the bench to think about Neil Adams. Why had she thought of him today? Well, it was natural he would be in her thoughts since she was going back to Egypt at long last. She had finally saved up enough money to take a trip back this summer. The school year was almost over, and she was going to take all of August to travel; first England and Europe and then down to visit the village once more. The trip to Europe would prove interesting. Ever since she had met a psychic last Halloween, she had become even more deeply involved in studying the Templars. One aspect of her studies had been the many buildings they had built, most especially the old Templar churches and the castles. Her brother had been equally fascinated in that aspect, as he was an architect and ancient building techniques had always interested him. If he didn't have the same passion and curiosity about the life of the Templars, at least she could talk to him about other aspects of the Templar time. Her fascination had not waned in any way. It was stronger than ever. Her unique experiences in the past two years had shown her how truly tied to the Templars she was.

As to Neil, well, she didn't think she would run across him at the village. From the press coverage, he was busy doing deals for the Carter Family businesses. The last she had seen he was in Buenos Aires with another rich glamorous woman on his arm. They had managed to talk fairly regularly for the first six months after she got home. And there had been the unforgettable trip to the Bahamas at Christmas that first winter. They had originally talked about going to Derbyshire so she could meet his family. At the last minute though, he had changed the plans and said he wanted time for just the two of them. So they had agreed on the Bahamas, which worked well for his travel schedule as he had to be in South America early in the New Year. She had flown down as soon as school finished. He had been in Singapore and arrived in the Bahamas the day after she did. They had spent a glorious week together, celebrating their first Christmas and rang in the New Year, filled with promises.

She let herself drift on the memories, from the first time she had seen him again when he walked into the apartment he had rented.

"Kelly? Where are you darling?"

Kelly was lounging on the balcony in the hot tub that gave her a gorgeous view out over the beach to the ocean.

"Neil? You're here? I didn't expect you so soon." Kelly leapt from the hot tub, grabbing her towel as she made for the balcony door.

"Come here, my love."

"I'll get your clothes soaked!"

"I don't care; they'll dry. I need you in my arms right now."

Kelly quickly complied and walked into his embrace. They simply hugged for a few seconds, then both pulled back a bit to gaze into each other's eyes. He lowered his head, to claim her lips in a kiss filled with longing and need. The passion they had shared in Eykel quickly flared to life between them. Kelly felt Neil reach down to lift her and started back into the apartment, heading unerringly to the master bedroom.

Once there Kelly felt the world tilt yet again, as he placed her on the bed.

"Neil, I'm soaking wet; the bed!"

"Don't worry, darling, the bed will dry too. And you're about to get a whole lot wetter."

Neil leaned over her, and gave her a sound kiss before pulling away to discard his clothes. When he was standing naked beside the bed, Kelly could see the evidence of his need and desire. She shivered with her own need. Neil came toward the bed, sat beside her, and reached out with his hand to caress her face.

"Oh, Kelly, I've missed you so much. I can't tell you how wonderful it is to see you again. I'm sorry to rush you into bed, but I need to make love to you."

"You're not rushing me, Neil. I need to feel you inside me again. Please, Neil, make love to me."

With no more encouragement required, Neil shifted and lay on the bed beside her. He undid the clasp of the bikini top she was wearing to expose her breasts. With one last tender look and caress of her face, he bent to take a nipple in his mouth. Kelly shivered at the flood of feelings coursing through her veins as he explored her breast. After thoroughly tasting and nibbling her left breast, he turned his attention to her right one. By the time he had studied both, she was wet and ready to feel him inside her. She reached out to encircle his erection in her hand. She heard him groan in need.

"Kelly, darling, please don't do that. I can't hold out if you do."

"Don't wait, love. Please, I need you now."

Neil raised his head, stared into her eyes, and then lowered his lips to claim hers. They continued to stare into their eyes, as they fought for the kiss. Passion, need and love exploded between them as it had in the summer. Neil shifted his body so that he was nestled between her legs, and slowly entered her body.

*****

"Hey, Kelly, great to see you and Sandy here today."

Kelly jumped and came back to the present with a jolt. "Oh hi, Sam. Um, sorry just daydreaming. You startled me. I wasn't expecting to see you until later tonight." Kelly hoped she didn't look as flushed as she felt.

"I worked from home, so was able to bring Buster out for a run. Thought I might as well wait 'til you were home. Sandy is still Buster's favorite play buddy. Just look at them."

Kelly looked over to see Sandy and Buster running around like little puppies chasing each other all over the park. It was good to see Sandy so active. She was getting a bit older so the activity was good for her.

"I see what you mean. They're up to their game of tag already. They are such a funny pair to watch."

"That they are. You still good for dinner and a movie tonight?"

"Yup, was just going to let Sandy run for a half hour, then head home to get ready. What time does the movie start?"

"At seven thirty. We can have a quick supper prior to the movie- maybe a drink and dessert after?"

"Sounds good. I haven't been to a movie in so long. I'll probably have to have some popcorn, just for old time's sake."

Sam chuckled. "Rebecca and I had movie dates every couple of weeks depending on what was playing. Popcorn was her favorite treat, smothered in butter of course."

Kelly glanced at her watch. "I better get going so I can get ready for tonight. I'll see you at six?"

"Yup, pick you up at six. See you then."

Kelly picked up Sandy's leash and called to her to come. Sandy looked once over her shoulder at Kelly, made one last dash after Buster, and then obediently ran to her. She attached the leash, and with a passing wave to Sam, moved off to the gate and back to the condo.

As she walked, Kelly drifted back to her memories of Christmas in the Bahamas those long two years past. How well she remembered the passion, as strong as it had been in the summer. She could still recall small details about the trip, like the day they had gone swimming with dolphins. But they had spent most of their time together just being with each other, lying on the beach, wonderful secluded dinners, and making love. Oh how good the sex had been. They had promised to try to get together by Easter at the latest. But their schedules had not meshed. When March Break had come, he had been back in the Middle East and unable to get to Canada. By Easter, she was dealing with her mother who had been ill. The calls started to be further and further apart. The time difference was simply too hard to coordinate. The emails had kept up for another couple of months, but they had gradually stopped too. Kelly was sure that her mundane details of daily life as a teacher had finally convinced him they lived in different worlds. Communication had completely stopped shortly after she had seen a couple of pictures of him with an Eastern European heiress. The press had been quite convinced that wedding bells were in the works for them. The two were from the same world and both were extremely wealthy. Those pictures, along with a few of him escorting actresses to the Cannes Film Festival, had been enough to convince her that there just couldn't be a future for them. Kelly sighed, she still had great memories of her time in Egypt, but the reality of life was that 'grand passion' just didn't seem to be part of her destiny. And frankly she was glad now; her heart had been broken three times already, she didn't think it could handle any more pain. That's why Sam seemed like such a nice option; steady, reliable and no sparks, exactly what she needed.

Later that night, Kelly and Sam were sitting in a bar enjoying a drink and listening to the band playing. He was holding her hand sitting beside her at the bar. She liked the feel of her hand being held by a man again, and Sam's touch was much like Ken's, comfortable and safe. Not at all like the sizzling passion had she felt when Neil touched her. She had dated a bit in the past year, but Sam was the first guy that she felt might have some potential as a longer term relationship.

"I see you're getting tired. Why don't we head home?"

"Thanks, it's been a long week. I had classes all week of course, but I received another positive response to the last query letter I sent on the Templar treasure. So, I now have to write that article. I spent my evenings doing research on the web until the wee hours trying to find new and interesting ways to address the Templars."

"You're getting quite a number of freelance gigs for the Templars, aren't you?"

"Yes, a few. But most of the freelance work has come from my work as a school teacher. It's amazing the number of magazines and online sites that want the input of an elementary school teacher on various topics."

"Think you'll ever give up teaching to write full time?"

"Not likely. The freelance work is paying for my trip this summer, but it doesn't give me enough yet to step away from teaching. I'm still paying off some of the debt that had run up before Ken died. I had no idea he had been spending so much money, but he apparently was into gambling and I knew nothing about it. Luckily when I sold the house and bought the condo I was able to reduce my housing costs and paid off a chunk of the loan."

"You mentioned that before, over coffee, that Ken had been a gambler. I didn't realize that he had left you so tight for money."

"It's not something I like to talk about. It seems unfair to Ken's memory. He was so sick toward the end, I don't know if he was even thinking straight. If I had to guess, I would say he was trying to *hit it big* so that he could leave me money to pay off the house. He was too sick by then to be eligible for any insurance. Unfortunately it didn't work out that way."

"Gambling never does. That's why I ended up divorced. My ex had a gambling and shopping addiction. She would spend everything she made at the gaming tables. Luckily I figured it out early on and separated my pay check from the main bank account. So, she was never able to gamble the household money. But enough of this depressing talk. How about one dance, and then I'll take you home?"

"Sure. They're playing one of my favorite songs."

Sam let go of her hand and slipped out of the bench. He offered her his arm as they made their way to the dance floor. Kelly stepped into his arms for the first time and was surprised by how strong and safe they felt around her. Actually, she was a bit shocked by how *safe* she felt. Sam guided her around the dance floor, gradually bringing her closer to him as they danced, so by the end they were almost melded together. *It feels so good to be held by a man again,* Kelly thought as she closed her eyes and let herself drift with the music. She didn't realize how much she had missed the physical contact of another human being. That was the major drawback of living alone as a widow, the physical touch and presence of another human being. How you learned to crave the sound of the door opening to announce their return home. Sure, Sandy helped some, but she never had learned how to answer Kelly when she needed someone to talk to. Maybe this relationship was something she should let develop and see where it went. No grand passion, but grand companionship, that was the answer she was looking for.

The song ended, and Sam escorted her out of the bar and down the street to his car. He walked to the passenger side to open the door for her. Instead of opening the door though, he pulled her into his arms once more and gently reached down to touch his lips to hers. The sweetness of the kiss was its gentleness and lack of demand. It was a safe kiss, not a passionate kiss. Kelly liked the feel of his lips on hers, but was feeling a bit disappointed that passion didn't flare to life between them. She shook herself, lightening was the last thing she needed. A steady, reliable relationship was what she needed. To be held in a man's arms again was enough.

"Thank you, Kelly, for a wonderful evening. I've wanted to kiss you now for months. I'm glad I finally got the courage up to ask you out."

"Me too, Sam. Thanks for a great night."

"I'd like to invite you to my place for supper tomorrow night. Rebecca is coming home for a few weeks before she heads off to her summer job. I'd like you two to meet."

"Um, are you sure? After all it's been one date."

"One date sure, but we've been friends for a lot longer than that; it's been a few months since you started to come to the dog park. So, yes, to answer your question, I want you and Rebecca to meet."

"Okay, supper it is."

Sam opened the car door and let her slip in, a Volvo; the car was much like Sam, safe and comfortable. Sam got in and drove Kelly home. When he got to her place, he parked in the driveway and immediately reached over to her to kiss her again. This kiss was much like the first, but slightly more demanding and searching. He moved his tongue across her lips, challenging her to explore with her own tongue. Of its own volition, her tongue met his in the challenge. The kiss quietly became full of promise.

Sam drew away from her. "I better let you go now. If I don't I may try to convince you to come home with me, so I can make love to you. I don't think either of us is ready for that yet. I know I'm not. I haven't made love to anyone in a long time. I need time to adjust to having you in my life."

Kelly lowered her eyes, partially in relief that he had pulled away. She knew that it would be unwise to make love to him yet. She was still not over her relationship with Neil. She didn't want to lead Sam into believing that more might exist for them.

"Yes, I agree with you. It is too soon yet."

"Hey, why don't you bring Sandy with you tomorrow? She and Buster can entertain each other while we talk."

"Sandy would love that. Thanks for thinking of it. She doesn't like it when I'm away so much. The only thing I don't like about traveling this summer is leaving Sandy behind. But my brother and his kids love her, so I know she'll be in good hands. Still I'll miss her terribly." Kelly contemplated the summer away and mentally shook herself back to the present, when her thoughts strayed to Eykel, and the possibility of seeing Neil again. "Okay then, I'll see you tomorrow. What time? And what can I bring?"

"Why don't you come over around five? The only thing I don't have in plentiful supply is wine. I'm a beer man, so if you bring wine you like, that would be great."

"Okay sounds good. And again, thanks for a great evening, Sam. I've enjoyed myself." Kelly then leaned over and gave

Sam a light kiss on the cheek, then pulled open the door and hurried toward her house.

Sam muttered to himself as she slid from the car, *well that went better than I expected. Buster buddy, I think I've found the answer to both our needs; Kelly and Sandy. I think we're going to have overnight guests tomorrow. I sure plan to have Kelly in bed tomorrow night; naked and slick with sweat.* Sam waited until she was inside the house before putting his car into reverse and heading the few blocks to his house.

II

A few weeks later

Kelly awoke in the morning and looked around, her surroundings feeling a bit dazed. *It always takes me so long to come to in the morning, especially in a strange setting.* She had finally agreed to stay overnight at Sam's place; the first time since they had started dating. Oh they had made love in the past few weeks, but she had always left before midnight; she hadn't been ready for the commitment of waking up with him in the morning. But last night, she had decided it was time to stay. After all she was leaving in just a few days for her summer trip, so she saw no harm in staying. She looked over at Sam. He was still sound asleep, sprawled out over half the bed. On the floor Sandy and Buster were laying curled up together on the dog bed in the corner of the room. *Funny how they have bonded so much in the past few weeks.* They were almost inseparable.

She wanted to avoid waking Sam, so she slipped from the bed as quietly as she could. Both dogs looked at her and rose. She gently padded from the bedroom with the dogs following. Buster looked longingly at the back door, with a pleading look in his eyes.

"You got to go, buddy? Okay, I'll let you both out."

She slid the back door open to allow them out and then turned back toward the kitchen. She knew that Sam loved coffee in the morning, so she set about to make that. She went back to the sliding door as she saw Sandy standing by it. Better get them before they started barking and woke Sam.

She contemplated Sam. How comfortable the relationship had become for her. It was easy going for both of them. It was a good one and didn't require either of them to make any major commitment, which suited her just fine. She was quite happy to maintain her own space and her own schedule during the week. Weekends they spent together for the most part. He had been helping her with some of her research work on the Templars too. Thinking of research, Kelly knew she only had time for a quick cup of coffee before taking Sandy back home, so she could shower. She had an appointment with her hypnotist at eleven am this morning. This would be her last one before she headed off to Europe. The work with the hypnotist had started as a lark after last Halloween and an unexpected meeting with a psychic. But since then, it had become a serious research tool for her. Turned out that her own subconscious held much of the knowledge and information she needed for her Templar articles.

Kelly wandered out to the solarium with her cup of coffee in hand and drifted back to that Halloween night, almost nine months ago now. She had become depressed again over the summer and fall. Looking back, she could see that she had retreated from life as she had when Ken had died. The pain of losing Neil had sent her right back into the same grief spiral that had threatened to engulf her in the past. Of course she didn't recognize it at the time, but now she knew the signs that should have alerted her to the situation. *Hindsight is twenty-twenty*, she thought. And that withdrawal was why she would never trust again in love and passion. She had proven to herself many times now that she wasn't destined for grand love. So why put herself through the agony ever again of trusting her heart. No, this grand companionship she had with Sam was exactly the right answer. Her thoughts drifted to that Halloween night.

*****

"Hey, Kelly, I'm so glad you're coming out with us tonight. I hate seeing you cooped up inside all the time."

"Thanks for the invite, Dan. I do appreciate it."

"It was Mary's idea to get you to come along. She thought you might be intrigued by the guy who's going to be there. He's a psychic. She knew with all your articles on the Templars that you might be interested in what he had to say."

"I've never seen a psychic before, so it will be interesting-especially on Halloween."

"Yes, I expect so, and that's why Wayne arranged it for tonight. The psychic is a friend of his. He usually doesn't do group sessions like this, but made an exception for Wayne."

"Should be fun."

They arrived at Wayne's house, and quickly all the guests were settled in the basement.

"Hey everyone, glad you could all make it for this party. I'm happy to introduce my friend Barry to you all. Barry is a great psychic and I thought it would be fun, on this All Hallows Eve, to open up the gates between our world and the spirit world with Barry's help. Barry, it's all yours."

"Thanks, Wayne. Hello to you all. Thanks for coming to-night. I don't usually work in such a large group, but I'm hoping that the spirits will still come to me and provide us all some insight to our futures. Just to let you know, when spirit talks through me, I don't have any recollection of what has been said. It's like my own personality is shunted aside, and the spirit takes over. Therefore, I record the sessions, so I have some inkling of what I've said. I hope this is okay with everyone? Great, so let me get started. Wayne, if you please, can you dim the lights."

The next hour flew by for the group. Barry's connection with spirit was incredibly strong, and he gave some interesting information to all about the power of love and how alike we all really were, souls inhabiting human bodies. About half way through, there came a change in Barry's posture, as if a new spirit had joined him. At this point he started giving some more specific information to people in the room. A few were messages from departed loved ones that were received in joy and tears by the guests. Then Barry grew extremely quiet, and his demeanor changed yet again.

"I'm getting a message for Kelly. Is she here?"

Startled, Kelly answered, "Yes, I'm here."

"This is a message from your father. He simply says that he loves you, and that he wants you to always remember to follow your heart. He hates seeing you so withdrawn from life. He says that you have a mission to accomplish, and you need to follow your heart, not your head, in order to move forward. Don't settle, he says. Grand love is worth the risk. Don't settle."

Kelly gulped and blinked back tears. Beside her Mary reached over and grabbed her hand.

"I know, it's quite startling to get a message like that, isn't it?"

"Yes."

"Kelly, I have further guidance for you," said Barry, but this time with a commanding voice and presence. Barry even looked different almost like he had become a soldier. For a brief moment as Kelly looked at him, she could see the image of a stern knight imposed on him or perhaps to her fancy the image of Archangel Michael.

"Kelly, you have the knowledge within you to unlock the treasure. Hunt for it. The time is now to reveal it to the world. Find your soul; find your mate. Together you will conquer that which felled you both. Trust your instincts to lead you to the Templar."

Barry subsided again and seemed to deflate a bit in stature. "I'm now being asked to provide a message to Kit Kat from her sister; is she here?"

Kelly sat back in amazement at the two messages she had been given. The first from her father was like most of the others; reassurance from departed loved ones that all was well, and that they were still loved. The second message was altogether different and had a distinct martial tone to it, along with an impulse to dig deeper. She had let her studies into the Templar life slide in the past few months. Somehow it hadn't seemed quite as exciting in the past six months, ever since she and Neil lost touch. She had decided there wasn't much purpose to continue the studies since she wasn't likely to ever go back to Europe or the Middle East again. Now here she was being told to pursue that work again; to find her soul? Conquer something that felled her? What on earth was that about? She shook her head; probably just Barry's way of adding tension to the session. She wondered why he had picked her for that particular role.

About thirty minutes later Barry was winding up his session. The final message to come through had been, "Love in its many forms is the core of the spiritual being. With love thee can leave behind the trappings and ego of the living world, thy schoolroom. Love can transport thee to the highest levels of consciousness."

The guests watched as Barry seemed to shrink before them again. Kelly blinked her eyes a few times, figuring the misty area around Barry was just a reaction from sitting in the darkened room so long. She turned to look at Mary sitting beside her, who was doing the same thing.

"Mary, are you seeing the same thing I am? Like a mist surrounding Barry?"

"Yeah, you mean it's not just me? I could have sworn I saw another being imposed on Barry a number of times. The one that impressed me the most, was almost like a knight or soldier when he was talking to you."

"Okay, now I'm spooked. I saw the same thing; a knight or even the image of Archangel Michael. Did Wayne burn some strange incense or other things down here prior to us arriving?"

"No way, not Wayne. He's completely straight up; doesn't drink or smoke, and I know he hates drugs. So, no, this must have been something we were both seeing. Maybe we should ask Barry about it."

"No, that's all right. I don't want to know."

"Well, I do, so I'm going to ask him."

*****

Kelly broke out of her reverie. She fingered the Saint Michael medallion that she now wore. It had been her father's, and she had found it again in her jewelry right after the Halloween party. It had seemed a strange coincidence that it reappeared so soon after the party. She clearly remembered her dad wearing it most of the times he went out to sea. It was a silver oval depicting Saint Michael slaying a dragon, with the words *Saint Michael, Pray for Us* embossed on it. She found great comfort when she wore it and felt the Archangel had become her protector. That fateful Halloween night had been the first time she had been given such strong direction to continue her pursuit of the Templar lore. Since then she had become immersed in Templar research, including seeing the psychic a couple of times, and at his suggestion she had visited a hypnotist that specialized in past life regressions. She had a nodding acquaintance with the notion of past lives from reading about Edgar Cayce after Ken had died. The theory had not provided her any comfort at the time of Ken's passing, and actually was totally opposite of her own education in the Catholic Church. She did find the concept much more intriguing now, but still at war with her faith. However, she had now done further research, most especially reading some of Dr. Brian Weiss's books and was able to admit that the subconscious held mysteries unknown to man. So whether past lives actually existed or if it was vivid fantasy created by the mind to protect itself, she was curious when it was suggested she try hypnotism. The first couple of sessions with Dr. Klein had been quite disappointing, at least from a Templar viewpoint. She had experienced only great sadness as a result of early death; both times in childbirth before her eighteenth birthday. But then about two months ago, she had experienced a brief glimpse into the Templar age. She had been a knight in about 1130 in France. She, or rather he, was being dubbed and admitted to a new order of chivalry that was just getting formed. It was the origins of the Knights Templar. She had quickly jumped from the scene of the knighting ritual to the death of that same knight. It had happened about ten years later, in a battle far from his home. His death had not been easy, but the peace that was felt after the end was truly amazing. She was still not convinced this was truly past life experiences. She believed that her subconscious was taking the threads of her research and providing a dream to give her some ideas of how to proceed.

That particular session had indeed spurred Kelly to complete more research into the origins of the Templars and especially the knighting ceremony. She now planned to put that research to the test when she visited England and the Middle East in a few weeks. She glanced at the clock and was startled to see it was already eight; time for her to get moving. She wandered into the kitchen, found paper and pen, wrote a quick note to Sam, then called Sandy and left.

III

Kelly was waiting in the reception area of Dr. Klein's office. It was eleven a.m. and she was relaxing while she waited for Dr. Klein to finish with her last patient. These Saturday hours were a boon for Kelly, as she didn't have to take any time from school to be able to attend. The door to the office opened, and Dr. Klein appeared escorting another patient.

"Cass, can you please take Mrs. Hollis here to the quiet room. I'm sure she would benefit from a nice cup of tea and a bit of relaxation before she leaves today."

"Certainly, Dr. Klein, and your next patient is here, Ms. Taylor."

"Yes, Kelly, good to see you again; it's been a while since your last appointment. How have you been in the past couple of months?"

After Dr. Klein shook her hand, she led her back into the office for her session.

"Dr. Klein, it's nice to see you. I've been doing great, just busy getting ready for this trip to Europe. I also wanted some time to assimilate what I learned in that last session. To dream of a Knights Templar in the 1100's was a bit startling. I needed to process the implications of it, especially as it relates to my free-lance work and research of the Templars."

"Yes, I suppose so. Have you garnered any further insight? Have you come to terms with past lives?"

"Not too much, although I did try to find some historical evidence to support what I saw and learned. But nothing concrete has come up yet. I did find a number of Templar records of who had been members, but there are so many with the same or similar names, it's hard to tell if any of them was the one I saw."

"Why don't we get settled for today's session and see where your soul and inner wisdom leads you. I admit I've been truly fascinated by the images you've been finding. They are more vivid than most patients have. I'm curious as to why that is."

"Really? They feel like normal dreams to me. I don't know, maybe that message I got through Barry has something to do with it? After that Halloween night I've seen a number of references to Archangel Michael. He seems to crop up in a lot of my work these days. Not to mention finding this Saint Michael medallion of my dad's."

"Not likely a coincidence in that. But let's see how this session goes. So, why don't you settle into the chair, and take a deep breath in and out, closing your eyes, and narrowing your senses to the feelings in your body. That's right, feel yourself sink deeper into the chair, calm your mind, and let your consciousness guide you to the images that you need to see. Kelly, I want you to let your mind wander free of constraints. You can travel to anywhere, anyplace or anytime you want. Awaken the memories of long ago to see what they lead you to."

"I'm in a church, walking down an aisle."

"Look at yourself, how are you dressed?"

"I am dressed for a wedding. My name is Eleanor Carter, and I'm from a prominent English family. My soon-to-be husband is waiting at the top of the aisle for me."

"What year is it?"

"I think it's around 1710."

"Okay Kelly, let the scene take you where it will. This is obviously a momentous occasion in your life as Eleanor, follow it along."

IV

1710 London, England

Eleanor looked down the aisle at her future husband standing tall and proud at the front of the church. How she had come to love this man in the past few weeks. He had been chosen by her father as the man she would marry, regardless of her own feelings. As he had been studying abroad when she made her debut last year, he hadn't been included in the round of parties she had attended. He had recently returned home, just before their betrothal was announced. But Eleanor had been raised from a young age knowing that she would have little choice in her marriage partner. Women were rarely given a choice, and she knew that considerations of connections would always play a role in her marriage. But she was content given her chosen husband was a kind and wonderful man.

She progressed down the aisle of Temple Church in London. How appropriate that she be married in this specific church. Generations of Carters had been married within these walls. With the recent death of her older brother, she was now the heir to the Carter family and its myriad secrets. She knew that her new husband was chosen specifically because of his long family ties to the Carter family and its Templar roots. His name was Robert Geoffrey Brock, soon to be Brock-Carter. He was the youngest son of Sir Raymond Brock a long-time friend and colleague of her father. The families had agreed that with the death of her elder brother Geoffrey, it was important to the continuation of their mutual Templar heritage that the families be joined yet again in marriage, and that Robert would take on the style of the Carter Family to ensure its continuation through their own children.

As she reached the front of the church she turned to Robert and listened with half an ear to the bishop as he started into the marriage ceremony. She raised her eyes to find him watching her intensely. She became lost in his gaze, as she always did. There was something about this man that spoke to her of long-held feelings; deep feelings that she had never experienced before. Eleanor was startled from her connection to Robert by the bishop reading the banns. She knew the ceremony was a mixture of Church of England and Templar rituals that would join her and Robert in the sacred vows of the Templars.

"Robert Geoffrey, thou hast come here today to be joined to this woman in the union of marriage. Doth thou promise to God and our dear Lady Mary to contract honorable marriage with this woman?"

"I do."

"Eleanor Katrine, thou hast been brought here today to be joined to this man in marriage. Doth thou promise to God and our dear Lady Mary to contract marriage with this man and join your purpose to his for the greater glory of God?"

"I do."

"By these words I acknowledge the commitments thou hast both made to the great glory of the work of God. I commend thee both for the good works thou shalt complete in the years ahead as a joined pair and in the blessings of future generations borne of this union. In the name of Lord Jesus and Lady Mary, may you continue to protect the future as man and wife."

Eleanor looked again at Robert, only to find that his gaze had drifted to her lips and his head was descending for the chaste kiss that was allowed them now as man and wife. Little did she expect the shock that went through her body at the mere touching of his lips to hers. Judging by his reaction, he too was feeling the power of the connection between them.

They progressed down the aisle to the happy congratulations of friends and family. They would all meet again at the Carter home in London for the rest of the day's festivities.

*****

Later that night at close to midnight, Eleanor and Robert were escorted by Sir Raymond Brock through the streets of London for one additional ceremony to finalize their binding to the ancient Temple Guardians. Eleanor had only learned of the fascinating history of her own family in the past few months since her brother had died. Imagine being able to trace their roots right back to the last days of the Knights Templar; a fascinating side to the family that had surprised her to no end. And tonight, she and Robert would be bound in honor to the same oaths those past generations of Carters and Brocks had taken. They were to be the Carter guardians and pass on that same loyalty to their own children.

"Robert and Eleanor, you are soon going to be bound to the heritage of the Guardians of the Temple, and by connection to the Knights Templar. This ceremony should rightly take place at your own chapel in Derbyshire, Eleanor, but we dare not wait for your return there. Your Father is very ill, and may not survive the trip to the country. So, we are going to dedicate you both here in the city and complete the full investiture when you arrive at your home chapel."

"Yes Father, you've explained that to us already. What I want to know, yet again, is why we are only learning now of this heritage of our combined families?"

"It has ever been that the heir is the only one provided such instruction. It was felt that divulging the true history of our families to more than one could lead to untold disaster. The secrets of the Templar treasure are simply too hard won to risk it falling into the wrong hands. You only have to study history, as it was written by the victors, to understand the implications of being on the wrong side of the Kings of Europe and the Vatican. Secrecy has always been our best defense to protect all that the Templars accomplished."

"So, my elder brother knew all of this?" queried Eleanor.

"Yes, my dear, he did, as does Robert's older brother Godfrey. Through him, and you two, the Templar legacy will live on after your father and I have passed on. At one time we thought to marry you Eleanor to Godfrey. But this union is proving to be the far better one for all concerned."

Robert looked at Eleanor. Eleanor looked into his eyes and couldn't agree more with that comment. Yes, Robert Brock-Carter definitely suited her as a husband. They all remained quiet for the next few minutes as the carriage continued to rumble through the streets of London. Shortly it stopped moving.

"It is not permitted for you to identify our location at this time. So, I will guide you each blindfolded into the building. Please trust that we do this for your own protection."

Both of them nodded their assent to the procedure. They were guided from the carriage and walked for a long time being turned left and right, and guided both up and down stairs to reach their final destination. As they stopped, the blindfolds were removed. Eleanor looked around the room they were in. It was evidently a chapel dedicated to Archangel Michael. His image was prominently displayed at four points around the room, which she assumed were the cardinal points. In the dim candlelight she could make out eight people standing around the room; four at those same places directly under the Michael images and the other four standing at one side, close to an altar.

"Masters all, I am Sir Raymond Brock. I have the honor to represent my brother in arms, Sir Richard Carter. We wish to present for dedication his heir Eleanor Katrine de Carter and her husband, my own son Robert Geoffrey Brock Carter. They have been joined in matrimony this day, as is our custom with a female heir. They are now prepared to dedicate their lives to the Guardians of the Temple and raise their heir to the service of God, the Lord Jesus, and his beloved Lady Mary. Will you accept these two as the heirs of the Carter Family?"

"Sir Raymond, we have studied the documents you provided to prove the legitimacy of these two, along with the formal declaration of Eleanor as the sole surviving heir to the Carter line. We are sorrowed to learn of the death of Sir Geoffrey Carter; he had much potential. It is the judgment of this council that Eleanor de Carter and Robert Brock Carter are suitable heirs for the Carter line. Please present these two for their dedication."

At Sir Raymond's prompting Eleanor and Robert moved forward into the circle of the four masters and knelt in the center facing the other masters.

"Robert Brock Carter, you have been brought to this place to confirm your dedication to be a Guardian of the Temple. This oath will place on you the burdens of secrecy and service to the great glory of God. Are you willing and able to provide such a dedication."

"I am and I will."

"Your recently espoused wife is the heir to the Carter line. Do you promise in faith to raise your heir to the same dedication the Carter family has shown through the untold years?"

"I am and I will, on behalf of my wife and I."

"Eleanor de Carter, you have been presented to us as the sole surviving heir to the Carter family. Have you been apprised of your role as mentor to the next generation of Carters?"

"I have."

"Are you willing to make the same dedication as your husband to be the mother of a Guardian of the Temple?"

"I am and I will."

"Then by the power of this council, and in the presence of Archangel Michael our patron and guardian, we accept the dedication of Robert Brock Carter and Eleanor de Carter as the heirs to the Carter line. Sir Robert, arise now and become a Guardian of the Temple. Eleanor de Carter, arise and join thy husband in the protection of the next generation of Guardians."

Sir Raymond then came forward to join Eleanor and Robert and led them through another door that exited the chapel.

"I am glad that's done. Now we can provide you all the information you need to complete your roles as Guardians. But,

I think more importantly, tonight is your wedding night. It's past time that I had you both home so you can consummate this marriage and get started on breeding those heirs we so badly need."

Eleanor found herself blushing as she looked at Robert. How well she remembered her mother's instructions regarding the marriage bed. It sounded like an uncomfortable business, but her mother assured her that the pleasures of the marriage bed after the first time were well worth the effort. Given how she had felt when Robert had kissed her earlier today, she wanted to see how it continued.

"Yes, Father, I will be most earnest in my duty to breed an heir; a part of the service to the Guardians that I will faithfully and frequently uphold." Robert gave a playful wink to his father, and then looked down at Eleanor.

"Yes, a duty that I'll have no trouble fulfilling with this woman at my side." He then stopped; pulled Eleanor into his arms, and bent his head to claim her lips in a kiss of searing passion. Eleanor felt her legs go weak as Robert pulled her close. She could feel his desire as it throbbed to life against her. She shuddered, oh yes; she was looking forward to the marriage bed.

"Come, Robert. I had best get you home with your bewitching wife."

Dr. Klein's office, present day.

"Kelly, listen to me, I think you have uncovered some important information for now. Can you review the balance of this life to see what else of significance occurs?"

"I can see her later in life, old and frail. Robert died many years ago, leaving her to raise three children. Now their son

Geoffrey is finally old enough to carry on the family traditions. Her dedication to serve the Guardians is almost at an end. She passes away gently in the midst of her family. I pause to review this life. I am satisfied in what was accomplished. Robert and I were together only for five years, but we had a truly loving relationship; soul mates reunited for a short time to accomplish a necessary mission. We were successful protecting the treasure and ensuring the continuation of the Carter family, vital to the service of Temple and Guardians. We have kept hidden the truth of the treasure until we are together once more, and the time is right to reveal all."

"Can you tell me more, Kelly?"

"No, the future is hidden from me yet, but I know that things are moving forward rapidly. Robert will soon be back again in my life to forge the next link in the broken chain. I think he might be Neil, another Carter man."

"Kelly, I want you to relax. There is no need to be agitated by what you have discovered. Let yourself sink deeper into your body. Allow your mind to detach from the emotion. Simply view what is before you as a movie. Breathe deep. It is time to awaken you from this session. Simply relax in peace and allow yourself to become conscious of your body again. Come back to conscious thought and awake refreshed."

Kelly drifted back to full consciousness and became aware of her surroundings again. She could feel the cool air of the air conditioning washing over her. She gradually opened her eyes to find Dr. Klein watching her intently.

"How do you feel, Kelly? That was an intense memory that you opened today."

"I don't quite know what to think right now. Is this truly a past life or is it just my subconscious pulling together fragments of my research with my upcoming trip back to the place where I first met Neil?"

"I can tell you from my experience that most vivid ones like this are truly past life episodes. But whatever the truth of the matter, you've been given special insight. How you choose to interpret it or utilize it is up to you, as it is for all my clients. The truth we will probably never know for sure, as it's almost impossible to find historic evidence of these insights. But the impact of the findings is no less concrete for being unable to confirm the true facts."

"I hadn't considered it in those terms. I suppose if it's real to me, then it's real. And what actions I take based on it are the true test of the knowledge I've gained, by whatever source it comes."

Dr. Klein simply waited for Kelly to process what she had just learned.

After a few minutes of silence, Kelly looked at her. "I just don't know what I think yet. I keep going in circles. My Catholic upbringing is so firmly entrenched; we live once and only once. Heaven is for our soul to pass on to once we have proven that we have completed good deeds in life. And yet the memories I have are so intense and clear, that I can't believe they aren't part of who I am. I guess I'll just let the information settle inside me, and see what actions I end up taking. I thank you for finding time for me today. It's been interesting."

"My pleasure, Kelly. Enjoy your trip overseas. I hope you come back with a new appreciation for the history that you've glimpsed."

"Thanks, Dr. Klein. See you when I get back from Europe in the fall."

V

A few weeks later

Kelly followed the young guide from the visitor center out into the Templar village. She had finally arrived in Egypt, and this was her first time back at Eykel. She had been surprised by the number of additional buildings that had been added to the model in the center. They had certainly been busy during the last two years in excavating the village. But something in the model didn't '*feel right*' to Kelly. She couldn't pinpoint why she felt that way, but something about the identity of the buildings just didn't seem right to her.

Jason, Neil's cousin, was her guide. She recognized his name from way back when she had talked to Neil. Jason had been just finishing up his masters at that time. That completed he was now working here rather than in a museum. Neil had mentioned that it would be a challenge for him to get a job in his traditional field as his theories weren't mainstream enough for the general public. The group wandered into what was dubbed now the 'Town Square'.

"From here you can see the three buildings that were critical to the life of the Templars at the time. Behind us is the Church, to the left is the old Abbey ruins, and to the right is the Banking Hall. Each of these buildings was a key element in the Templar daily life. The Templars themselves lived in the Abbey. They were considered a monastic order, so were celibate. The Abbey provided them living quarters where they could live in their monastic isolation. However, a village this size required many people to operate it. So, there were a number of housing developments. Some occupied by husbands and wives. Others were more barrack style to house unmarried people. We don't have concrete evidence yet, but we believe that both young men and women served different duties in the village."

Kelly nodded in affirmation at that last piece of information. She knew that young girls had worked in the village. Again she was struck by the positive vibration within her that knew this to be true.

"Let's move forward from here. As this is an introductory tour, we will not visit the buildings in any detail at this time. You all are scheduled for at least a week's stay. There will be plenty of time to visit each site in depth. So, let's move onto the next major avenue that we have been excavating since the first part was exposed by a wind storm a couple of years ago. Please follow me to the main street of commerce here in the village."

Jason turned and moved down a street between the Abbey and the Church. This had not been uncovered when Kelly had last been here, but she remembered Neil telling her about the find when they had talked. As she moved down the street, she saw that more buildings had been uncovered behind the church. These were all one or two story buildings that looked like they had been shops of some sort in the past. As Kelly passed the third building in the group, she suddenly had a vision of a butcher shop in the 'window' of the building. The next shop to her mind was a leather shop, including boots. Kelly shuddered as she passed each building. She had the strongest feeling of déjà vu as she moved down the street. As they paused in the middle of the street Jason continued.

"As of yet we haven't identified any of the uses for these buildings. The speculation is they may have been residences for the senior administrative people in the Templars."

Kelly held up her hand, "Could they have been shops? I get a strange feeling that the one behind us was a butcher shop and the next one was for leather-making. Is there a smithy farther down here? It seems like there should be one."

"I'm sorry, I'm just bad with names, and you are?"

"I'm Kelly Taylor."

"Kelly, we haven't figured out for sure the use of these buildings, but you raise a viable consideration. In fact, our head Neil Adams also feels these are shops, but the archeologists aren't yet convinced. As to a smithy? You are correct; the last building in the street is a smithy. We found evidence of all the necessary tools of that trade, including the forge that would have been used to heat the steel for the horse shoes. This last building is on the edge of what we feel was the village proper. The stable would have been an easy walk from here around the outskirts of the town. Why don't we walk around that way to the stables? They are an incredible structure, hardly surprising since a Templar Knight's life frequently relied on the ability and training of his horses."

Jason led the way farther down the street. They continued to pass more 'shops' that fed the imagination of what they would have housed when the village was a going concern. As they got to the end of the street, Kelly felt another powerful feeling of déjà vu. She 'knew' this place. She walked right up to the door of the smithy and looked inside. She blinked in confusion and looked away. Turning back, her 'vision' wasn't improved; right in front of her was a large horse's head. She could smell the sweet aroma of hay that the horse was contentedly munching. Further into the smithy she saw a young man working bellows to keep a fire going at the forge. Another man was bent over a horse, with a foot between his legs, pounding away with a hammer.

Kelly stepped back in shock. She couldn't imagine where that image came from, but it had been like she was seeing ghosts of people inside the smithy. She shuddered in fear and apprehension. The rest of the group took a quick look at the smithy and then moved on down to the end of the street and turned left to walk toward the stables. Kelly started to lag behind the group. As she walked she could feel a rope in her hand. The rope pulled to the right as if something beside her stopped suddenly. She turned to see what was behind her. She got the sense of a large war horse stopping to scratch his side. Then the horse turned back to her, nuzzled at her shoulder, and then buffeted her with his big head. She could feel the breath from his nostrils, as he searched her for a treat. Or rather him? She felt like a young man. She staggered feeling dazed; *what is going on? I don't know this place, and yet? I've been here?* She stopped, shaking in her shoes, and tried to take some deep breaths to steady herself.

Jason looked back at her. "Kelly, are you all right? You look so pale."

"I don't know. I'm having the strangest feelings of déjà vu. More than I felt in London. It's like nothing I've ever experienced before. I can almost feel and see things around me, that aren't here?"

"Déjà vu? Like you've been here before?"

"Yes, exactly like that. I know this route. It leads around the back side of the village, past a couple of small hotels, past the barrack residences for the boys, and then to the stables just inside the west gate of the town."

"Kelly, you're describing exactly where we're going. How did you know?"

"I've no idea, Jason, but I'm pretty scared right now. I don't know what's going on. I've never been in this section before. I only visited the church, abbey, and banking hall last time I was here."

"Okay, I'm going to call Kendra to get her out here. I think this is important for her to hear. Can you make it to the stables? There's what we think was a head groom's office where you can sit down until Kendra gets here."

"Yes, I can make that."

Jason escorted Kelly the rest of the way to the stables with the balance of the group. "Everyone, if you can just wait here outside the stables for a minute. Kelly is feeling a bit unwell. I'm just going to take her to the groom's office so she can rest a few minutes. I've already called for another guide to take you on the rest of the tour."

Jason helped Kelly into the cool of the stables. Kelly leaned on his arm in disbelief. "This isn't an office; it's the main tack room. The office was upstairs. We kept all the saddles and bridles in here."

Jason looked at Kelly and helped her sit down on a bench at the side of the room.

"This is where I did minor repairs to tack. Anything major we took to the leather shop, but here we could do some work.

We were all expected to know every stitch in the tack and inspect it for wear every day. The lives of our knights depended on the tack being in good repair."

"It's okay, Kelly; tell me more about your life here."

Kelly continued as if in a trance. "I'm young, no more than 15. My name is Gerard. My older brother is here with me, well not actually my brother, but we were raised as such. It's his gear I attend to. I had begged him to take me with him when he joined the Templar order. At first he refused and left our home to come here by himself. But his father and my mother died a few years later. I was left to the care of his father's brother, but he treated me as a slave since I wasn't of his blood. I was just another mouth to feed, and he didn't want me around. My brother came back a year after my parents died. I begged him again to take me with him. He was now high up in the order, having progressed fast. He was being sent here in order to be groomed as the new Commander. I asked him to take me on as a squire. As I was not nobly born, I knew I could not be knighted, but I could still serve in the Templars as a squire. I wanted this more than anything. He finally agreed to bring me. I've been here for more than two years now. I love the life in the village. I love tending to Godfrey's horses. They are so gentle with me. I'm happy in this place."

Kelly returned to the present to find that she was making motions like she was cleaning a piece of leather. She looked up at Jason and found that Kendra had come in while she was lost in another lifetime.

"Oh my god. What is happening to me?"

"Hi, Kelly, I'm glad to see you back here. I knew when you and Neil hit it off so well, that you had to have a Templar background somewhere in your past. I think it's resurfacing now that you're back in what I'll call 'familiar surroundings'. Jason, this is Kelly Taylor, the woman that Neil talked about so much a couple of years ago. I knew they had lost touch. Kelly, this is Jason Carter, one of Neil's cousin's boys."

"Kelly, I'm pleased to meet you. Cousin Neil talked of you for a very long time. He still mentions you every once in a while when he comes here. I think he stays away 'cause the memories here are too hard for him."

"Jason, sshhh, Kelly doesn't need to hear all of that right now. What we need to do is give her some time to recover, and then find out how we can work with her to help uncover more of the mysteries of this place. Like the cemetery for the knights and the horses. We still haven't located those."

Kelly closed her eyes to see the picture of the village in her mind's eye. "The cemetery for the Templar Knights was outside the east wall. It was closest to the route to the Holy Land. The knights' best horses were buried in the same general area, out the east gate. The rest of the villagers were buried outside the south wall; mass graves in some cases when disease went through the village."

Kelly watched as Jason and Kendra looked at her and then each other. She could tell they were silently communicating between themselves.

"What are you two thinking?"

After a moment, she saw Kendra nod. Jason spoke up, "Well, you are the first person to give us any concrete ideas about the village. Perhaps you have an old soul that actually lived here and are unconsciously taping into those memories?"

Kelly gaped at them in disbelief. "An old soul? What are you talking about?" But inwardly, Kelly was frightened. What had Barry said to her last fall? '*Trust your instincts to lead you to the Templar.*' Could this be what he had been talking about?

Kendra reached over to place comforting hand on her shoulder. "Kelly, I think you've had enough for one day. I've never experienced the déjà vu that you've just had, but I've been around a couple of mediums in my time. They always end up exhausted after their sessions. I suspect that you're going to feel fatigue settle quickly. I think we should get you back to your hotel. Are you staying at the Foundation's place?"

"No, I'm at the little one that is down in the town square. I fell in love with it when I was here two years ago. I wanted to come back to it. But before I go there, and I agree, I am starting to feel some fatigue, could I go visit the church? Neil had shown me the view from the tower when I was here. I think I can pinpoint the location of the cemetery for you from that perspective."

Jason replied, "Sure, Kelly, I can take you up the tower. Cousin Neil took me up for the first time a year ago when I started working at the Foundation after I finished my masters. I know the power of the view from up there. As long as you're sure you're up to the climb. It's a long way up."

"I remember. I'm sure it's easier now. Neil had talked about getting the stairs repaired for easier access to the top. I'll make it up. Besides I do want to see that view again."

"Yes, it is ready for tours now. It's taken almost two years to get a stone mason to rework the stairs and to have the tower completely cleared for safety concerns. Why don't we go there now, then I'll take you back to your hotel myself. Assuming Kendra that you can find someone to take the rest of my tour work today? I think it best that I make sure Kelly is okay after her experiences today."

"Yes, I agree. I'll clear your schedule for the rest of the day. Make sure Kelly eats when you get back to town. She'll likely need it."

The three of them moved out of the stables and back into the main streets of the village. The stables were on the farthest reaches of the walled portion of the town. The walk back to the town square took them a few minutes. Once in the town square, Jason guided Kelly toward the church.

Kendra turned away towards the main office and commented, "Kelly, I hope you'll excuse me, but I've a couple of calls to make. Jason will escort you up the church and back to town when you're done. If you need anything from us in the next few days, please call me. I haven't seen your itinerary for the week, but I'll look it up. I'm probably going to shuffle some things around. I think you need to have Jason with you at all times. If you have more of the déjà vu, it's important to have someone with you who'll recognize what is happening immediately." Kendra gave Jason a significant nod. He understood the underlying message. One of the calls was going to be to Neil. He just hoped Neil dropped everything and came as soon as he could.

"Thanks, Kendra, for everything. I'm still in shock over what I can only describe as memories. It's a bit more than I've ever encountered before. I don't quite know what to make of it all."

"My pleasure. I'm sure I'll see you over the next few days. Enjoy the view from the church tower."

As Kendra moved off, Jason escorted Kelly toward the church. Kelly had more memories crash over her. But these were her own memories of the time she had spent in the church with

Neil two years ago. The memories were as fresh as if they had happened yesterday. How could she have forgotten the incredible peace and holiness of the church? She was again caught by the resemblance to Notre Dame in Paris. She had just visited that great cathedral again and taken many notes about its architecture. Her brother had taught her the things to look for. She would have to pull her notes out when she got back to the hotel. But first glances told her all she needed to know. The Templars had designed Notre Dame and modelled this one after it. Or perhaps all of their great churches were of the same model, just different sizes to reflect the wealth of the city and the depth of the local church coffers?

Kelly put her reflection aside as Jason led her to the stairs at the back of the main altar. There was a new door at the base of the stairwell.

"We had to install a door with a lock to satisfy the safety people. They only wanted guided tours of small groups to be allowed up the tower. We tried as best we could to make it look like it belonged here, but there was only so much we could do."

"I remember the stairwell was steep and very poorly lit."

"It's still steep, but safety required us to put lights up and handrails. We opted for LED's in the shape of candles as you will soon see. Let me just call into the tour desk to let them know of our ascent."

Jason clicked his walkie talkie system and talked to the desk, giving them his name, the name of the guest, and the time of the door opening. A passcode was provided allowing him to open the door.

"Kendra must have stopped at the desk on her way through to give her approval for the passcode release. Let's go.

The door will close behind us, but it doesn't require a code to exit, just push the electric release inside."

Jason moved inside the open door and gestured for Kelly to follow him. He started to climb the stairs to the tower. Kelly was surprised by how different the stairwell was now that lights were on the wall and a handrail. The work on the stairs was excellent. There were no crumbling steps left, and they had still managed to retain the uniqueness of the steps that were in good repair.

"Your stone mason did a first rate job on these stairs. It must have been so hard to blend the new with the old and keep it looking like a restoration instead of a renovation."

"Yes, the work took a long time. The masons we hired were excellent, but because of that they were in high demand, and slightly temperamental to work with. Cousin Neil and great grandpa spent a lot of time here during the work to make sure it got done."

"Well, the result is wonderful. Oh, I can start to smell the fresh air from the opening."

"Yes, we're getting there. How are you doing?"

"I'm okay, getting a little fatigued, but adrenaline and anticipation are keeping me going."

"It's just a little farther."

They continued up the stairs for another few minutes. The light kept getting stronger the closer to the top they got. With one final spiral, they came out on the landing of the tower. Kelly looked up first into the bell area. She was surprised to see a small bell hanging in the space.

"Oh wow, where did the bell come from?"

"Great grandpa found it in one of the old churches that he visited in Eastern Europe. The church had a supposed link to the Templars, and that bell was found in the basement gathering dust. He purchased it from the rectory and had it moved here. It took some doing, and a lot of approvals, but we got it installed. We are allowed to ring it only twice a year. We chose to do so on October thirteenth to commemorate the arrest of the Templars in France, and on August twentieth the date of the death of Bernard de Clairvaux, the patron saint of The Templars. So, we are planning on ringing this bell later this week. I hope you can be part of those festivities."

"I didn't know about that part. I do plan to be here all week. I'm not flying back to Canada until August twenty fifth."

Kelly lapsed into silence as she turned her attention to the views out of the sides of the bell tower. She became engrossed in the incredible beauty of the view and the vantage point it gave of the surrounding area. She could easily imagine standing here and sounding an alarm at an approaching army. She shivered. There was something there in her memories; she pushed that aside. Enough for one day she decided. If there was something else for her to see, let it be another day. She would concentrate on what she could see with her eyes, not her clairvoyant sight. She shivered again. Where had that thought come from? She never considered herself clairvoyant before. But things were happening to her she didn't understand.

She gazed out the east opening of the tower. Her gaze clouded over, and she could see a procession of Templar Knights moving along an avenue on the east side of the town. They were following two 'hearses'; one carried a man, the other a dead warhorse. She could see the armor of both laid out on a third wagon.

They were moving to the cemetery. She looked beyond the town walls, and saw the cemetery about a mile out of town in a little copse of trees.

"The cemetery is on the east side of town, outside the east wall, about a mile out into the desert. It's at a small oasis that was consecrated by the Grand Master many years ago. All of the great Templar Knights that die here are buried there, along with their favorite warhorse. The horse is killed when the master dies, so that it may carry the knight into his next life."

Jason looked at Kelly in wonder again. He pulled out his phone so he could jot down the notes on what she was seeing.

"Kelly, can you tell me anything else you see? There is no oasis that I can see. You said about a mile east of the town? If is straight east and right on the road?"

"No, the oasis is about a thousand steps to the north of the road. It is a beautiful place to visit, filled with the presence of the Templar Knights that permanently reside there."

Kelly's gaze cleared and she could only see a sea of sand out the east side of the tower.

"I'm sorry, Jason, the vision is gone now. I can't give you any more details."

"That's okay, Kelly, you've given us more in the past hour than we've been able to uncover in the past few months. But now it's time to get you down those stairs before you pass out from fatigue. I can see the toll that those visions are taking on you."

"I won't argue with you on that. I feel drained now. I definitely need to eat something and then sleep away the day."

"I can certainly help with that. Let's get you down to the visitor center and back to your hotel, with a lunch stop on the way."

"Perfect, lead the way."

Jason turned back to the stairwell. Kelly took one last look out the east side, and could only marvel at what her vision had shown her. There would be time enough to figure this all out after she had some food and sleep.

VI

That same day, Spain

Neil opened the door to his hotel room. He knew he had a few hours to rest and do some work before heading out to the benefit ball tonight. Yet another round of endless, meaningless talks with potential investors. He was getting tired of the travel and the dinners. He knew that there would be more photographers again trying to get pictures of him with Hannah. They were all waiting with baited breath for him and Hannah to announce an engagement. Truth was that he had no intention of marrying Hannah, or anyone for that matter. And Hannah knew that, and was actually grateful that up front he had been honest with her. She too was under a lot of pressure to marry. She was the heiress to an immense fortune, so of course she was always in the press's eyes, wondering whom she would marry. She had a boyfriend and Neil was camouflage for her. The boyfriend was uncomfortable in the glitter and glam of the world of the "rich and famous" as he liked to put it. Neil genuinely liked the man and hoped that Hannah and he would eventually get married.

Neil sighed; he picked up his cell phone and noted that he had a number of missed calls, a couple from the village. He wondered what was going on that they were calling him. His cousin Jason was in charge at the site, so what was up that Jason couldn't handle? He checked the voicemail, surprised it was from Kendra and not Jason.

Neil sat down, powered up his laptop, and dialed the number to Kendra's office.

"Hello? This is Kendra. How may I help you?"

"Kendra, it's Neil. You called? What's up?"

"Neil, I'm glad you called. I think you better come down here as soon as you can."

"What's going on? Can't Jason handle the situation? I'm absolutely buried in the fund raising here."

"I know you've been avoiding the village, but this time, I think you need to come. We've found something that you'll find intriguing. Or rather one of our guests has found something. One of Jason's group today had what I can only describe as a past life remembrance. While in the stables, she fell into a trance is the best description I can come up with. I only caught the last part of what she said, but she talked about being a squire to Godfrey. So, I knew you needed to hear about it. Jason took her up to the church tower, at her insistence. From the quick note I got from Jason, it seems she has located the cemetery for us."

Neil came to full attention with Kendra's narrative. He wondered who could've known about the church tower and the view from up there. His heart leapt in possible explanation. He wondered. Kelly? Could it be her?

"Who is she?"

"It's Kelly Taylor. I recognized her as soon as I saw her in the stables. In her trance, she called herself the brother of Godfrey."

Neil sat in silence for a few seconds. Kelly, the woman he still loved, whom he had lost touch with through stupid circumstances. She was back. He let out a great sigh. "Where is she now?"

"Jason has taken her back to her hotel, with the intention of getting her settled and with some food. She is scheduled to be here for a week in one of the intensive courses. She was only registered as K. Taylor, which is why none of us picked up on it being Kelly. And of course Jason had never met her. But as soon as she said her name, he knew who she was."

"Kelly," Neil sighed her name. He had an immediate vision of her before him. How she had looked when he last saw her as he watched her walk away from him to climb on that damn plane back to Canada. Then he saw her as she had looked when he had made love to her that first time. He felt his body responding to the memories of her.

"Okay, you've got my attention. I'll be out to the village tomorrow by the end of the day. I can't skip the fund raiser tonight, but I'll damn well clear my schedule for the week. How long is she in town?"

"She's scheduled to be here until August twenty-fourth."

"I'll be there sometime tomorrow. Let Jason know that I'll be staying with him at the penthouse, and that I intend for Kelly to stay with us."

"Will do, Neil. I look forward to seeing you again. It's been too long since you were here."

"I know. See you tomorrow."

Neil thought about Eykel. He had been avoiding it for the past eighteen months. The memories of his time with Kelly were too painful for him. He had immersed himself in his work with the corporation and less on the needs of the foundation for the past year or so. When he lost touch with Kelly, he needed to distance himself from everything to do with her. This time he vowed, she would stay with him.

Neil turned his attention to his laptop. He wouldn't be resting this afternoon. He had to cancel a number of appointments and meetings and get Charles and Lawrence up to speed with the change in itinerary for tomorrow. They would probably enjoy a week off once he got to Egypt. He knew he would be staying until Kelly left.

*****

Twenty-four hours later Neil stepped off the plane in Eykel. The plane would be back on the twenty-second to take him to another benefit event in London; one that he couldn't back out of. But he was hoping Kelly would be with him on that trip. He headed into the terminal to grab a shuttle to the hotel so he could pick up a vehicle to head out to the site.

"Hey. Neil, glad you made it."

"Kendra, I didn't expect to see you here."

"Charles called in the arrival time, so I could pick you up here. Jason already has the truck down at the village, so we figured you could ride home with him or Kelly in her rental."

"Thanks for picking me up. Where is Kelly?"

"Jason is with her down at the church today. She wanted to study it in detail. Apparently she had been at Notre Dame earlier this month and took a lot of notes. She wants to compare some of the structural elements of the two churches."

"Funny, I remember talking to her about Notre Dame when she was here the last time. I guess I shouldn't be surprised that she'd do that. I assume you haven't told her I was coming?"

"No, as you asked, I didn't mention it to her, nor to Jason, since he can't always keep his mouth shut. By the way, it's great to have you back here. It's been way too long since you were here."

"I know, but you know why I can't be here. Everything reminds me too much of her. When she walked out of my life I just had to leave this behind too. I couldn't take the memories of what we had. I don't intend to let her leave this time, without being at my side. She is the one woman in the world for me. And I don't care that she lives in Canada, and I live, well, I guess I don't have a home right now. I'm hoping that together, Kelly and I can create one for ourselves."

"I know, Neil, and I can truly say that I'm happy for you that you've found the one woman that is right for you. I know you Carter men find it hard when you don't have your true soul mate at your side. It's been like that in the family for years. We women are much luckier, as we don't lose our way if we don't find them. I just hope Jason finds his woman soon. I'm already seeing the signs in him of that restless energy."

"I know, but he'll find her."

They lapsed into silence for the short drive down to the village's Visitor Center. Neil sat back and relaxed as he contemplated what Kendra had said. It was true. Carter family men were doomed to a restless life if they didn't find their true soul mate to marry. It was something that had been true in the family for generations. There were multiple stories of Carter men who had lost their way when the right woman didn't appear. And there were the remarkable stories like his grandfather, of finding his soul mate in the most unlikely places. Just as Neil had done almost exactly two years ago, when he stumbled across Kelly that day; this time, he vowed the result would be different. This time, he would keep her by his side, no matter what he had to do to convince her that her future was with him. This time, he knew that they would be together, forever.

VII

Kelly sat on the refurbished pews at the front of the church. She couldn't help but remember the last time she had sat in this place, with Neil Adams at her side. That had been the start of the two day romance that had left her feeling dazed and confused. And more deeply in love than she had ever been in her life. That love, she realized, hadn't died off. As much as she had convinced herself that the distance between them had eventually killed it, she knew that was just an excuse. She had been scared of his whirl-wind life. She could tell by the short amount of time they had spent together that he was always on the move, flying all over the world for business. This had only been reinforced by the number of the pictures she had seen of him in the papers and on the internet. The conversations they had about his travelling, the benefits he attended, and the various models and actresses that graced his arms had highlighted the gulf between them. The glamor of that life in comparison to her own had eventually scared her enough to make her pull back ever so slightly on her responses to his emails. Eventually he had just stopped sending them. She had been happy and sad all at the same time when communication ceased between them. And now, here she was, sitting in exactly the same place as two years ago when she had first fallen in love with him and this village.

She looked down at the extensive notes she had taken about the church. She was trying to use techniques her brother had suggested for viewing the church with an analytical eye. One thing that she didn't remember seeing the last time she had been here was the significant presence of Archangel Michael. It wasn't that his image was prominent in the room, but she could see the many small references to him. It was hardly surprising, as he was the protector of knights and police officers, which essentially was the role of the Templars. She fingered her medallion. Her own connection to St Michael had only grown in the past eight months. When she had been standing close to the nave she had seen in the floor an embossed image of the St Michael sigil or seal. From her memory she had a clear image of it, a unique looking seal with the words Michael, Athanatos, Saday and Sabaoth around the outside, and many symbols on the inside with the initials SM prominent in the center. She had seen the sigil many times in her research, and it had even showed up in a couple of her nightmares too. It surprised her to find it yet again here on the floor of the church. It was much worn, but with a little imagination, it was unmistakable. She wondered at the significance of the seal being in the floor of the church, partly covered by the altar right now.

She heard the door at the back of the church open and close.

"Jason, are you back with that water? I'm parched."

"No, I don't have water with me, just arms that are desperate to hold you again."

Kelly felt shock when she heard Neil's voice. She knew that voice in the core of her being. She stood up and turned to look down the length of the church. In the blazing light of the sun, she could barely make him out at the entrance to the church. Still her body and heart reacted as if they had been given a shot of adrenaline.

"Neil?"

"Yes, it's me."

They closed the distance between them, as if drawn by a magnet. Kelly looked up with a shy smile and greeting into his eyes. She didn't know if she should shake his hand or give him a little kiss. Neil answered that for her, by reaching out with his arms. She stepped into them as if she had been doing that all of her life. She wrapped her arms around his body and cherished the closeness that they had.

Within a short time, Neil pulled back a little to look deep into her eyes. He could see the tenseness around them and her uncertainty about his appearance in the depth of them. But she couldn't hide the yearning for his touch that he knew was but a mirror of what he felt. There was no point in resisting that siren call. He bent his head to claim her lips in a searing kiss. He held nothing back of his longing or desperate need for her. His body responded to her contact as it had those two long years ago. He was hard and throbbing. It was like coming home. He knew this was his home. Wherever this woman was, that was home.

Kelly could feel his erection against her and the need that welled within her matched the passion that she knew he was feeling. The same electricity and passion that had flared between them from the first time they had met. She knew that whatever other relationships she had in the past or would have in the future, none of them would ever match her love and passion for this man.

"Kelly, I can't believe you didn't let me know you were coming back here. Kendra called yesterday to let me know you were here, and about the remarkable experiences you've been having. I need to hear more about them, please."

"I didn't think you would care that I was coming back. We lost touch so long ago, and all I see of you are pictures with models, stars, and heiresses. The papers have you all but engaged to that eastern European heiress, Hannah. She's beautiful."

"Hannah and I are friends. We're useful foils for each other. She's in love with a doctor working in London who comes from a working class family. They know that the press would be all over his family and friends to find dirt on them. So, Hannah and I attend functions together to keep the press occupied. As for me, I'm also deeply in love, with the woman standing before me now. And I have been for two years. I'll never find a more perfect match for me than you. You've been the only person to occupy my heart in the past two years."

"Neil…you stopped writing and calling me over eighteen months ago."

"You were the one who didn't respond to the last email I sent. I've the email memorized. I asked you to meet me in London for a benefit. When I didn't hear from you, I lost all hope, but not my love."

"Neil, Kelly, it's getting close to closing time. We want to fire up the security system if you don't mind?"

Startled by the intrusion, Neil and Kelly drew apart and turned to see Jason walk into the church.

"Hi, Jason, thanks for taking care of Kelly for me yesterday and today. I'll be with her from here on, so you can go back to your normal duties."

"My pleasure, Neil. I'm glad you got here. I can see what Kendra meant when she said that Kelly was the perfect match for you; the one woman that a Carter man needs to find. I sure hope mine shows up soon."

"She will, Jason, you just have to stop looking for her. She'll arrive when you least expect it."

With that bit of advice for his young cousin, Neil turned to Kelly to escort her from the church and out into the town square to return to the Visitor Center.

"So I've heard from Kendra a little bit about your experiences yesterday, but I want to hear more and if anything else happened today. We'll have dinner together at the hotel in our suite. That way we can talk privately. Where are you staying Kelly?"

"At the same place I did last time. I loved that little hotel."

"Would you think about moving into the suite with Jason and me? I want to have you near me."

Kelly paused musing about the risks of being around Neil full time, "I'll think about it."

"That's all I can ask for now, after being apart for two years."

They continued up to the Visitor Center.

"Neil, I'd like to head back to my hotel to freshen up before dinner. What time should I come over?"

"I don't want you to leave just yet, but I understand you need some time. So, why don't you come to the place at seven? Then we can have a nice dinner and a long talk."

"Okay, I'll see you then. Thanks, Jason, for a great day today. I'm learning so much more about the life of the Templars."

"No problem, Kelly, I'll see you tonight. I know Neil is going to want both of our perspectives on what happened the last couple of days."

"Jason, tell Kendra I'll be right back. I'll just take Kelly to her car."

"Will do."

Neil offered Kelly his arm and led her out the main door of the Visitor Center into the car park.

"My car is that blue one, just over there."

"Kelly, I'm not ready to let you go without me. I've finally just got you back."

"Neil, please, I need some time. I haven't seen you in two years. I'm feeling a little overwhelmed right now, especially with all the visions I've been having the past two days. I need to rest a bit before dinner. And to get my own thoughts in order about what I've been seeing."

"Okay, I can accept that. But don't plan on being out of my sight for the next few days. I have you back, and this time I'm not letting you go."

Neil reached down once again to claim her lips with his own. He put into the kiss all of the longing and desperate need that he had for her. Kelly responded to the kiss with the same passion that he felt. It wasn't long before both were looking for more. Kelly broke the kiss with a gentle push back on Neil's chest.

"Please, Neil, give me some time."

Neil dropped his forehead to rest against hers. "Okay I'll let you go for now. But I can't make any promises about tonight."

Kelly opened the car door and jumped in before she could change her mind. Her emotions were reeling, and she needed to take a few breaths before she was calm enough to start the car and drive away. She watched Neil walk back into the Visitor Center and wondered what the future would hold for her.

She drove back to her hotel thinking about Neil and Sam. Sam was a wonderful man. The relationship had no pressure on her; they lived their own lives and came together to enjoy weekends when they could. It was a safe, stable relationship that didn't push her to expose her heart to anything that might break it. She knew that she had come perilously close to major depression less than a year ago. Neil on the other hand evoked a deep passion and need within her that she had never felt. It was unnerving in some ways, and exhilarating in others. The emptiness she had felt when they parted ways had been numbing. She knew that she couldn't live through another major breakup like that. Best that she keep her heart and soul tucked away.

Sam was expecting her to call him today. They had been talking every couple of days since she had left Nova Scotia for her trip. He had actually tried to persuade her to cancel the trip, in favor of spending time with him on a trip through the Maritime Provinces. But she had wanted to do this trip for years. So, she had come on her own. And now, having seen Neil again, she knew that she had made the right choice. Neil was the other half of her. She knew that. Even if the relationship couldn't last, she wanted to have another few days with him, living in shared passion and interests.

Kelly got to her hotel and set up her laptop. She was still a few minutes early to call, so she spent the time looking through her wardrobe for appropriate clothes for tonight. She wanted to look her best. And she knew why. She wanted to be in Neil's arms again, to feel the passion they shared. Already her body was humming with the desire that she knew would flare to life the next time Neil kissed her. She longed for that moment. Kelly moved back to the computer and punched in her Skype details to open the call to Sam.

"Kelly, it's so good to hear from you today. I've been longing for this call for a couple of days. So, how is it in Egypt?"

"Hi, Sam. I'm settled here nicely in the hotel. I've been over to the village both yesterday and today. I've been assigned a great young guide. He wasn't here the last time I was here as he was still in University. And the best part, he is a Carter, so I'm actually getting some phenomenal information about the Foundation's plans for this place."

"I know you're interested in the church and comparing it to Notre Dame. How has that gone so far?"

"I just spent time in the church today. I'm taking my brother's advice and just making notes as I study the place on its own merits. Then I'll review the notes I took at Notre Dame and compare them. I suspect I'm going to have great information for a travel article from this trip."

"Sounds good. And I have an envelope here for you from Zoomer. Should I open it for you?"

"Oh, Sam, yes please. I sent them a query letter about an article based on my travels in Europe as a single female."

"Okay, here goes. It says, 'Dear Ms. Taylor. The article proposal you sent us is quite interesting. We would like to discuss this with you in greater detail. Please contact me at your earliest convenience via email.' Oh honey, this is great news. Congratulations."

"Thanks, Sam, it is great news. Can you give me the email address so I can respond to them later?"

"Sure thing. Just remember, I'm leaving tomorrow for PEI with Rebecca. I won't be touching your mail for another week. Hope you aren't expecting any more of these letters."

"There are a few more outstanding, but they can wait for a week. If this one is as positive as the letter sounds, I'll likely only be able to do the one article. They're a demanding magazine to write for."

"Well, I hope it turns out for you."

"Me too. Sam, I hate to cut this call short, but I'm meeting with some of the other visitors for supper tonight at the Foundation's hotel. They're all staying over there. I've met some very interesting scholars, and I want to take advantage of talking to them before they leave."

"Well, I can't say I'm not disappointed to not have more time to talk, but I guess with the time difference and all. So, enjoy your supper hon. I can't wait for you to get back home. I want to talk about taking our relationship to the next level. I think we're both ready for that."

"Sam."

"No, Kelly, don't say anything right now. But please think about it. I'm missing you more than I thought I would. Please consider it over the next week. We can talk about it when you get back."

"Okay, I'll think about it, but I'm making no promises to you."

"Understood."

After an awkward pause Kelly continued. "Sam, I've got to get going. The group wants to meet for drinks first."

"All right, Kelly, have a good couple of days. Let's talk again in three days. Same time?"

"Yeah, that'll be fine. Talk to you then."

"Bye, Kelly."

"Bye."

Kelly closed Skype and contemplated the discussion that Sam wanted to have. If Neil hadn't shown up today, Kelly was sure her reaction would have been different. Sam was a wonderful man, and she enjoyed his company. He was a good replacement for Ken. But there was none of the passion that she had with Neil. But on the other hand, she wasn't sure that the fireworks she felt with Neil would make for a lasting relationship. Surely a steady and placid man like Sam would be a better bet for a long term, stable relationship. Kelly would have to consider all of that- but later, much later. For now she wanted to have a shower, then dress in the best clothes she had with her. She knew that she would be spending the night with Neil. Her excitement was clear to her. She intended to make love to Neil again tonight, to see if the passion was as good as her memory had it. Humming to herself Kelly moved to the washroom to shower. Then she would rest and get ready to see Neil at seven.

VIII

Kelly pushed the elevator button that would take her to the penthouse suite of the hotel. She stood filled with nerves and excitement at the thought of seeing Neil again. The elevator seemed to take forever to get to the top floor. When the door slid open she saw Jason waiting for her in the foyer.

"Hi, Kelly, Neil asked me to let you in. He's on a call with London, but should be finished very shortly. Come on in. Can I get you a drink? Wine? Or something harder?"

"Red wine would be lovely, thank you."

"Come and get settled in the living room. We ordered the food about ten minutes ago. It'll be here in about a half hour. Give us a chance to relax before dinner."

Kelly walked toward the living room and caught a glimpse of Neil in the office; he was on the phone. He had changed into jeans and a shirt. He looked sexy as hell. He waved to her when he saw her. She could see his eyes open wide. Guess her selection of the little black dress had been a good thing. She moved into the living room and waited for Jason to appear from the kitchen.

He came back with a glass of red wine for her and a beer for himself. He leaned back into the cushions of an easy chair, and they chatted quietly, waiting for Neil to finish up on the phone.

"Neil is talking to the London office. Neil bailed out of a couple of important meetings in order to come down here. Not surprising, given that you showed up. Now he has to organize people to fill in for him."

"I remember from a while ago how busy he always was. If it wasn't Foundation or Carter Corporation business, it was the charity work the family does. I must admit, I have come to admire the dedication the entire Carter family shows to the charity cause. Not every wealthy or influential family cares as much for the world around them."

"I think it's a heritage of our Templar roots. As maligned as the Templars were, they also did a great deal of charity work, as was and is carried on by both the Freemasons and the Knights Hospitaller. Both groups had extensive roots built on the Templar demise in the early 1300's."

"I don't know much about either of those groups, but the Carter family certainly does support a lot of charities, especially Children's' hospitals."

Jason chuckled at that. "How do you know about the Children's hospital work? That's something we try to keep quiet from the press."

"Please, I am a teacher and freelance writer. I absolutely know how to do my research."

"That's obvious."

"What's obvious?" Neil asked as he came into the living room. "Sorry I was on the phone when you got here." He reached down and gave Kelly a firm kiss, filled with the promise of later passion.

"Kelly and I were just talking about some of the charity work that you do. She knew a fair amount more than I expected. She told me it came from her work as a teacher and freelance writer."

"Yes, she's good at her research for sure. I saw a couple of the articles you wrote over the past couple of years. I imagine the freelance writing is taking off for you?"

"Not yet actually. I can only write a lot in the summer months. My school year is pretty tight by the time I do anything with the kids after school. I've written a couple of articles during the year, mostly for teachers' magazines. The true freelance work I confine to the summer months. In fact I just heard today from *Zoomer*. They want to talk to me about a piece I proposed to them about traveling in Europe as a single female, or rather as a widowed female traveling alone again. I can't wait to talk to them about it. I emailed them back tonight, so I hope to have some conversation with them over the next few days."

"Darling, that's great. I can't wait to read that one too. I'm sure it will be as good as the one you did about traveling here two years ago. You should actually approach them too, about a follow up article based on your trip this year."

"Thanks, Neil, I do love the work. Probably even more than I love teaching, which I didn't think would be possible."

"I think your experiences this time would make for a great study and article."

Kelly laughed. "I don't know about that. I suspect many would be ready to measure me for a straight-jacket if they heard me talk about Eykel like I lived there. I still can't quite credit it myself. But the visions I have are too clear to be anything but real."

"I want to go over all of what you've learned in detail. But dinner will be here soon, so why don't you just give me a brief overview of what happened."

"Well, I'm honestly not sure where to begin."

"Kelly, why don't you let me tell Neil about what I heard from you, from my perspective?"

"Sure."

"The first I had any indication that there was something strange going on was when Kelly told me that she thought those 'offices' were actually shops, like a butcher shop and then talked about the smithy at the end of the street. We hadn't yet been down the street, so I knew she didn't know about the smithy from seeing it before. She was then able to describe exactly the way to the stables."

"I don't think I mentioned it at the time, but when I glanced into the smithy, I could have sworn that I saw two horses tied up and two men working there- one at the bellows and the other working on a horse. Then as we walked along the back avenue, I felt like I was being followed by a big horse and could feel a line in my hand holding the horse."

"No, you didn't mention that."

"I thought I was going crazy actually. I wasn't exactly going to mention visions in front of ten strangers," Kelly chuckled.

"No, I imagine that would have been awkward for you," said Neil. "So, Jason, what happened when you got to the stables?"

The elevator buzzed.

"That must be the room service. I'll let them in." Jason got up, leaving Neil and Kelly alone. Neil waited for a brief second and then rose to hold his hand out to Kelly.

"I can only imagine how you must have been feeling, such strong déjà vu and visions coming to you unexpectedly. I wish I'd been here with you to hold you while you struggled with them."

"I know. But Jason was great. He made sure that I sat down in the stables as soon as I got there. It was like he knew that I'd be feeling exhausted."

"Yes, he would've understood that."

Neil reached his arms around Kelly. "I want a proper kiss now, while Jason is occupied in the dining room." And he lowered his head to Kelly's lips and seized them in a passionate and deep kiss. Kelly responded to the need in Neil's kisses with a matching need of her own. She met his passion kiss for kiss. She was soon breathless as they battled for it.

A discreet cough from the direction of the dining room reminded them they were not alone. Neil pulled back from Kelly with a deep sigh. "Soon," he promised her, "soon we will be alone."

Kelly just whispered back "please". Neil understood her message to him in that simple one word. He released her from his grip and took her hand to lead her to the dining room.

"Would you like some more wine?"

"Yes, thank you. That'd be lovely. It's a wonderful vintage. But I recall that you always did have the best wine around."

The three of them settled into the dining room. Kelly was hardly surprised to find that the food at the hotel was excellent. She had heard from a few of the other visitors about how good it was. Now she would definitely agree with them.

They passed the meal in good conversation. It was evident that Jason and Neil were two of a kind, and that probably explained why Jason was working at the village. There was noticeably a great deal of affection between these two and a respect for the accomplishments and knowledge of each. Jason, it seemed, had studied history at university and so was well versed in all of the ancient history of the world. Kelly privately suspected that much of the information he had was from sources that weren't as academically accepted as the mainstream universities. But he had managed to integrate the accepted versions of history with many of the alternate views and created plausible explanations. Kelly found herself listening to the two men talk with rapt attention. She filed away much of the discussion for later review and further talk with both men.

"I'm sorry, Kelly; I hope we're not boring you with our discussion."

"Not at all. I'm finding this fascinating. I'm a school teacher, and the version of history that you two talk about is so different than what we teach in the school system, at least in Canada. I wonder what the academics would think if their cherished views of history were so disrupted."

"We actually do know in some cases. The academics label anyone that is outside the norm as either delusional or conspiracy theorists. But Galileo and Copernicus were both labeled as heretics in their times. It's amazing how the truth will eventually come out," said Jason. "I know when I was working on my thesis; I had to overcome a lot of the suspicions and disbelief of my advisors."

Neil looked at Jason affectionately. "And still do. I know you had wanted to work at one of the major museums. Your thesis was just a little too controversial for some of the Boards to accept."

"True, Neil, too true. But in reality, I'm far happier working here at the village and doing the Foundation work. You and Dad were both right. This is where I belong. Guess I am another of those throwback Carters that the family talks about. You and I together."

"Yes, there seems to be a few of us in each generation that are meant for the current equivalent of the Templar life. It comes with the territory. In time you'll understand even more as you reach farther into your Templar roots."

Kelly listened to the men in fascination. Neil had mentioned something in the past about the Carter family having deep and ongoing Templar connections. She was just beginning to understand how deep they were. From the conversation she suspected that the Carters were far deeper into Templar lore and studies than she had originally thought. Kelly needed to think about it and tie all of that into her own experiences and recent visions, especially as it related to the hypnosis she underwent a few weeks ago. That had obvious ties to the Templars. *Wasn't that woman's name Eleanor Carter? Could that be coincidence? Or is my subconscious trying to tell me something about the Carters?* Kelly mentally shook herself. *Plenty of time to digest all of this later.* She sat back and just listened as the men continued their discussions on the Templars.

*****

Much later that night she stood at the living room windows gazing out into the night sky. She could see the moon as it was rising and illuminating the village. The view was just as beautiful as she remembered it from two years ago. She was waiting for Neil to return. He said he had to follow up on a call from earlier today with some people in the United States. He said it should only take a few minutes. Kelly mulled over the evening. After finishing supper they had gone back to the living room where they continued to discuss Kelly's experiences of the prior couple of days. Neil was as fascinated as Jason had been when she was describing the dimensions of the village and what she could recall of it from her visions. The 'ghosts' pressing in on her had been disturbing her all day, but so far she had not had any more visions.

Kelly sipped at her wine and wondered how the rest of the evening might lead. Jason had left a short while ago. She was eager to have Neil to herself and figured that privacy would be a good thing for the next couple of days.

"I'm glad that's all done, and now we can have some privacy, just you and me."

Neil came up behind Kelly and wrapped his arms around her from behind. He leaned down and nuzzled on her neck where her dress had left it bare. Kelly shuddered at the fire that flared to life within her at his merest touch. Neil turned her around in his arms. They gazed at each other and saw passion sparkle in their eyes.

"Kelly, I promised myself that I'd give you time to adjust to me being back in your life. But I need to make love to you now."

"Neil," Kelly let out a breathless sound, "yes, please, make love to me. I need you." Kelly reached up to give Neil a searing kiss. The passion exploded between them as it had that night two long years ago.

As he had done the last time they were in the apartment, Neil picked Kelly up and carried her to the master bedroom. She felt herself tilt back to upright as he lowered her feet to the ground. He looked into her eyes again and then leaned down to claim her lips. Kelly reached up for the buttons on his shirt and started to open them so she could run her hands over his chest. How she wanted to explore again every curve and inch of this man. The passion and need were building inside her as Neil explored her lips. As she brushed her hands along his bare chest, she heard a muffled groan come from him.

Neil reached behind Kelly and pulled on the zipper, gently easing it down the length of her back. As it released, the dress fell to the ground in a heap of black. Kelly looked at him as he pulled back wondering if he would think that the black lace bra and panties she wore were too much.

"Hmm, I approve the look, but I'll approve more if we remove them."

Kelly reached up and undid the bra, then slipped the panties to the ground. She stood proudly in front of him, as he drank his fill of her naked body. "My god, Kelly, you are so beautiful. Even more so than I remember."

"No, I'm not, but thank you for saying so. I feel beautiful when you look at me the way you are now."

Neil pulled her close. Kelly moaned as her breasts were crushed against his bare chest. Neil moved her backwards until her legs were pressed against the bed. She lowered herself to the bed and moved to the center, holding her hand out to invite Neil to join her. "Please Neil, make love to me."

Neil quickly divested himself of his pants and socks and followed her onto the bed. She patiently waited as he spent the next few minutes exploring her body with his hands and lips. When he took her breasts into his mouth, she could no longer contain her excitement and groaned in need and passion. Soon she wanted more and reached out to encircle Neil's erection; to encourage him to enter her. He went slowly to allow her time to adjust. The passion grew swiftly and soon Kelly felt her body spasm. He held himself away from her as she quivered around him. The look on her face told him all he needed to know of her love and need for him. As she opened her eyes to look at him, he could feel his own orgasm building. He moved within her and then exploded.

After he was spent, he rolled onto his back, taking Kelly with him so she could lay cuddled in his arms. Kelly was awed that the passion of two years ago erupted between them just as quickly and strongly. *This was what it feels like to make love to your soul mate. The one you are meant to be with.* Kelly intended to hold this memory deep within her. She knew that as much as she and Neil might love each other, that the possibility of them remaining together was remote. *We live in such different worlds. There is no way I could live the life he does, forever on a jet, gallivanting around the world. And he would get so restless living life in a small town in Canada.* She sighed. *Better to get this restless passion out of my system now. I'll have the memories for the years ahead, but it just can't work between us. He'd leave me alone again; just like I've always been left alone.*

"Such a big sigh. What's that for?"

"Nothing. Just relaxing. It feels wonderful to be in your arms again."

"Yes, I know you belong here with me. And I intend to keep you. Do you want to sleep now, or talk some more about your visions?"

"Right now, I could use some sleep. Tomorrow is soon enough to explore the visions I have."

"Okay let me go turn off the lights in the living room, and we can fall asleep holding each other." Neil slid out of the bed to go take care of that issue. By the time he got back to the bedroom, Kelly was sound asleep. He watched her for a few minutes while she slept on his bed. He could feel himself harden against her. He groaned. As much as he needed her, she needed the sleep. There is time enough to make love to her in the morning. He slid into bed beside her. She moved a touch, and slid her body close to his to spoon as she slept. He slid his arm around her, kissed her neck, and settled down to sleep.

IX

The twentieth of August arrived faster than Kelly had expected, only a few more days until she was due to leave. She quickly dismissed that thought. *There is time enough to worry about that later.*

She was standing in one of the rooms of the ruined abbey, its bare outline still visible. She remembered from the last time she was here that the general consensus was that the abbey had been dismantled when the nearby town had been built hundreds of years ago and before the sandstorms buried the Templar site. It would have been a good source of cut stone for the new buildings. She consulted the guide in her hand. Someone had laid out a scale drawing of what they thought the abbey would have looked like. It was called an abbey, but actually it was the living quarters of the Templar Knights; kept alone in their secluded, austere lifestyle.

Kelly consulted the map again. She believed that she was standing in the Commander's office and living quarters. They appeared to be the largest in the ruins, so it made sense they would belong to the Commander. She looked around the area and moved to what would have been the outside wall. She could feel once again the strange sense of déjà vu that she had been encountering throughout the village, perhaps even stronger here. The persistent 'knowing' assailing her was still so powerful. It was spooky and left her feeling very unsure of herself, and of her place in the world. She wondered what was taking Neil so long. He had said he would be right back.

She glanced at her watch. They were supposed to ring the bell today. This was the anniversary of the death of the Patron Saint of the Templars, Saint Bernard de Clairvaux. It was just before noon, and they were hoping to gather in the town square for the ceremony. She wanted to stay here in the abbey and explore the eerie feelings she was having. Plus she had a great view of the church from here. There was no need to be amongst the others.

"I'm back. Sorry that took so long. Here's your water."

At that moment, the bells of the tower started to ring.

Kelly felt her consciousness fade away as she was transported back in time. *Ringing bells? The alarm was being sounded! I must run!*

"Kelly, what is it? Tell me what you see?"

"I'm in a panic. I'm in the office of Godfrey, the man I serve. The bells aren't supposed to be ringing. It can only mean one thing, we are under attack. It had been expected; Arwad had fallen, so how could we stand? My Commander is sending me to the stables to prepare his horse for battle. I don't want to go. I want to stay with him. He is firm. I am to prepare his battle stallion and his travel mount for me. He is giving me strict orders to flee. I must leave to warn the order of the fall of the village. Thank God. He says that we had moved the treasure long ago. We can see through the window of his quarters. There is panic in the street as everyone realizes the significance of the bell ringing. He insists that I go on my way. I move to the door I look back. "Godfrey", I say. "Go little one," he says, "I must stay to defend the order. Go! Find freedom and safety. Take this with you as a sign that you come from me. Give it to the master in England. He'll know what it means and what to do. It is my last order to you. Be safe my brother."

Kelly felt the scene recede as she became aware of her surroundings again. She was now standing at the entrance to the quarters. As she looked back at the center of the room, she saw a double image before her. She saw Neil, but overlaid was her remembrance of Godfrey as she had seen him in her vision, full armor and his Templar surcoat crisp and white with the red cross standing out in stark contrast.

She whispered, "Godfrey," and started to fall in a faint. Neil moved as fast as he could to catch her. He barely made it to her in time or her head would have hit the ground. He pushed his communication button. "Get me medical assistance out here. I'm in the abbey. Kelly has passed out."

Kelly had regained consciousness before the medical person arrived. She was thankful that Neil had been there, or she would have hit her head when she fainted. She had never done that before. She felt a bit silly as the medical staff gave her a quick going over, taking her blood pressure and other vital signs.

"I think you'll be okay. I'd suggest that you stay well hydrated and take it easy. I suspect the heat of today coupled with lack of water and food has caused a sugar imbalance. Please take it easy the rest of the day."

"Thanks, Tom; I appreciate your getting here so fast."

"Hey, it's why you guys have me on staff here. Kelly isn't the first guest that didn't realize the impact the heat here would have on them. Plus there are always a few cuts and scrapes."

Tom packed up his supplies and moved to head back to his office. "I recommend that you bring her back to the Visitor Center so she can cool down in the air conditioning."

"Actually, I'm going to take her back to the hotel. That way I know she'll lie down and rest."

"That'd be best." Tom left them.

"Neil, please stop fussing. I feel fine now. It was silly that I didn't even think to have water with me."

"Sorry, Kelly, but you had enough water. This wasn't a simple heat stroke. You dropped after you turned back from the door and whispered 'Godfrey'. Tell me what you saw."

"It was almost as if you and Godfrey were standing in exactly the same place, like you were one person or overlaid on each other. It was a dual image of you and him looking at me. The look on his face was pained and desperate. He knew he was sending his servant on a dangerous mission, but it seemed the only way to save him."

Kelly shivered at the memory of the dual image of Neil and Godfrey. It spooked her.

"So, that's what the visions are like for you? I'm amazed at the detail that you remember when you're having them. I assume the bell ringing triggered the scene?"

"That's my guess. It transported me to another time and place for sure, much stronger than the one I had in the stable. This time I could actually 'see' Godfrey, I think that was his name. I can only give you a few details about this office and the square; the intensity of my reaction to the bells caused me to focus on Godfrey. Who was he?"

"Neil, Kelly, you guys okay? I just saw Tom and he said Kelly had fainted from heat exhaustion?"

"Hi, Jason, no, it wasn't the heat. Kelly had another vision when the bells started ringing. She was transported back to the day the village fell. The bell must have rung that day to signal the arrival of the invasion force, much as we'd always been led to believe."

"Are you telling me that the 'Godfrey' she mentioned in the stables as her 'brother', was actually the last Godfrey to command this facility and our ultimate great uncle?"

"Yes, it appears that way."

Kelly looked at Jason and Neil in confusion. "What are you guys talking about? Ultimate uncle? I don't understand."

"I think it's time that we told you the entire story of this village, the Carter family roots, and how we knew of this place's existence. But I'm not doing that here- too many ears. This is something for family only. Jason, come to the penthouse tonight for dinner with Kendra. I think we need to sort some of this out and fill Kelly in on the details she's missing right now. In the meantime, I'm going to take Kelly back there so she can relax and rest before dinner."

"Neil, I told you I'm fine."

"I know, but please humor me. I want you to rest."

With an exasperated sigh Kelly agreed to let Neil take her back to the hotel. However, she had other ideas than resting on her mind.

*****

Three hours later Kelly was feeling rested and refreshed. As much as she hated to admit it, Neil had been right about her needing to sleep. But perhaps that had also been due to them making love shortly after getting back to the hotel. Kelly had deliberately seduced Neil when she got to the bedroom. It hadn't taken much to convince him to make love to her. After they finished, she had cuddled into his arms and promptly fell asleep. She had awakened two hours later feeling refreshed and eager to hear the full story of the village. She had a quick shower and walked out of the bedroom to find Neil. He was in the office, on the phone again.

"Yes, Gramps, I know the implications of this as well as you do. But I think it's important that we give her all the details now and not wait for two days until we are in London. Her visions are incredible and can mean either her soul is the re-born brother of Godfrey or she is clairvoyant. Either way she is now tied to us." He paused, listening to his grandfather. "Yes, Gramps, we will be in London early that day. I will fly out first thing on the twenty-second. We should be in London by eleven a.m. or so. That will give us plenty of time before the banquet to talk. We'll see you then. Bye, Gramps."

Kelly shuddered a bit at the implications for herself in Neil's comments to his grandfather. Re-born soul? Clairvoyant? She didn't understand how either of those could be true. She had never believed in reincarnation and still hadn't come to terms with her last hypnotism session and the implications of it. And as to clairvoyance? Unlikely. Sure she had her fair share of déjà vu moments, but didn't everyone?

"Kelly, there you are. I'm guessing you heard the last part of my conversation with my grandfather?"

"Yes, I did. Three things confuse me: London, re-born souls, and clairvoyance."

Neil chuckled as he stepped away from the desk and moved towards Kelly, "I can easily answer the first one. I have a charity benefit on the twenty- second in London. It was the only thing I couldn't cancel on my schedule when I flew here to be with you. It's for a Children's charity, and you know the importance of those. So I had planned to ask you to come with me on another mystery flight. 'Surprise!' This time we would be going to London. And I know before you say anything that you wouldn't have anything to wear, Mom was going to have a few dresses delivered to the apartment and you could choose which one you wanted to wear. We were going to guess at size, but since you know, I need it so Mom can complete the arrangement."

"Neil, umm, I don't know what to say."

"Another simple, 'yes, Neil, I will come with you to the benefit', will suffice. We can deal with the rest tomorrow before we fly out the following morning."

Kelly laughed at him. "Yes, Neil, I'll come with you to the benefit."

Neil laughed too and pulled her into his arms to give her a sound kiss. "That's what I love about you, Kelly, so easy to persuade."

Kelly looked at Neil and could see the passion sparking just below the surface again. She knew her own eyes reflected the same thing. He had said he loved her. Sure it was slightly off the cuff, but he had said the words.

Neil reached down to kiss Kelly again. This time it was a deeper, more passionate kiss. He knew it was time to tell her how he felt.

"Kelly, I meant what I said. I do love you, with all my heart and soul."

"I love you too, Neil, as I've never loved another in my life."

"That's all we need. Our love for each other will carry us through anything that life throws at us."

They heard the chime of the elevator. "That'll be Jason and Kendra, meaning dinner will be only another few minutes as well. We will continue this discussion tonight, in bed, after I make love to you again."

"Promises, promises."

Neil swatted at her as she moved away from him. He walked to the wine fridge to pull out a fresh bottle of red. Jason and Kendra walked into the penthouse, just as he opened the bottle.

"Hey you two, we're in the kitchen opening a bottle of red. Want a glass?"

Two voices echoed, "Yes."

Neil poured the glasses, gave two to Kelly to carry, and moved into the living room.

"So, Kelly, I hear from Jason that you had another vision today. I'm surprised that this is your first since that day you arrived."

"Hi, Kendra, yes, I was surprised not to have more concrete reminders as I did that first day. But this one was triggered by the bell ringing. I heard the bell start, and the next thing I know, I'm being pulled back in time to another day in that same room."

"Kelly, why don't you let me tell it from my perspective of what I saw? That should take us until dinner arrives. We can then tell you the story of this village and the Carter family after dinner."

"Okay, sounds fair."

Neil related to Jason and Kendra what he had heard Kelly

say during her time in trance. The only things that surprised Kelly was that he mentioned that she had been moving around the room in great agitation. She had no recollection of moving from the center to the outside wall and eventually to the door. She did recall that when she saw the overlay of Neil/Godfrey that she had been standing on the opposite side of the room. So she must've moved around as Neil described.

"When she whispered 'Godfrey', she then fainted. I grabbed her as quickly as I could. When she came to, she told me that I must've been standing exactly where Godfrey had been when she turned to say good-bye. She saw an image of Godfrey exactly where I was standing."

"Neil, it was more than that. It was almost as if you were overlaid on each other. Almost like you were him, or vice versa. It was the weirdest thing I've ever seen. It was different than the other ghost images that I've seen around here. This one was more concrete. It is the only description I can come up with right now that seems right. Does that make sense?"

She looked at Neil, Jason, and Kendra, and found them looking at her with a knowing and understanding look.

"Okay, now I'm spooked. What is it that you guys aren't telling me? What's going on here?"

"Well love, it's something that comes around in the Carter family fairly regularly. I don't know your beliefs on reincarnation or about souls coming back to life again and again. The truth is that my soul, the one inside me, is the same soul that inhabited Godfrey those many years ago. I'm not the same person. I have my own distinct personality and experiences. But the soul at my core is the same one. And I've lived in other bodies over the many years in-between."

Kelly looked at the three of them to see if they were joking and pulling her leg. They all looked back at her in earnest belief that what Neil said was true. She shuddered when she remembered her session with Dr. Klein. Hadn't she felt that Neil was Robert, the husband?

"Souls reincarnating again and again? You're trying to tell me that there is such a thing as reincarnation?"

"Yes, Kelly, we are," said Kendra. "I know it's hard to digest when it's thrown at you like this; but that's the reality. We are all souls that have lived many times in the past. You're being privileged at coming back to the site of a very old soul memory for you. It's my belief that you definitely were Godfrey's brother as you've seen in your visions. I don't think this is simple clairvoyance. The detail is too clear. You're reliving a past life."

Kelly sat in disbelief staring at the three of them. Sure she had been doing some reading about soul journeys first after Ken had died and most especially in the last eight months since that Halloween party. But she continued to discount the theories as wishful thinking by people in grief as a way to keep the memories of their loved ones alive. Or in her case, as if they were dreams. Her subconscious was bringing forth the answers to her research questions. Now she was sitting with three people who evidently believed in the concepts of reincarnation. They believed they had really and truly lived as these people in the past. She was unsure of what to think.

They could hear the elevator bell go off, indicating the imminent arrival of someone.

"That must be dinner. Jason, why don't you give me a hand," said Kendra.

As Kendra and Jason left, Neil moved a bit closer to Kelly and grabbed her hand in his. "Hon, I know this is a lot to take in, especially if you haven't been exposed to these notions before. I would've preferred to take a slower approach to all of this, but your visions won't allow that. You're going to have to jump into the deep end with us."

"I've seen books on past lives and things. Some were recommended to me when Ken had died. I've read a few of them. But my upbringing was staunchly Roman Catholic. So I've been taught from the cradle that there is no reincarnation." She wasn't going to mention yet to these people her experience at Halloween or the hypnosis work she was doing. Time enough for that once she understood more about what they were talking about.

"I understand that all of this goes against what you were raised to believe. Will you trust me enough to let me show you a different possibility?"

Kelly looked at Neil. She could still see the traces of Godfrey in his face from this afternoon. And she could even catch echoes of Robert Brock Carter. She shuddered when she recalled the visions she'd been seeing in the past few days. She'd seen more ghosts that she hadn't mentioned for fear of sounding crazy. Now she wasn't so sure.

"I'll trust you, Neil. I can't promise anything, but I will try to keep an open mind."

"That's all I ask of you, keep an open mind."

"Neil, Kelly, dinner is laid out and ready to eat. Should I open another bottle of wine?"

"Yes, grab another bottle. We've still much to talk about tonight."

X

A few hours later, Neil and Kelly were sitting together on the sofa while Jason and Kendra had taken chairs to the side. They were all relaxing after dinner. Kelly was enjoying the company of these three truly interesting people, who had lots of things to talk about. They were sipping after-dinner drinks as they watched the setting sun through the living room windows. It was another beautiful night here in the desert.

Neil put his arm around Kelly and had her nestle into the crook of his arm. She was content to just relax.

"All right, Kelly, I guess it's time to tell you a bit of the history of the Carter family, so you can understand the deep connection we feel to Eykel and the Templars. Jason, you were the last of us to study our archives and have delved further now with your history Masters. Why don't you tell the story?"

"Sure, Neil. Where do I begin? I guess the best place is the demise of this village. Kelly as you've surely guessed by now, Godfrey was the last Commander of this village. As near as we can tell it was ransacked somewhere around 1303 to 1305. No one survived the attack so we have no history to fall back on. But the pieces we put together suggest somewhere in that time. The fall of Arwad occurred in 1302. We know that a few escaped from there and made their way to Eykel. In 1301 Godfrey became concerned about the safety of the town and decided to pack up all of the treasures and valuables in the village and send them to Europe for safety. He enlisted his second in command, William of Lothian, to lead the mission. They were transported by camel train to the nearest port where the Templars had sent ships to carry it from there to Scotland. In Scotland, William took the treasure to Godfrey's brother, Geoffrey. Yes, there was another, older brother. From our family history, he had left home just before Godfrey left for the Templars. He was also training to be invested in the Templars, but had been injured in battle and could no longer fight on the front lines. As a consequence he had been sent to Scotland to set up what we would now call 'safe houses.' The Templars knew they had many enemies in the world, and so they were building up castles around Europe where they could safely hide the priceless treasures they had uncovered in the Holy Land, as well as the great wealth they had amassed over the years. Geoffrey had been entrusted with one of those places in Scotland. William arrived in Scotland sometime in 1302."

Jason paused for a minute to sip at his drink. "A few years later the mass arrests of the Templars occurred. Geoffrey ostensibly had distanced himself from the Templars in the intervening years and moved from the highlands of Scotland down into the more settled regions of England. There he married and had three children, all girls. The eldest daughter married into a de Cartier family who originated from France, but had migrated to Portugal to evade the Templar downfall. Yes, the de Cartiers had also been Templars. That's why Geoffrey had his daughter marry into the family. All three girls married into Templar families who had escaped Europe. Of the treasure that had been here, all traces of it were lost. Geoffrey, together with other Scottish-based Templars had been part of the plan to send the Templar fleet to safety with all of the treasures of the Templars on-board. As you know, that Fleet never returned to the known world, so the whereabouts of the bulk of the treasure is still a mystery."

"I know about the Templar Fleet and its treasure. There are many that believe it's buried on Oak Island, which is just a few miles from where I live. There is a place there called 'The Money Pit'. The legend that surrounds it suggests that there is a vast treasure buried on the island. One account has it as being the Templar treasure. The shaft entrance keeps flooding, so no one has been able to go down far enough to see what does lie there. Of course there are many natural explanations for the caves too. All in all, it is a perfect place for a conspiracy theory to come to life."

"Yes, that's one of many theories that exist about the treasure. It's in Scotland at Rosslyn Chapel, or hidden in Spain or France, or Oak Island. The search for the lost Templar treasure has been the basis for many books and treasure hunts, but so far it has eluded mankind. What baffles scholars as much is what the treasure actually is. Is it the Arc of the Covenant or the Holy Grail? Is it the truth about Jesus and Mary Magdalene? Is it the gold and silver that the Templars had accumulated over the years as Europe's first bankers? And of course there is the possibility that there is no treasure at all. As you said, it is a perfect recipe for conspiracy theorists."

They sat in silence for a few minutes, Jason and Neil contemplating what they 'knew' to be true and wondering how much they could tell Kelly at this time. They looked at each other and Neil shook his head almost imperceptibly. Jason nodded in understanding. Another day would be better to reveal all they knew. They were aware that Kelly was still skeptical. There would be time enough to tell her the real story.

Jason continued. "But getting back to our family history, Geoffrey's daughters married about the mid 1320's. The eldest had three sons and two daughters who survived. Her eldest son was born in the late 1320's. During the first generations the marriages were always selected to bring together the various Templar families that had escaped Europe. So, Eleanor's son married a girl with Templar roots as well. The Carter family can trace directly through this eldest son down to great grandpa and through him to Neil and me. Up until the last few generations, the Carter family secrets and history have fallen upon the eldest son and heir. But in the mid 1700's things changed. The eldest male and only son died before he married, so the legacy had to fall to the only daughter. There was real concern amongst the few families that still honored the Templar heritage. When it was realized that the Carter family might die off, they were united with the Brock family and the daughter was married to a younger Brock son. Thus the Carter family continued on. This is about the time that the first of the Carter businesses was formed. Since then the corporation, now run by great grandpa and great uncle Geoff, has grown into one of the biggest and most successful businesses in Britain. The Geoffrey name runs true in the family. Each generation has at least one. The name Godfrey fell out of use and hasn't been popular in years. Many of the males have it as a second name, as Neil does. The charitable foundation was formed by great grandpa's father. He was an only son himself, with only one sister. He loved the Templar history of the family and vowed to carry on that legacy. He established the Foundation first as a charity organization, but his second calling was to uncover the truth of the Templars and find some undiscovered aspect of the Templar life. We had the ancient records from here, and that seemed like a good place for him to start. For the past hundred and fifty years or so, we have been tracking down as much Templar lore as possible. Great, great granddad was the one that determined that the Foundation should fall to the family members that had the closest calling to the Templars, which was granddad and now Neil, and Kendra and me. My dad, also Geoff, is running the corporation, along with Kendra's dad. Neil heads up the Foundation. There you have it, the Carter family and its links to the Templars."

"That's a fascinating history. Imagine being able to trace your family roots back so far, with such clarity."

"We are proud of our long heritage. We had our tough times during those early years, with all of the changes in the political climate in England, but we managed to keep clear of the worst of it. Titles came and went, but the family endured."

"Yes, I've studied English history through the middle ages. It was a turbulent time for sure. It is amazing that your family has remained intact through all of that, right back to the 1300's and even farther. But what is the connection to this village?"

Neil took over the narrative at this point. "As Jason said, Godfrey, the last commander here was the original Geoffrey's brother. Geoffrey with William of Lothian's help had recorded all of the information and history about the village. This was passed down through the family over the years. As the records deteriorated, they were recopied into the latest technology. They are now in the process of being completely input into computers for digital storage. We knew that the village existed, and an approximate area to search. It was granddad who really became obsessed with finding the village. He had been to this area a few times, thinking that it should be around here, and maybe right under the town itself. We finally unraveled some of the mystery when I took a trip with him when I was still in high school. In the church, we found some stone that was not like any of the other ruins in the whole village. We asked around and found that there was a theory in the village that the stones had been part of another structure that was scavenged to build the church. We got permission to carbon date the stones and they came back as being from around the 1200's to 1300's. This excited Grandpa and he felt that he was close. Then we found out about some folklore about ancient sandstorms that had come through the area in the middle ages. The pieces fell together for Gramps, and he started to believe the village was right there just buried under the sand. We brought in sonar technology and stumbled on it. We started excavating and have gotten to this point so far. We're learning more and more about this place almost every week. And now you're bringing us even more information with your visions."

"So, why are you three so intimately connected to the village?"

"Well, this is where the more esoteric part of the conversation comes in; the part that will probably conflict the most with your Catholic beliefs. This is where I ask you to keep an open mind, and consider your own experiences of the past few days. Maybe that will help you consider the truth of this. Actually, let me start a little further back than this current generation. One of the theories that abounds about the Templar treasure, is that it contained the Arc of The Covenant, the vessel that stored the original version of the Ten Commandments. As well, there is speculation that there was also a box containing the original teachings of Jesus."

"The teachings of Jesus? Isn't that the Bible?"

"Not really," said Kendra. "The Bible was first written in its current form, some three to four hundred years after Jesus actually died. It wasn't the direct words of the man known as Yeshua but stories passed down via word of mouth, and then heavily edited by the powers of the time so they reflected only what they wanted the people to think and know. The Bible, as we know it today, first came into being about 400 AD. Many of the true and original meanings and words have been lost through the multiple translations over the years. Of course each translation has its own spin, depending on the beliefs of the sponsor of that particular version, and I include the current King James Version as an example of that. The real words of Yeshua, as he spoke them in Aramaic, are purported to have been buried at Mount Solomon not long after he and Mary Magdalene escaped from the Holy Land and went to France after the supposed crucifixion. One of the theories of the treasure is that the Templars found the teachings and used them to bribe the Vatican into silence, and hence how they became so powerful and rich in such a short space of time."

Kelly gaped at the three of them. "That's a pretty far-fetched theory isn't it?"

"No, actually, there's plenty of evidence that the Bible isn't the original teachings of Yeshua. There are many scholars who acknowledge the gaps in the Bible and are even now searching for missing gospels, and original tablets to confirm the words in the Bible."

Neil continued. "Whatever the truth of the matter, the
Templar families had a different set of beliefs than was traditional in the Roman Catholic Church, and the subsequent churches
that came about like the Church of England. So while we paid
lip service to the church of the day, we kept our own faith within
the walls of the family homes. This has continued right through
the years until now. One of the things that we accept as faith
has to do with the rebirth of the soul. Our faith is based on the
premise that the human body is simply a wrapper that a soul
chooses at birth in order to move about on the Earth. The soul
is immortal and returns time and again to this earth in order to
learn lessons and grow. That is why the three of us have such a
connection to the Templar village. We are all souls that did live
in the village at one time or another. Jason is a current incarna-
tion of William, the second in command who took the treasure
to Scotland. Kendra is a former commander of the garrison at
the village. As for me, the reason you felt that Godfrey was overlaid on me earlier today, well, I was Godfrey. Or rather the soul
that is the core of me was also the soul that occupied the body of
Godfrey. I know this seems like a real stretch, but it is the strong
belief in our family of the immortality of the soul."

Kelly stared at the three people in front of her in some
disbelief. She sure was trying to keep an open mind, but her
staunch Catholic upbringing was preventing her from doing so.
Souls being reborn again and again? The Bible wasn't the real
words of Jesus? Jesus didn't die on the cross? That was against
everything she had believed all her life. She did believe in the immortal soul, but that there was only one life cycle, and if you did
good you went to heaven, and if you did evil, you went to hell.
That was the simplicity of it. Now, here she had three extremely

intelligent and well-rounded people telling her that her beliefs were wrong? Kelly took a deep breath, '*open mind*,' she reminded herself, '*open mind*.'

"Okay, let's say I suspend my Catholic upbringing and consider the possibility of past lives. What makes you all think your past incarnations are the people you say they were?"

"Good question," said Kendra. "We've each done past life regressions with trained therapists, who didn't know of our family heritage and connection to the Templars. That's something the family has kept pretty hidden for the past centuries. As you can imagine, after the dissolution of the order, you didn't want to go about advertising that you were connected to them. Most families kept the secret and passed it on through the generations, only when the heir came of age. It has been thus since the 1300's. A few of the families ceased the practice of informing the heir. Thus many have lost the knowledge of their own Templar roots. It's a shame really, but given the political and religious times, it is hardly surprising."

Kelly took a minute to digest that information. How it echoed her hypnosis session. Wasn't that the information her subconscious was trying to pass on? Eleanor's brother had died and only just prior to her wedding had they informed both her and her husband of the Templar roots they shared. That Eleanor was the sole surviving heir to the Carter family in the 1700's? She still wasn't convinced that it was a true past life regression. She was convinced it was her own subconscious taking the research work she was doing and turning it into stories that she could use as part of her writing. But then again, she had to consider her experiences of the past few days. Either she was hallucinating and going crazy or she really was experiencing some past life or clairvoyant episodes. She preferred not to think of herself as ready for a straight-jacket. This left her considering the possibility that past lives were truly real?

"Kelly, there is one more thing that you need to consider here too. It's our connection. Have you ever fallen in love with someone the way we did? It was a matter of hours and I knew that you were the woman I wanted with me. You can't tell me that our connection is something you've encountered before."

"No, Neil, I've told you that. I don't understand why I feel so strongly how I do with you. It's something new to me, this love at first sight concept." She trembled as she remembered her 'dream' of Robert Brock Carter and the sizzling reaction she had. Could he really have been Neil in a prior life?

"But, add in the visions you've had and the possibility that you might have been Godfrey's servant. From what you and Jason have told me of what happened in the stable, it seems that Godfrey and his servant shared a special and close relationship. Certainly when Godfrey ordered him to flee the village when it was attacked was a sign of the deep love they shared. So, consider the possibility that what we share is a soul-deep knowledge that we're supposed to be together. Two souls reaching for the bond that is embedded deep within what we each are."

Kelly sat in quiet contemplation for a few minutes. Suddenly she recalled the nightmare that had awoken her two years ago, when she had first arrived at Eykel. How had she forgotten about that? If she coupled that with the image she had of that same badge in Godfrey's hands, how could there be any doubt? The image of St Michael, the seal and sigil, were these memories of some kind coming to the surface? She weighed what Jason, Kendra, and Neil had said to her, plus her own experiences in the village. *Maybe, just maybe there is something to be gained in further study? But this goes against everything that Mom and Dad had taught me as a good Catholic. But what harm could come from at least suspending my disbelief for a few days? Maybe I get a whole new perspective and understanding of life as I know it. Yes, what harm could come of it?*

"Okay, you make persuasive arguments that all of this could be plausible. I'm not saying I believe everything that you say, but I'm willing to at least consider the possibilities. That's all I can commit to right now."

"That's all we ask you to do. Whatever the source of your knowledge, the reality is that you have access to information on the village that no one else has been able to bring forth. That's what we need to work with you on, bringing that knowledge out. Then we can work to restore the true Templar heritage to the world."

"Well, there is the added thing that I don't want to be hauled off in a straight-jacket either. So the alternatives of either clairvoyance or past life memories are an infinitely superior outcome."

Jason, Kendra, and Neil all laughed at the image that Kelly had conjured of them all being rounded up in strait-jackets. The laughter broke the tension.

After a few minutes of silence, while they all contemplated the long history of the Templars and the Carters, Kendra spoke up. "I think we've covered the details of what we needed to here. I've an early start tomorrow with the tour groups, so I'm going to head out to get some sleep. Jason, let's head out."

"Sounds good. I hope we haven't overwhelmed you with information, Kelly."

"To some extent, yes. There's lots to think about that's for sure. Imagine you all believe that you're not only genetic descendants of the Templars, but soul descendants too? That's a lot to grasp at one time."

Jason grinned at Kendra and Neil, "You know I like that; genetic and soul descendants of the Templars. I like the sound of that."

Jason and Kendra said their good-byes to Kelly, and headed to the elevator. Neil followed to have a quick word with them. Kelly got up and moved to the large living room window. The sun had set while they had been talking. The moon wasn't up, so the village was only partially visible. It had a faint glow tonight. Kelly looked in the direction of the church and tried to determine what she believed of the narrative she had just heard. The genetic descendants she was prepared to believe. She imagined that any Templars that had escaped the massacre of King Philip would have gone into hiding. She could imagine a number of them throwing off the bonds of their oaths to the Templars and starting "normal" lives amongst the nobility of the time. That part she had no trouble with, including the ability to trace their roots back eight hundred years.

But, past lives, and souls reborn? She thought, *I'm not so sure of that.* But a small part of her whispered; *why can't it be true? I know things I shouldn't, in those visions. I'm not making those up. How could I have any subconscious memories like that?* She was seeing ghosts in many corners of the village. She hadn't shared with anyone the number of them she had seen. She figured she was hallucinating. But maybe she wasn't. Maybe she was sensitive to the power of the village. Maybe she was responding deep within herself to this place. She had to acknowledge that she did feel at home here; like it was familiar to her. Her déjà vu was strong and uncontested. *Maybe, just maybe, I need to reconsider and re-evaluate my long held beliefs? Maybe.*

Neil came up behind her and wrapped his arms around her.

"Penny for your thoughts, my love."

"Just going over what you all said tonight. I don't know what I believe anymore. All I do know is that I want to understand what's happening to me; both down in that village, and when I'm here in your arms. I am at a loss to explain any of it. Maybe your explanation is my answer? I don't know."

"It's a lot to take in at one time. I wish we could've gone slower, but the images and visions you're getting are too strong to ignore. Most people first encounter déjà vu when they visit a new place for a short time. Like someone being in Notre Dame and getting that 'spooky feeling', or in a castle anywhere in Europe. It happens all the time, but most people ignore it. You can't. You're getting bombarded by images all the time. And sometimes, something triggers it to come to the surface."

Kelly hesitated for a minute; *do I tell them what I've been seeing? If anyone will believe me it's these people. Do I risk it?* "I guess it's my turn now. I haven't told you about all the things I've been seeing. I've seen more of what I can only call 'ghosts' than I've probably mentioned."

"Why didn't you say anything to me? No, don't answer, I know why, fear, simple fear."

"Yeah, fear that I was going crazy. Fear you would think I was crazy; whatever you want to call it. But I can't deny it. I know my way around that village. It calls to me all the time, a siren call. I *need* to be there."

"Yes, you have the same call that I do to the place. You can't imagine how hard it has been for me to be away from here for the past eighteen months. But the memories of you here were too powerful. I couldn't be here without yearning for you. You were ignoring me and had pushed me out of your life. I just had to stay away. But you're here with me now. That's all that matters. We're together. We're here."

Neil turned Kelly in his arms to look deep into her eyes. He tried to touch her soul. He knew if he was open enough that he would be able to link with her at their core. The deep connection between them flared. He knew who she was to him, the other part of his soul. He reached down to touch her lips with his own. The passion that was always there flared to life between them. He pulled her close so she could feel his desire as it came alive. He kissed her thoroughly for a while, then pulled back to look at her again. He took her hands in his and kissed them. Then holding one, he walked with her to his bedroom, where he planned on making love to her for the rest of the night; sealing her fate to his for the rest of their lives.

XI

The next day had been a whirlwind for Kelly. She had spent it at the Templar village, completing her own investigations that had brought her here, plus opening up some new ones with Jason, Kendra, and Neil. One of the three had been with her at all times while she wandered around the site. They wanted to be sure that she shared any experiences that she had while looking around. There had been a number of them for her, but nothing as traumatic as the episode in the abbey. For that she had been thankful. The evening and night had been spent with Neil. They talked, they laughed, they shared their lives, and they made love. Every moment with Neil was special to her. She was deeply in love with the man. And now, here she was once again on the corporate jet winging her way to London to meet with his parents and grandfather and to attend a charity benefit tonight.

Her agitation grew with every mile that she drew closer to London. She didn't know what to expect from any of today's events. Her nerves were jangling and she had to take many deep breaths to keep herself calm. *What am I doing? Why did I agree to this? Good thing I called my brothers and Sam.* She wanted to make sure they were aware that she was going to be in London and might be photographed with Neil at the benefit. She knew that the cameras would be there, as it was at a benefit that she had first seen the picture of Neil with Hannah. She was apprehensive about meeting all these glamourous people that Neil knew and most especially his family. She was pretty sure she was going to feel like a fish out of water. Sam had been particularly understanding of what was going on. Their last call had been sad, but comforting at the same time.

"Honey, I know you're tempted by this new world that he can offer you. He is rich and famous and everything I'm not. But, from what you've told me of your past, it's just not something you see being a future together."

"I've told you about our past history, and I know that, long term, there are significant hurdles to overcome. I won't deny that the glamor of flying to England for a charity dinner is intriguing, but I know deep inside me that it's all show."

"Well, I wish you a good evening. Know that I'm here for you whenever you are ready to settle down. I love you, Kelly. Remember that."

He had hung up on that last comment. How sad she had been, seeing that lost and sorrowful look in his eyes. Perhaps he did care for her. She tried to remember the comfort she had felt being with him; but all that came to her mind was the passion and energy she shared with Neil.

"Are you still nervous about tonight?"

"Of course I am. Not to mention meeting your parents and granddad. I'm petrified right now."

"Take it easy, love. My parents and gramps are going to love you, mostly because I love you. I suspect Gramps will be singing for joy that I finally found my other half. He never liked Patricia and was happy when we split up."

"Yeah, but I'm nobody from Canada. That can't be what they expect from you."

"They expect me to love the woman I'm with. They want me to love deeply and forever. Call it a tradition in my family. We marry for love only, not for material considerations. And yes, I did love Patricia when we got married. But I had no idea what the feeling of a true soul bond was, until I met you. So while I loved Patricia, it was not the deep love that I have for you. Please relax. My family will love you. Just remember you've already met and spent a great deal of time with my family. Jason and Kendra are family, and they care for you and like you already. So, please….relax."

Kelly took a deep breath and tried to exhale her dread. What Neil said did make sense. In point of fact, she liked Kendra and Jason. They were his family, so maybe everything would be okay.

"Why don't you go to the back and lay down. We have a five hour flight, and it will be a long day today, even if it's only a two-hour time change. The benefit will go until well after midnight. So a rest might do you good."

"Sounds like a good idea. Join me?"

"In a while. I've a bit of work to take care of first. But I'll come back in about an hour."

Kelly leaned over and gave Neil a kiss. She poured all her love and longing for him into it. He responded to her as he always did. She pulled away breathless after a couple of minutes.

"Don't tempt me, my darling, or you'll join the mile high club right here and now."

Kelly chuckled. "Promises, promises."

"It is a promise, love. Now go get some rest. I'll be back shortly."

Kelly moved past Neil and felt him caress her back and butt as she slipped by him. She smiled to herself. Work be damned, he better come back soon. She moved past the little galley into the neat bedroom at the back of the plane. It was as she remembered it from two years ago. She didn't expect to sleep, but lay down just to relax; within minutes though she was fast asleep.

Neil looked in on her about thirty minutes later and saw that she was sleeping peacefully. He didn't want to disturb her. He simply closed the door and went back to the captain's chairs. They reclined nicely, and he was soon relaxing and meditating.

*****

Four hours later, the plane landed in London. They taxied to the private jet hangers and were picked up by a limo just outside the plane. They quickly left the airport behind and drove to the Carters' apartment. Neil had explained that he didn't have his own place right now. The family had a few apartments scattered around the world, and he stayed in hotels when those weren't available. Here in London they had a couple of small apartments as well as a home outside the city, which had been the seat of the De Cartier/ Carter family since the 1600's. Neil hoped to have time to take Kelly to the family home in Derbyshire. With her understanding of the Templar ways and architecture, she was going to love the place.

Kelly and Neil had both slept for more than two hours. Kelly had been surprised when she woke up to discover that she had slept so long. She was a little upset that Neil hadn't joined her in bed. When she asked him, he had said she was so sound asleep, spread across the entire bed, and he hadn't wanted to disturb her. She had laughed at the picture he painted of her sleeping like a princess. She knew that Ken had said the same thing that she liked to hog small beds. This was why he insisted they buy a king size bed, in order to have his own space.

Kelly found her apprehension had returned in full force now that she was on the ground and heading to the city. She knew that Neil's parents and granddad were waiting at the apartment. Neil reached over to hold her hand.

"Relax. They'll love you."

Kelly laughed. "Am I that easy to read?"

"For me, yes."

"Darn, I had hoped to maintain a seductive elusiveness for a little longer."

Neil laughed too. "Around me, that'd never be possible. Ah, here we are. Let's head in."

Kelly looked up at the imposing building in front of her. She thought she recognized it as Albert Court. She was impressed, but of course the Carters would have an apartment in this exclusive part of London. Neil stepped out of the limo and reached back in to give his hand to help Kelly out. She looked up at the imposing red brick building and felt a tremble course through her body.

"Relax, it's just an apartment building."

"I suspect that your 'little place' is bigger than my entire home back in Halifax."

"Come, let's grab our bags. I suspect my granddad is pacing the floor waiting to meet you."

"Oh thanks, that helps….NOT!"

Entering the building, they went up the elevator to the third floor, to the Carter apartment. They opened the door and crossed the threshold into the entry foyer. Kelly was not surprised to find the grandeur inside met the level of the outside of the building. Obviously this was an exclusive and luxurious address in London.

"Mom, Dad, Gramps? We're here."

"They're in the family room, so glad you made it. And this must be Kelly, please be welcome to our home."

Neil's mom reached out to pull Kelly into a close hug.

"I imagine you're both tired after that flight and want some time to freshen up."

"Actually, Mom, we slept most of the way, but I'm sure Kelly would like to freshen up a bit. We'll just pop in to say hi to Dad and Gramps, and then I'll take Kelly to my suite."

"Okay, I held lunch until you two arrived, so I'll get it served up in thirty minutes. Will that be enough time? And, Kelly, the store delivered three gowns for you to try on for tonight. I hope they fit you. Neil did give me your size, but you never know how some of these will fit. Perhaps after lunch we should try them on and see what we have."

"Mrs. Adams, I'm overwhelmed. It all sounds so 'Cinderella' to me."

Katrine laughed. "I guess it's a bit over the top isn't it. And please, call me Katrine. Now off with both of you. Dad and Christopher are waiting for you."

Neil led Kelly further into the apartment, through the formal entertaining area. She quickly glanced around at the elegant room. There was a unique round table at one end with ten chairs around it. The wood gleamed in hues of red mahogany.

The chairs were covered in a pretty green and white pattern that was echoed in the tile surrounding the huge fireplace at the other end of the room. Close to the fireplace there were ornate chairs and a small sofa. Glancing up she could see the coffered ceiling with elaborate details that spoke of the history of the building. On the walls were massive pieces of art work. Unless she was mistaken, many were originals by the masters.

"This is the formal room that we have for our more intimate but traditional dinner parties. We all prefer the cozier parlor and kitchen eatery at the other end of the place. Come, I'll show you the way. Then we can go to the bedroom and you can take a quick look at the dresses Mom ordered for you."

Kelly felt her feet dragging as they moved to the west side of the apartment. Neil walked ahead of her into a sun-filled room that held comfortable looking and relaxing furniture. Neil greeted his dad and granddad with heart felt hugs and back slaps.

"Dad, Gramps, I want you to meet Kelly, my date for tonight. Kelly, this is my father, Christopher Adams, and my grandfather, Sir Robert Carter."

Christopher was the first one to hold out his hand to Kelly. "Kelly, it's a pleasure to meet you. Neil has spoken much of you over the past couple of years. I'm happy that you're finally able to join us here in London. And please, call me Christopher."

"Christopher, it's nice to meet you."

"Young lady, you've led my grandson on a grand chase for the past two years. Well I remember that first night after he met you and how much he talked about showing you the church tower. I knew then that he had finally found his Abigail. I am happy that you finally recognize the connection between you two- about time in my estimation. I'm happy you finally are here."

Kelly was taken aback by the greeting from Neil's granddad.

"Gramps, really."

"Just saying it like it is, my boy, no point in beating around the bush amongst family."

"Mr. Carter, I am pleased to meet you finally. Neil has told me much of you."

"There she goes, calling me Mr. Carter. Out with it, girl. I'm Gramps to everyone around here. That includes you too."

"Gramps, please, give Kelly a chance to catch her breath."

"Neil, my boy, she is your Abigail, so that makes her family."

Neil sighed in exasperation at his granddad's excessive greeting. "Kelly and I are just going to go freshen up. Mom said she'd have lunch ready in a few more minutes. We'll join you shortly."

Neil guided Kelly down the hall toward the bedrooms of the apartment. "Sorry about Gramps. He tends to get a bit enthusiastic about things. Kind of puts the cart before the horse sometimes."

"No problem. He actually seems like an adorable old man."

"Adorable? Not many would call him that. But I love the old man and all that he means to the family. He'll settle down in a bit. I'm sure dad and mom will talk to him, and get him to lighten up a bit."

"Who is Abigail?"

"She was my grandmother. She passed away ten years ago. Gramps met her when he was seventeen and she was twenty. He liked the older women in his day. He tells the story that he knew within a few minutes of meeting her that she was the only woman for him. He loves to talk about how it took him five years to convince her of the same thing. But he finally did, and they married when he was twenty-three. They had three children, my mom and her two brothers. One of my uncles, Jason's granddad, is running the corporation. My other uncle escaped the family business and is an architect running his own firm in the U.S. He was the reason I wanted to go into architecture in the first place. Gramps had other ideas for me, and eventually I came to believe in his vision of my future."

"As I said, adorable old man, but still a firecracker."

"That he is. Here's my suite. It's got a bathroom and small sitting area so I can work away in here when I'm in town. I don't come here often, but it's nice to have this place as a base. I'm sure my mom has put those dresses in the wardrobe in the dressing room. Why don't you check those out, and I'll freshen up in the bathroom."

Kelly wandered in the direction he had indicated and opened the wardrobe. She found three gowns that were all more elegant and glamorous than anything she had ever owned in her life. She stood staring at them in awe. How was she going to choose any of these? She quickly closed the wardrobe door and decided to wait until later before making a choice. Time enough for that, after all it was only one p.m. London time, but to her it was three.

Twenty minutes later, she and Neil went back to the kitchen to have lunch. She felt a bit more relaxed having at least gotten the introductions out of the way. Now she could settle into her day as Cinderella.

Lunch passed quickly in easy conversation. They were all interested in Kelly's past and her life in Canada. She was surprised to find that Katrine had studied to be a teacher too. Although she had met Christopher during her studies, and instead of becoming a teacher, she had joined Christopher in his business prior to amalgamating it into the Carter family empire. Christopher had then gradually learned all of the Carter's far flung enterprises, and was now working with Katrine's brother on running the entire operation.

Grandpa Robert had been particularly curious about her writing and had asked to see her work. Neil printed the article she wrote two years ago and showed it to them all. They were impressed at her writing style. Grandpa had been quite taken with her description of widowhood, and they chatted a bit about that bond they had in common.

After lunch was over, Katrine had suggested that she and Kelly repair to the bedroom to try on the gowns for the evening's benefit. She was of the opinion that Neil could wait with the other men and see the effect of the dress in full when she came out of her room. Kelly was starting to feel like Cinderella now. She wondered what would happen when midnight came.

Katrine and Kelly moved the gowns into the main dressing room off the master bedroom. Kelly tried all three on. One was a pale green ball gown that was a halter top crisscrossing over the front and then billowing down to a full length chiffon skirt. The second one was a sexy red form fitting dress that had small capped shoulders and a plunging neckline that revealed a lot of cleavage. The final dress was a blue or, more correctly, azure chiffon dress that was strapless. The bodice was form fitting with small crystal accents. The skirt billowed down in a chiffon drape over a silk underlay, extending down to ankle length. Kelly tried on all three, but was particularly taken with the vibrant blue and the way it fell from her waist to the ankle length skirt.

"I think this blue one is perfect for me."

"I agree; the color is perfect for you. The rich jewel tone sets off your skin, hair, and eyes. The red gown does the same thing, but I think it's a bit too sexy for tonight's affair, and I suspect you'll feel a bit 'over revealed' in it, and uncomfortable. I think we should have your hair done up and swept up off your face. I know I have the exact necklace and earrings that will complement the dress to perfection."

"Katrine, I have a nice necklace with me that will work on this."

"No argument, the one I'm thinking of will suit this dress. It was one of my mother's sets, and I rarely wear it. Dad would love to see it on you."

Kelly looked at herself in the mirror and was amazed at the glamorous look that she presented. A small piece of her was waiting now with anticipation to see Neil's reaction. She suspected he would approve of the gown.

"Now, I would suggest that you have another nap and relax for a few hours. The benefit will go on until all hours tonight. I suspect that you've had enough stress already meeting us. So I suggest you head off to your room. I'll send Neil in to you. You can relax together until it is time to get ready to go."

"I think that'd be a good idea. I'm tired again, what with the trip and the time difference and all. I think a rest would be a good idea."

"Okay, I will see you at six so we can get ready to go for dinner and the benefit."

****

Kelly looked at the clock in the atrium of the Grosvenor House Hotel. It was getting close to midnight. She was making her way back into the main ballroom after having a few minutes to herself. She had been disconcerted by the whirlwind evening. They had left the apartment just after seven and taken a limo to the Grosvenor. There they had been photographed by multitudes as they descended from the car and moved across the red carpet into the hotel. She had been shaking in her shoes as they entered the hotel, and only Neil's hand on her waist had prevented her from bolting into the crowd and running away. The flash bulbs had gone off in rapid succession with a number of calls of "Neil this way, please. Who's the lady?" They had also taken a group picture just inside the hotel for the charity to advertise the attendees at this grand gala event.

Neil had been holding onto her possessively as they moved across the threshold and into the ballrooms. They were stopped a number of times by people the Carters knew and she was introduced to more people than she could even come close to remembering. There had been a few dukes and duchesses, some princes and princesses, and a number of stars, some she recognized and some not; as well as the who's who of corporate leaders in England. With the approach of midnight she was feeling increasingly like Cinderella, and figured she had better make an escape soon, before the gown she was wearing turned back into rags.

She let her mind wander back to earlier in the evening when Neil had first seen her in the gown as she left his mother's dressing room. The azure looked stunning on her, she knew. She couldn't believe how the color and cut flattered her so well. Katrine's maid had styled her hair for her, sweeping it up off her face and into a bun at the back of her head. A few stray locks had been left down to soften the look around her neck. The necklace and earrings that she borrowed from Katrine had turned out to be a glittering confection of sapphires and diamonds. When she saw it, she had protested that it was far too expensive and precious for her to risk losing. But Katrine had insisted that the combination was perfect for the gown, and had placed the necklace around her neck. When Kelly had looked at the finished product in the mirror, she had been stunned. Who was this glorious creature staring out at her? This wasn't she; there had to be a mistake.

When she and Katrine had left the dressing room, they had met Neil, his dad and granddad in the sitting room. Neil had stood when they entered, and the look in his eyes was all that Kelly needed to see. He moved toward her and took her hands in his. "My god, Kelly, you look stunning. If I wasn't already head over heels in love with you, I would have fallen the moment you walked in here. Mom, thank you, the gown is perfect for her."

"My dear, you look beautiful. And I'm happy to see Abigail's sapphires on you. It was her favorite gem. I know that Katrine prefers emeralds, so I'm very happy she gave them to you to wear. They're perfect on your skin."

"Thanks, Grandpa Robert. It is an incredible necklace and earrings. I figure the earrings themselves cost more than all of the jewelry I own. I feel like Cinderella tonight."

"My love, you look more beautiful than Cinderella could ever hope to. And your coach doesn't turn into a pumpkin at midnight. And your prince already loves you with all his heart." Neil reached down to kiss her with his heart in his eyes.

"Neil, don't muss her up. Besides, we need to get moving to the limo."

"Yes, Mother. I'll behave…for now."

Neil and Kelly looked over to his parents. Kelly noticed that Katrine and Christopher were looking at them with a clear look that said, 'at last'.

"Well, my boy, you've definitely found her. Seeing you together reminds me of the many times Abigail and I dressed for dinner. And the look in both of your eyes is the same as your Mother had when she and Christopher first started dating."

"Thanks, Gramps, I know I have. Now I understand what you and Mom and my uncles were talking about when you described meeting 'that perfect one'. I knew it the minute I saw her. Now, it's a hundred times stronger and growing every day."

*****

Kelly walked back into the main ball room still thinking about the look in Neil's eyes when he had made the last remark. It had been the most intense and loving gaze she had ever seen. It had penetrated to the depths of her being and connected to her inner soul. She looked around for Neil. He had said he would still be at the table, and there he still was, talking to his mother. They had been dancing much of the night away and had just stepped off the dance floor when she excused herself to go to the ladies' room. A stunning brunette, who was dressed in the highest fashion in bright red, was also with them. She gulped as she recognized her from the pictures of Neil last year and realized this must be Hannah. She grew nervous again. She couldn't hope to compete with this glamourous woman.

Kelly joined them. "Kelly, there you are. Hannah, let me introduce my girlfriend. This is Kelly Taylor, from Canada. I know I mentioned her to you. Kelly, this is Hannah Wagner, from those pictures you saw."

"Kelly, it's a pleasure to meet you finally. Neil spoke of you so many times in the evenings we spent together. I'm happy that you've finally managed to get here to London for one of these events."

"Hannah, it's a pleasure to meet you too."

"Neil Adams, finally we get you to one of these little soirees. I'm happy to see you here darling."

This was from a woman who barged her way into the tableau and cut Neil off from the other three women. Hannah rolled her eyes at Kelly, while Katrine looked pained.

"Neil, darling, it is past time for you to move back here permanently. I know my daughters will be most happy to join you in any of the events that we host. It is time for you to marry again. And of course, the most eligible women are all here in London. It is time to come back to your roots in the English countryside."

"Lady Davenport, it is nice to see you again. Let me introduce you to my girlfriend. Kelly, this is Lady Davenport. Lady Davenport, this is Kelly Taylor from Halifax, Canada. And of course, you already know my Mother and Hannah Wagner."

"Oh yes, I am well aware of who Hannah Wagner is. Katrine, as always. And why should I care about a nobody from

Canada? Neil, let us repair to our lounge so you can mingle with the people who count and who can help your Foundation."

With this Lady Davenport pulled Neil's arm and commandeered him to move into the lounge to the side of the main hall. This had been set aside by the Davenport family as a separate salon where they would not be disturbed by the masses, as they liked to call them. Neil moved along with her, conscious that he needed to meet with these people, as they were supporters of the Foundation. He knew that mom would explain the situation to Kelly. This invitation from Lady Davenport could not be ignored, or he risked the funding that he needed.

Kelly looked around in silence at Katrine and Hannah. She knew that she looked perplexed.

"Just ignore her. Lady Davenport and her group deem themselves to be aristocrats that can ignore the 'unwashed masses', as they call them. They look down their snotty little noses at anyone that can't trace their roots back to Elizabethan times. But, unfortunately, they are either wealthy themselves or have access to or control great wealth. So, The Foundation has to appear to work with them. They have to some degree decided to overlook Neil's roots, probably since he is considered a wealthy bachelor. I guess they figure if one of their daughters marries him then they can cut him off from the 'low life' family he has. Fat chance any of them has in any attempt to marry. Neil is permanently taken now by you, Kelly."

"Yes, Kelly, just ignore them. They are old farts who can't see that the world has changed. But Neil will be some time with them, so I'm going to introduce you to the people Neil, my boyfriend, Trevor, and I hang out with. Come with me, to the fun side of this party."

Hannah beckoned Kelly to follow her to another room that had been opened for the ball now that the dinner was over. They moved to a large table set part way into the room that was crowded with about twenty people. Kelly recognized a few of them from pictures that were in the tabloids as some of the young wealthy set that visited all of the hot spots around Europe. Were these the people that Neil normally hung out with? If so, she was sadly way outside her element with these glamorous people.

"Everyone, this is the mysterious Kelly that Neil has been moping about for the past year. He finally convinced her to come to London to attend one of these soirees."

There was a chorus of 'Hi Kelly' from the group at the table.

"Let me introduce my boyfriend, Trevor. I finally convinced him to come to one of these evenings as well. He is feeling a little like a deer in the headlights, as I'm sure you are too. But in reality, Neil and I normally don't hang with this crowd too much. We both prefer to be out of the limelight. Neither of us is of the "wealthy playboy" set that is always in trouble in the tabloids. Still at these things, they are the most fun to hang with."

Kelly sat down where Hannah indicated on one side of Trevor, while she sat on the opposite side.

"Hi, Kelly, nice to finally meet you. And I'm so glad that I'm not the only one here that doesn't have a six figure 'play' fund."

Kelly chuckled at the image Trevor presented. "Yeah, I feel completely out of my element here. I'm an elementary school teacher in Canada. These earrings I'm wearing probably cost more than all of the jewelry I have at home. It's intimidating to say the least. But Neil and his family have been by my side all the time, so they've cushioned some of the blow."

"Let me guess, Neil was co-opted by the "assistocats". That's my name for those stuck up snobs who are forever looking down their noses at the unwashed or the 'noveau riche'."

"Yeah, a Lady Davenport barged into our group and hauled him off for a discussion. Hannah was kind enough to rescue me from being left on my own. I know Neil's mom was planning to leave soon with her dad, and Hannah has kept me from being a wall flower."

"Kelly, Trevor, I'm just going to see what I can do to pry Neil out of the clutches of Lady Davenport and her ilk. Maybe then the four of us can go find something a little quieter and more in our taste to do. Sounds good love?"

"Yes it does, I want to get out of this monkey suit. I think I've done enough for the fund raising cause now."

Hannah smiled at Trevor. "One of the many things I love about you, Hon; you see right to the heart of the matter. Yes, we've done enough here for this gala. You know it is one of the charities that is near to my heart, but I prefer to be more hands on with the kids, than attending these types of fund raisers. Let me get Neil, and then maybe we can spin by the hospital to see the real beneficiaries of this."

Trevor smiled at Hannah. "The kids would love to see you and Kelly all dressed for the gala. They'd love to think that at some time they could be dressed so elegantly and look so beautiful. Sadly, most will never see their twentieth birthday."

Kelly looked at Trevor in question as Hannah left. She watched as he marked her progress across the room. She could see how very much he loved her.

"Trevor, I knew this was a children's charity ball, but I didn't get any more details than that."

"I'm not surprised; most of the people here wouldn't even cross the threshold of some of the charities this Foundation supports. The one I work at is a children's hospital. We are much like the U.S. Shriners hospitals in that we take all children regardless of nationality and ability to pay. Most of our cases come from third world countries where the standard of care is so poor that most of them would've died far too quickly. We can't save all of them, but we try. I'm a doctor, a pediatrician. I did a stint with Doctors without Borders, and that's how I found the hospital I work at now."

"Oh wow, I had no idea you were a doctor. Neil had mentioned that Hannah had a boyfriend, but nothing else about you."

"I keep my professional life quiet amongst this set. They wouldn't understand my need to work with the underprivileged. They don't even have a concept of what it is to be hungry or to not have medical care. It's enough to make my blood boil when I realize how most of these people give lip service to helping the poor by attending these types of galas. Most of them would never step into a hospital room to hold a child that was scared. That makes me sick."

Kelly looked at Trevor with understanding. "Yes, it is sad how so few of the world's truly rich people give any care for the rest of the world."

"I'm sorry. I didn't mean to preach to you. I sometimes get carried away, especially when I'm at these functions. I normally don't come with Hannah to anything like this. I don't want the publicity that comes with being with her in public. Don't get me wrong, I love Hannah with all my heart. I just don't like the public side of all this."

"I know what you mean. This is the first time I've attended and event like this with Neil. I don't even own a dress as
glamorous as this one, let alone these jewels. I live a quiet life in
Canada. I wasn't prepared for the hundreds of pictures that were
taken when we got here. I'm glad I told my family I was coming,
or they would have been really surprised."

"Yes, my family is one of the main reasons I keep out of
the limelight with Hannah. I don't want them subjected to the
intense scrutiny that comes from being even remotely involved
with an heiress. It wouldn't be fair to them. So I keep as low a
profile as I can. This is one of the few galas that I do attend.
As a doctor at the hospital, I can justify being here to support
the charity."

"You two, like Neil and I, are from such separate worlds.
How did you meet?"

"We met at the hospital. As Hannah said earlier, she likes
to be hands on with the charities she supports, especially children's hospitals. She was at the hospital the first time I saw her.
I had just gotten back from Africa, returning from a Doctors
without Borders stint. I was doing my rounds and checking on
the new patients I was going to be working with. I came into one
of the play rooms and found a beautiful woman telling a tale to
all of the kids. They were all lost in rapt silence as she recounted
a tale of a beautiful princess who was looking for love. I stood by
the door and just watched her. As she came to the end of her tale
she happened to look up toward me. As soon as our eyes met,
I was a goner. I fell head over heels with her in that moment. It
wasn't until a few weeks later that I found out who she truly was.
She introduced herself only as Hannah that day. Imagine my

surprise to open my paper one day to find her on the cover of the fashion section- attending a ball with Neil as it turned out."

"Oh, I understand that one. Neil had warned me about the pictures and tales that would be in the papers. It didn't prepare me for seeing a picture of Neil with Hannah and a full article about how they were supposedly engaged and would marry in the summer, 'uniting their fortunes', as the paper put it. I was in Canada then, and hadn't seen Neil in six months. So, I imagined the worst, and we ended up losing touch."

"Kelly, Trevor, sorry that took so long. It was surprisingly hard to pry Neil from their clutches, but here we are, and I already told Hans to bring the car around. It should be out front now."

"Sorry, love, I didn't expect that to take quite so long."

"It's okay, Neil, I understand. Besides it gave Trevor and I a chance to get to know each other."

"I don't know about you all, but I've had enough of this. What say we leave here and go see if any of the kids are still up? I doubt it, but you never know with them. Then we can go find a nice quiet pub to have a couple of drinks and relax the rest of the night."

"Dressed like this at a pub?"

Hannah laughed. "Don't worry Kelly, there are a few galas tonight, and we won't be the only ones over-dressed for a pub."

The four of them went to the foyer in order to leave the hotel. On the way to the car, more photographers flashed pictures of them. "Hey, Neil, and Hannah, this way please the two of you. When are you going to announce your engagement?"

"Who knows? We aren't planning anything in the near future."

"Come on, Kelly," said Trevor, "this is our chance to escape to the car, without having a lot of pictures taken."

"Dr. Abbott, did you enjoy the ball? A little outside your budget isn't it?"

"Thank you, I did enjoy my night. I was fortunate that Neil and Hannah saw fit to invite a few of the doctors from the hospital to attend. It was nice to be able to thank these people in person for their generosity. The hospital and its associated charities always appreciate the support the people of Britain give us. But I must be going; I have an early surgery tomorrow morning."

Trevor then escorted Kelly down the boulevard to a line of cars that was waiting for them. Trevor moved her toward a blue and grey sedan parked at the end of the row.

"Dr. Abbott, I see Hannah is fending off the photographers again."

"Yes, Hans, she is, and allowed Kelly and me to escape. This is Neil's girlfriend. They will be joining us for the rest of the evening."

"A pleasure Miss. Why don't you both hop in the car, while I get Hannah and Neil?"

"My thanks, Hans."

Kelly and Trevor climbed into the car. It wasn't many minutes later that Hannah and Neil joined them. The car edged away from the curb and into traffic as soon as they were all settled.

"Well, looks like I made it past midnight and the gown didn't turn to rags, nor the car into a pumpkin. Maybe I've escaped poor Cinderella's fate?"

Trevor, Hannah and Neil all laughed.

PART 3

I

"Gerard, wake up."

Gerard was dimly aware of a hand shaking him. The insistence in the voice was enough to interrupt his dreams. He cracked his eyes open, to find William of Lothian standing over his bunk.

Groggily he looked at the Second in Command and stirred enough to sleepily say, "Sir, I'm sorry, did I sleep in?"

"Shh, no, it's still the middle of the night. Be quiet, we don't want to wake the other boys. We are going to finish the loading of the camels now and get underway before day break. Godfrey asked me to wake you so you could assist with the final preparations."

"Yes, sir."

Gerard got up, quickly dressed, and followed William out of the barracks, moving quietly to avoid waking the other stable boys. They went into the silent streets of the town and headed toward the town square. No one was about yet, although Gerard could catch the faint whiff of bread baking. The cooks were up at least. His stomach rumbled.

"I know, the smell from the bakery is hard at this time. But you had best keep an empty stomach for this morning's work."

Gerard made a turn toward the banking hall, but felt a hand on his shoulder leading him toward the other side of the square, in the direction of the church.

"Come this way, Gerard, there is something in the church to attend to first."

Puzzled, Gerard fell into step beside William as he entered the church. Both briefly bowed their heads to the Lady Mary statue hidden to the left of the church entrance. As Gerard raised his head, he could see Godfrey and three other senior knights at the altar, one he only knew by reputation, Sir Rai Bin Hassan, a Knight of supreme standing. He was reputed to have deep lore and magic. The stable boys had been abuzz yesterday with speculation about why he had arrived. Gerard had been in the stables when he arrived on his beautiful black Arab mare. She was a delicate creature, but strong from all evidence. Sir Rai had headed directly to the Abbey after dismounting. He had been closeted with Godfrey and the senior commanders all day. The three were standing on the seals of the cardinal points close by the images of Archangel Michael. He felt William move to take his position at the unfilled cardinal point.

"Come forward, Gerard, into the center of the circle." Godfrey beckoned him forward to the middle of the knights. He knelt in the center as Godfrey gestured for him to do.

"Gerard, this is an unusual ceremony that we are invoking tonight. There is reason to believe that our enemies will be upon us sooner than later. As you know, we are sending the bulk of the treasure with William this morning to safety. Yet, there is some that we simply cannot risk in transport, so they will be hidden here to remain safe until the time comes for them to be revealed. We wish to bind you and your soul to the protection of this as a

Guardian of the Temple. The ceremony this night will bind you to the service of the Temple for all time. Are you willing to make such a commitment?"

"I am, my brother."

"Gerard né Laney de Cruce you have been brought to this place to confirm your dedication to be a Guardian of the Temple. This oath will place on you the burdens of secrecy and service to the great glory of God. Are you willing and able to provide such a dedication?"

"I am and I will."

"Do you promise to God, and to our dear Lady Mary, to observe all your life long, the customs of our Order, and to uphold the secrecy placed upon you this night to only reveal that which is given to you in faith to another whom dutifully provides you the required codes?"

"I am and I will so commit."

"Then by the power vested in me as the Commander of Eykel, I welcome you to the ranks of Guardians of the Temple. Uphold thy commitments with honor and faith."

Gerard looked at his brother as the sword in his hands was raised and descended to his shoulders. After it had touched both of his shoulders, he sensed the other four knights move toward him.

"Rise now, brother Gerard, and join us in the hiding of the treasures of our Order."

Gerard rose and was drawn aside from the center of the church into the area close by the side of the altar. There was a small room to the side that Gerard had never seen before. He could see a dark and narrow stair leading down.

"Come, Gerard, be not afraid. This entrance was built into the church many years ago in the expectation that we would require a safe haven at some point. We will wall it and seal it now to be revealed again when the two who dedicate the seal through a blood bond are reunited and the time has come for all this to come to light again. We are to be those two. Please join with me my brother to be a Guardian."

"Godfrey and Gerard, please join thy hands together and stand at the sides of the entrance." Sir Rai Bin Hassan directed them, joined by the other knights.

Gerard did as he was directed and joined his hands to Godfrey. Godfrey looked at him once more.

"Although you are not my brother by blood, you became my brother when my father did marry your mother. And in truth we were raised together and love as brothers should. And you have joined me as a brother Guardian. Please pair with me now in the blood bond that will seal our fates together as the Guards of the treasure hidden within this church. Never shall we reveal the treasure concealed within until we are reunited again as souls bound to the same fate. Are you willing to make such a blood oath?"

"I am, brother of mine."

"Then I ask these four knights to witness our vows and to consecrate this blood bond with the dagger descended from our founders and seal our fates to each other and to the treasure hidden within."

Gerard felt a knight grab him from behind, as one did to Godfrey. The other knights clasped their hands tightly together. Fascinated Gerard watched a dagger materialize in Sir Rai's hand.

"By the power and protection of Archangels Michael, Gabriel, Raphael and Uriel, we, the Guardians of the Temple witness and commit this blood oath between Godfrey de Cruce and Gerard né Laney de Cruce to seal this wall against intrusion and detection until such time as their souls are reunited in love and harmony and in the presence of these four souls to lift the burden placed on these two. In the name of God, our Dear Lady Mary, and the Lord Jesus, let it be done."

Gerard watched in fascination as the dagger was lowered to come into contact with his and Godfrey's hands where they were joined. Pain exploded in his hand as the dagger made contact.

*****

Kelly jolted awake, shaking all over and soaked in sweat. Sandy was licking her face, trying to comfort her. Already the threads of the nightmare were disappearing as she came fully awake. What she could remember was the fear and pain she felt as the dagger descended. But yet there was also the compassion she could feel coming from Godfrey and the mysterious knight. This dream was nothing like her past experiences in Eykel. It was entirely new to her. The shock was immense. She reached for the diary she kept at her bedside to write down what she could remember. She had been doing this for a few weeks now, ever since her return from London. The dreams or nightmares were becoming more frequent now. It was disturbing her sleep to no end.

Why had this nightmare come tonight of all nights? She had broken things off with Neil earlier that evening. How vivid that was still in her mind. She let her mind wander back to the call.

*****

"Kelly," Neil said with rising anger in his voice, "I can't believe you're saying this to me now. After everything we've been through together. How can you possibly break it off?"

"Neil, it's for the best. I don't fit into your life. I have a life here in Halifax. I can't be the person you need to have beside you."

"You are my soul, you are my heart. How can you not be the person I need?"

"Use your sense, Neil. I'm not cut out to be the globe-trotting girlfriend you need, the high profile hostess to grace your arms at those balls."

"But that's not my life. My life is with you."

"Be serious. Your life is everything that is The Foundation. You are the face of it. You have to do this work. I'm just not part of that scene and can't live that life with you."

Neil groaned in frustration. "I can't let you continue to jerk me around like a marionette on a chain. First you want to be together, now you don't. My heart can't take this yo-yo life. If you break if off now, I don't ever want to see you again. This time, it's forever. I just can't do this again- get my hopes up, to have you splatter them all over again when you get scared."

Kelly looked at Neil and could see both the anger in his look, and the unshed tears in his eyes. "I know, Neil. But this is how it has to be for me. I just can't do this. I'm sorry. Good-bye, Neil. Be well."

And Kelly had hung up the Skype connection, turned to Sandy, and bawled her eyes out.

She had finally fallen asleep well after midnight. And now she was awakened by this nightmare? What was going on? Kelly took a deep breath to center her mind, and let her hand wander over the page, writing the details that her conscious mind was already trying to erase. She had experimented with this writing method the last few days and found it captured the most details of her dreams, when she just let the pen flow and try to tap the subconscious mind.

A few minutes later, she was satisfied that she had captured all the details that were pertinent. She knew better than to reread it at this time, and simply closed her book, then tried to settle back to sleep. Sandy nestled in beside her. She placed her hand on the dog's warm body, closed her eyes and tried to relax. Too bad this was the Thanksgiving weekend, and she couldn't call Barry or Dr. Klein tomorrow. She knew they would be able to help her sort out the many dreams she had been having. Hopefully she could get some time with them in the coming weeks. With a deep breath and a sigh, Kelly drifted back to sleep.

II

Christmas Break

Kelly sat at her desk and stared into the classroom. It was a few days before Christmas, and she was about to dismiss the class for the break. She was looking forward to the two weeks off. It had been an incredibly tough term for her. The kids weren't the problem. She was still nursing her broken heart and fighting the recurring nightmares that disturbed her sleep regularly. She hadn't seen Neil since she had left Europe at the end of August when she came home for the school year. As the last time, they had had great intentions of getting together as regularly as they could, but soon she realized that it simply wasn't going to happen. Her life was in Canada, and his was around the world. As much as her soul longed to be with him, her logical mind enumerated the many ways that they were different, and so could never be together. He was rich, famous, and a globe-trotting billionaire, who moved with a fast set and was constantly in the limelight for either charity work or at Cannes or other such world-wide festivals. She on the other hand was a simple elementary school teacher from small town Nova Scotia. Her "globe-trotting" was confined to the globe in her classroom, and the closest she got to Cannes was to watch the odd film that had made its debut there when it came to Canada. Her one foray into that fast paced world at the charity ball had left her feeling dazed and confused. Cinderella attending the grand ball with her prince. However this story didn't have the "happily ever after." No, on the contrary, after the brutally difficult call with Neil in October, she was left nursing a broken heart. She knew that after the heartbreak of losing her dad and Ken, and now splitting with Neil, that it would be a very long time before her heart healed fully, if ever.

All she wanted to do at Christmas was to sleep and rest and work on her manuscript about the Templar village. The article she had written in the fall describing her travels and the adventure in Europe and Africa had been a great success, and this book was a natural progression from the article. She hoped it would help her put behind her the images that still haunted her of the village when it had been attacked those long years ago. She could still see the village in her mind's eye as it had looked when it had been occupied in the 1300's.

Ah Neil, how she still loved that man, and would for the rest of her life. After the gala ball, she had been shocked to see all of the pictures of her and Neil published in the tabloids. There had been big question marks about who she was, and some enterprising reporter had managed to dig up a few facts about her, but much was left to speculation. She did admit that she looked stunning in the blue dress and sapphires that she had borrowed from Neil's parents.

That day she had gotten an email from Sam questioning her about Neil and her feelings for him. She had ignored that one as she hadn't been quite sure what to tell him about her current state of mind. She didn't want to break it off with him over the phone or via email, so she had just ignored it. She had returned home as scheduled in late August, although Neil had wanted her to stay for another week. She had compromised and agreed to stay until the thirty-first, which made her a bit late in getting ready for the school year.

The week with Neil had been wonderful and overwhelming. By the time she got home, she knew that as much as she loved Neil, she wasn't cut out for a long term relationship with him. She hadn't heard from him since October, other than the many pictures she saw of him escorting women to all sorts of functions. He had gone right back to the high flying life he had always lived.

She glanced at the clock, only a few minutes until dismissal; time to wish the kids a 'Merry Christmas,' and remind them of their assignment.

"All right class, it's almost the end of the day and the end of the term. Christmas break is here. I wanted to wish those of you who celebrate a very Merry Christmas and to all of you a Happy New Year. I will remind you all of your assignment for the New Year. You are to find something 'new' to do. It can be a new habit like eating more fruit, a new food you will eat like broccoli or mushrooms, or a new sport or hobby you want to try, like knitting." Here the classroom broke into laughter at the thought of any of them knitting. "It can be anything that is new to you that will expand your normal daily routine and change your daily habits. We will discuss them in class in January and see how long we can all manage the new habit. I will tell you mine now, so you can think about what you want to change. My new thing is going to be to eat more vegetables. So I'm going to bring vegetables with me to class every day, and eat them here in the class, so you can mark down and watch my progress in this new habit. Here is the board we are going to track this on. I'll put my name on it now, with my new habit, and then we can see how many days in the New Year I manage to honor this commitment to myself." Kelly marked her new habit on the cardboard she had obtained for the task. All twenty of her kids' names were already included on the board, with hers at the top. She marked in her 'eat more vegetables' goal and then closed the marker. The bell rang indicating the end of the day.

"All right class, you are dismissed. Enjoy the holidays, and see you all in the New Year."

The kids all packed up their desks and exited the room quickly. They were all as eager as she to get started on the holiday. She went to her desk and pulled together her notes and things she wanted to take home with her. Just as she finished wrapping up her tidying, Dan poked his head into her class.

"Hey, Kelly, all wrapped up for the break?"

"Yes, Dan, all finished up; time to head home for two weeks of relaxation."

"Not too much of that for Mary and me, we have all the kids home this year, so it will be a busy week. Would you care to join us for Christmas Day? Mary would love to have you over. With all of ours being boys, she doesn't get much chance to have a woman's voice in the commotion. Although this year, Jason is bringing a girlfriend with him, so that will be new. We haven't met her yet."

"Poor thing, meeting all of your family at Christmas? What was Jason thinking? She'll run away fast."

"Yup, but on the other hand, if she fits in, she'll have seen us all at our worst, so maybe there would be hope if she sticks around."

"True. And thanks for the offer, but I've already planned to be with my brothers on Christmas. I'm going to drive over to Kentville to get Mom and everyone will be at my brothers on Christmas Day. Should be fun."

"That's great, as long as you're with your family. We're also planning a small gathering for New Years. Please come over and enjoy that with us. I've invited Sandra and a few of the other teachers to come too."

"That sounds like fun. I'll be there for that. Thanks for inviting me."

"Okay, sounds good. We'll see you on New Year's Eve. I imagine any time after eight we'll have the party ramping up."

"Okay, see you then."

Dan left the room, followed by Kelly. In the hall they found Sandra just coming down the hall.

"Hey guys, ready for the break?"

"For sure. I have so much work to do on that book over the holiday. I'm looking forward to a few days of uninterrupted writing to see if I can finish the first draft, and get it ready for my editor."

"Can't wait to read it. Everything you've said about it is fascinating. Imagine all of those experiences you had in the village."

"Yes, it was a heck of an experience. But will make for a good book."

"Want to come have dinner with Reg and me over the break? We'd love to have you over."

Kelly looked at Dan and Sandra. "Okay, what is all of this? Is this a 'let's not let Kelly be alone over Christmas' conspiracy?"

Dan and Sandra looked at each other, Sandra with a slightly perplexed expression on her face.

"I had invited her over for Christmas and the New Year's party already."

Sandra laughed. "No actually we hadn't even discussed that, but it's a good idea none the less. But really, Reg and I would just like to have you over; anytime over the holidays."

"I'll see how my writing goes- maybe between Christmas and New Year's? I'll give you a shout after I get back from my brother's place."

"Perfect. Have a great Christmas with your mom and brothers."

"I will. I'm heading down tomorrow and coming back up here on the twenty- seventh. Sandy will love to spend time with my brother and his kids. They always have a great time together."

"Take care, and we'll see you after Christmas, and if not, at least at Dan's party on New Year's."

"Sounds like a plan. Have a great Christmas, both of you. See you on the thirty-first if not before."

"Merry Christmas," echoed from both Dan and Sandra, as the three moved off toward their cars.

Kelly watched Sandra and Dan as they pulled out of the parking lot. They had both been wonderful and supportive of her over the past few years. She had moved to this school in the year following Ken's death. She had known Sandra for years, and she had been the one to encourage Kelly to make the change. Dan she met her first day on the job. Sandra had clearly briefed all the teachers on her situation, for none had thoughtlessly asked about her husband. They had both been great people to talk to not only about her struggles after Ken died, but lately as she nursed her heart over Neil. Kelly shrugged off the melancholy thoughts, started her car, and drove out of the lot. Time to get home to Sandy and some dedicated computer time to write her book and then Christmas with her brothers and mom. The holidays looked to be a nice break.

III

The following morning Kelly was sitting at her computer attempting to write some more of her book. She couldn't maintain her attention on Eykel and kept drifting back to her last few days in England in the late summer. They had been whirlwind days with Neil traveling around London and his home in Derbyshire and magical nights spent in his arms. Neil and his granddad had taken her on a tour of London that had nothing to do with the traditional English history, and everything to do with the history of the Templars and the Carter family. It had been a fascinating education for her in the difference between the history as written by the victors, and the true history as passed down by the generations. Although Grampa Robert did acknowledge that even they had lost much of the truth. There had been some generations who had ignored the traditions of family mostly due to the political times they lived in. Britain had seen such turmoil over the years; it was hardly surprising that much of the Templar history was lost.

They had stopped into Temple Church during their tour. Kelly still remembered the shock she had felt when she walked in again. She had not been back to the Church on her tour of a few weeks prior, so had not been inside since her therapy session with Dr. Klein when she had dreamed of Eleanor and Robert. They had approached the church from Tudor Street and were dropped off right at the entrance to the Gardens.

"Welcome, Kelly, to the Temple Church grounds," Grandpa had said.

"Thanks, Gramps, I'm so glad to be back here. I had loved this place two years ago, and now I'm anxious to see it again, with my new perspective on the Templars."

"Well why don't we go right to the church then, since it's what you came to see."

They walked around the Inner Temple Hall and approached the main entrance just to the right of the Round Nave, walking past the statue of the Knights Templar. As Kelly crossed the threshold she felt like she was being catapulted back in time. She knew this place, knew it in her soul. As she gazed at the Round Nave, she could feel the ancient call of the building as it bid her to remember her history within this exact church. The Knight Effigies in the floor seemed to urge her to reach into her past and embrace all that she was.

She shook off the gentle stirrings in her soul and tried to concentrate on what gramps was telling her about the history of the church.

"It was built by the Templars back in 1180's as a tribute to the Church of the Holy Sepulchre in Jerusalem. This was one of the most cherished and vibrant areas of the Templars here in London. The surrounding area became the central banking district as well, where wealthy Crusaders and pilgrims could bring their wealth for storage, and take letters patent with them to withdraw when they arrived in Jerusalem. This was a very active section of London at that time. Over the years, as the Templars were exterminated, this became the property of the Crown, and, in time, passed into the hands of the lawyers. They have maintained the Church on these grounds through all the turmoil over the years, including the Blitz."

"Gramps, that's the history that we all know. What about the connection to our family? What can you tell Kelly about that?"

"Well, for many years all of the heirs were married in this church. Due to the turmoil over the years, it did skip a few generations, but always we maintained in our home chapels the documents that tied our family to this church. When each heir was dedicated to the service of the Templars they were given the historical records that tied our fates to the Templar legend. Unfortunately many of the records were lost due to fire and frankly were neglected by some of our ancestors. By the time my father qualified for the inheritance, much of the true connection to our roots had been lost. I've spent most of my years trying to recreate those lost records."

"I know, Gramps, and I've helped you many times especially as we get the records stored on computers now. Hopefully with proper care, we'll never lose them again."

"Yes, today's technology should ensure that we don't lose what we have found. And, as we now don't rely on a single heir to keep the traditions, at least it's not lost when that heir is killed before the knowledge is shared. Sadly it has happened more times than was necessary over the years. Thankfully other Templar families like the Brocks, Nicolauses, and Mounfords- plus all the others who settled in Hertfordshire- were able to provide support to the de Cartiers and Carters when such ill events took place."

While they had been talking, they had wandered around the Round Nave looking at the Knight Effigies. As Gramps finished up, they had moved to the center of the Nave. Kelly looked up at the roof with Neil standing by her side and felt herself heeding the call of the building once again. She could hear voices around her echoing dimly:

> *"Eleanor Katrine, thou hast been brought here today to be joined to this man in marriage. Doth thou promise to God and our dear Lady Mary to contract marriage with this man and join your purpose to his for the greater glory of God?"*
>
> *"I do."*
>
> *"By these words I acknowledge the commitments thou hast both made to the great glory of the work of God. I commend thee both for the good works thou shalt complete in the years ahead as a joined pair, and in the blessings of future generations borne of this union. In the name of God, our Lady Mary, and the Lord Jesus, may you protect the future as man and wife."*

Kelly shook her head. Had that been one of those times Gramps was just referencing? An heir killed off early, leaving Eleanor as the sole surviving heir? She shuddered; was she hearing things now?

"Are you okay, Kelly?"

Kelly looked at Neil, and thought that her eyes were playing tricks on her. She could swear that she saw the echo of another man in Neil's manner, voice, and eyes. She shook her head to clear the cobwebs.

"Yeah, I'm okay. Just tired. I think this building has so much history in it, I seem to be tuned to the vibrations coming from it."

"Like in Eykel?" Neil asked in concern.

"No, it is not that same kind of connection. This is more muted, like I'm hearing voices from afar. It's almost a ghostly image, but not nearly as vivid as I get in Eykel."

"Maybe, my dear, you are picking up echoes of your past in here. I've always felt tied to this building. But then Abigail and I were married in this church many years ago. I've a bond to this building that goes back many lifetimes."

Kelly looked to Neil. "Were you married here?"

"No, Patricia was raised in Bristol, so we got married there." After a brief pause while Neil watched Kelly from the corner of his eye, as she continued to wander around the center of the Nave. "Gramps, I think we've explored enough around London for today. I think I should get you and Kelly back to the apartment for a rest. I want to be on the road early tomorrow to Derbyshire. I want to show Kelly our home."

"Yes, I agree, we must get Kelly home. I'm sure she will love the grounds there. And I can't wait to show her the chapel and the old ruins there."

"Kelly, are you ready to leave?"

Kelly turned back to Neil and Gramps, and had to again blink her eyes to clear her vision. Staring back at her had been two different men. Two men she had never met before, and yet she knew them both. Standing in front of her were the images of Robert Brock and Raymond Brock as she remembered them from her session with Dr. Klein. Her head started to spin and she felt light-headed.

"Neil." She gasped as she started to wobble on her feet. Neil moved as fast as he could to catch her before she fell. He cradled her to his chest, as he frantically checked for her pulse.

"Kelly, what happened love? Please tell me what is going on?"

"I don't know. I must have turned too quickly toward you. I could just feel my head start to swim as I turned. Maybe I've just not had enough to eat, and I'm tired."

"Are you sure? Please tell me if this is another episode like Eykel? Were you seeing other people?"

"It's just that for a brief second I thought I saw others here, but I think it was just my imagination. I'm pretty hungry and thirsty too. I suspect that's what caused me to feel wobbly."

"I don't know, love. I'm growing concerned about you. That's twice now that you've turned quickly and felt off balance in the past few days. Are you sure it's nothing?"

"Yes, Neil, it's nothing. Just fatigue today. And we know what caused it last time. I'm not worried. Honestly."

"Okay, but I think we've done enough for today. It's time to get you and Gramps back to the apartment to rest for the day. Tomorrow I'm taking you home with me. We'll stay there until I have to put you on a plane back to Canada."

*****

Kelly's musing was interrupted by her cell phone ringing. She looked down, and saw her brother's number.

"Hey, Simon, how are you today."

"Doing great, Kel, how are you?"

"Great thanks. Everything all ready at your place?"

"Yup, we are set. Just wanted to call to find out when you were planning on getting here. What time are you picking up Mom?"

"I should be in Kentville by eleven and to your place by one all going well."

"Okay, sounds good. We'll have lunch set out for you when you arrive."

"See you tomorrow."

"Sounds good, Kel. Bye."

Kelly turned back to her computer and stared at the screen at the unfinished work in front of her. She had better try to put her writer's cap on for a few hours, or she would never finish this book. That proved to be far more difficult than she imagined.

She had been haunted by so many images that she had seen in the Templar village and London. But nothing haunted her quite as much as the portraits she had seen at the Carter home in Derbyshire. She remembered her shock one day as she was wandering through the Portrait Gallery. Neil had been showing her some of his ancestors, when they had come to the portraits from the 1700's.

"And this is Eleanor Carter and her son Geoffrey Carter. They are one of those examples we hold of why we will never again risk the heritage of our family by keeping our secrets too closely guarded. Eleanor's older brother, also a Geoffrey, was killed before he married and had children. The family heritage was left to Eleanor and her husband Robert Brock Carter. That's his portrait just over there. Eleanor became the sole heir, and of course as a woman, she couldn't legally hold land in her own name. The family agreed with the Brocks that in order to continue the line, their younger son should marry into the Carters, and style himself a Carter."

Kelly remembered gasping in surprise when she had looked at the portrait, for this woman was straight from her own dreams. This was the same woman she had pictured earlier in the summer. She trembled, then turned to look where Neil had indicated the picture of Robert Carter. Kelly gasped in surprise. Here was the man from her dreams! And from her vision just the other day at Temple Church. She felt herself sway and gulped.

What is happening to me? Why are my dreams so accurate? I've never seen these portraits before, and yet my dreams are exactly of these people. Why?

She had quailed in fear at the implications.

"Kelly, Neil, the limo is here to take you back to London. Kelly I wish you didn't have to leave so soon, but I understand you need to get back to your school."

"Yes, Katrine, I have commitments back home. I know you Carters understand honoring your commitments. Therefore I must leave. But I want to thank you again for your hospitality over the past week. I've had a wonderful time."

*****

That had been the end of her summer romance with Neil, but was not the end of her problems. The nightmares had begun shortly after she got home and occurred so regularly all fall that she decided to go visit Dr. Klein again. She had been hoping to get more insight into who she had been, and why she was experiencing so much déjà vu. It had taken a number of sessions with Dr. Klein before she was catapulted back into the 1300's in

what is now Egypt. At first she had been unsuccessful in returning to any past life. Dr. Klein had attributed that to the various
nightmares that she had been having. He surmised that her subconscious was protecting her from any further trauma associated
with her past lives. It had been thoughts of Neil prior to her
session, that particular day, that she believed finally triggered her
return to Eykel.

She let her mind wander back to that day in November.
It had been unseasonably warm, close to fifteen degrees Celsius.
A few days prior she had seen yet another photo of Neil with another new woman on his arm, attending some function in south-
ern France. It still hurt every time she saw him with someone,
and always made her recall the anger in his voice when she had
broken the relationship off with him in September. She could
still clearly recall his words from that day.

*"I can't let you continue to jerk me around like a marionette
on a chain. First you want to be together, now you don't. My heart
can't take this yo-yo life. If you break if off now, I don't ever want to
see you again. This time, it's forever. I just can't do this repeatedly-
get my hopes up, to have you splatter them all over again when you
get scared."*

Kelly shuddered. She still knew that she had made the
right decision to break it off with Neil. They just weren't meant
to be. And although she knew that he didn't really enjoy the
rounds of social engagements he was required to have, he had to
maintain them for the sake of the Foundation. The Carter family
relied on Neil's charisma and charm to keep the donations roll-
ing into the Foundation. They were engaged not only in historic
education work, like the excavation at the Templar village, but
also in extensive charity work for children's hospitals worldwide.

It was part of Neil's job requirements to attend these functions as the play-boy to keep raising the money. A typical 'you pat my back, and I'll pat yours'.

When Kelly had arrived at Dr. Klein's office, she had been a few minutes early, and went for a short walk around the block. Her mind had been completely pre-occupied with Neil and how much she loved him to the core of her being. When it came time for her appointment, she fell into a trance instantaneously and found herself opening her eyes in familiar quarters. She was inside the office in the abbey at the Templar village. Even now she shivered in remembrance of the emotions she felt in recognizing that place. The hypnotist had asked her what she saw.

"I'm in an office in an abbey. There is a large desk in front of me. I'm sitting on a small stool. I'm doing some work on a piece of armor. The commander of the garrison is due back here at any moment, and I want to have this armor repaired for his return. We are expecting an attack in the next few days. The enemy army was spotted a few days ago on its way to our village. We know that we won't be able to hold out for long. All the other Templar fortresses in this part of the world are already gone. We are the last holdout as far as we know. I hear the approach of my commander. Good, the work is almost done and I can finish putting his arms on. Then I will head to the stables to make sure the horses are ready in case they are needed. I feel great affection for my commander; he has been like an older brother, the man who saved me from a drudge's work on my uncle's farms. He had rescued me after my parents had died. We are also now blood brothers, sealed in oaths to protect the secrets of this village. I can see the scar on my wrist from the ceremony we did a few years ago. They are healed now, but are a stark reminder of the commitments I made. The door opens, he enters, and he turns to me. I see his eyes, oh my god, it's Neil!"

Kelly recalled the shock she had felt when she recognized Neil. And not just as the Neil/Godfrey overlay that she recalled from the visions in August. This time she had seen directly into his soul. Neil and Godfrey were the same soul, not the same man, but the same soul.

"Kelly, refocus on the scene. This must be a momentous time. You've gone directly to this memory. Let the scene unfold for you."

When she had refocused on the scene, she had heard a bell ringing urgently in the background. It had taken her back to the August day in the abbey when she had been about to faint.

"I hear a bell ringing stridently in the air. It's the alarm for an approaching army. They are here already, far earlier than we had expected. My brother orders me to return to the stables and saddle his battle stallion and his courser for me. He orders me to await him to mount, and then to mount and flee from the village. I protest that I won't leave him to certain death at the hands of the invaders. I want to stay and protect him. He laughs at first, and then looks at me urgently. I hear him say, 'little one, I want you to escape this. Please run and live another day. I will rest easier in my grave if I know that you have escaped and can continue to live. Remember our vows before the seal in the chapel. We are bound together for eternity. So although we will be separated now in death and life, we will live again together.' With such a plea, I am sent on my way to the stables. He follows me and gets to the stable just after I have finished getting the horses ready. Just before he goes to mount his horse, he pulls me into an embrace.

"You are closer to me than my own brothers. By blood bond we have committed our souls to protect the treasures hidden within. Take this token of our guardian Archangel Michael. This will assure you safe passage to Scotland and our brethren in hiding there."

Godfrey held out a badge. I recognize the seal of Archangel Michael that had been used in the ceremony two years ago. He then turned to mount his horse. He reaches once again for my hand and with great affection tells me of his love and how we will find each other again in many years in Heaven. I watch him move off to the eastern gates to confront the invading force. I then mount my horse, and flee toward the western gate as he ordered me to escape. I leave the village behind, and give the little courser her head. She's swift and sure of foot. But I make it no more than a mile down the road when I'm spotted and chased. The little horse gives all she can, but we've been trapped in front. They kill the poor beast under me. I'm dragged by my captors to a picket line, where I'm chained with others who had tried to escape the village. I recognize many of the other young boys, undoubtedly sent away for protection. The battle for the village didn't last that long, perhaps eighteen hours. Then the captors looted the place for any valuables. The invaders then packed up the field and took their captives to be sold as slaves. This would be the true value they recouped from taking the village. All of the young boys that had been captured were chained together and forced to walk the long route to the homeland of these invaders. As we passed the eastern gate, we could see the carnage that had been committed by these men. On the walls were the bodies of many who had valiantly fought to hold the village. I saw my brother's body amongst them. I had watched them kill him earlier when he refused to divulge any of the secrets. I could still feel the pain from the lashes they had applied to my own back, to try to break him. We had both held fast to our oaths. I wept knowing that he had died defending this place, when he should have been escorting and guarding the treasure on its way to its final home."

Kelly remembered that the hypnotist had asked her to jump ahead in her life to the next significant incident. It had occurred not too many months later. The boy had survived the trek to the slave sales and been acquired by someone looking for field labor. She had described being abused and used by the other men who were slaves. He eventually died after having been flogged, collapsing in the field after a particularly bad night of abuse. The boy had died from the wounds of the flogging which had become infected. Death had been slow in coming and very painful. Many times he had wished for the swift death in a field of battle instead of the slow one he endured. Kelly had recalled a final vision just before he had died. Staring at the moon late at night, he could swear he saw the image of his brother beckoning him to come with him and escape the world. He followed his brother and left his pain-wracked body behind.

Even now, six weeks later, Kelly could still feel the terrible despair that the young boy had felt and what her soul had felt when she had left the village behind and later died. Such loss and pain she hoped to never feel in her life ever again. She could also remember very clearly the love and devotion he had felt to the older brother Godfrey, Commander of the village. And now she recognized him as Neil too. All of this was powerful confirmation of the information that Jason, Kendra, and Neil had told her back in August. Over the past few months she realized that her old doubts had little by little washed away. She could no longer pinpoint the exact moment when her views changed, it had happened so gradually. But now, she truly did believe in the immortality of the soul and the ability to reincarnate again and again. What that would mean to her future, she didn't know. But she looked forward to her future, a new beginning with the New Year.

IV

London, England, 1715

"Sir Raymond Brock, we recognize your right to present to this council. Please state your business."

"Masters all, I am here on behalf of my late son Robert Carter and his wife Eleanor de Carter to present her son as the heir to the Carter family. My son was recently killed in the Battle of Preston, protecting the English Crown from the Jacobite Rebels; otherwise he would be here to present his son himself. These two were invested a few years ago to become the Guardians of the Carter heir. After two female children, they now have the honor to be parents to Geoffrey Raymond Carter who is the sole male heir to the Carter family. May we present this child to you for affirmation?"

"The Council has reviewed the documents that you did forward to us. We do recognize the legitimacy of this child as the heir to the Carters. We sorrow with you both that the father will not be around to raise this child. Please bring him forward to be dedicated to the service of the Guardians. Are you both willing to reaffirm your oaths to this service?"

"We are."

Eleanor moved toward the center of the circle formed by the Masters of the Temple. This time she paid more attention to the circle around her. There were four seals in the floor of this room. She recognized the ancient seals of the Archangels Michael, Gabriel, Raphael and Uriel. She knelt holding her son Geoffrey close to her. The Head Master reached down and beckoned her to place Geoffrey on the floor between herself and Raymond.

"Eleanor de Carter, you are presenting your son to confirm your dedication as a Guardian of the Temple. This oath will place on your son the burdens of secrecy and service to the great glory of God. Are you willing and able to provide such a dedication?"

"I am, as a means of honoring my late father, brother, and husband."

"Upon your wedding day, you, together with your late husband were confirmed as the heir to the Carter line. We acknowledge your service to the line in the infant now before us. Do you reaffirm your promise in faith to raise your heir with the same dedication the Carter family has shown through the untold years?"

"I am and I will."

"Then by the power of this council, and in the presence of Archangel Michael our patron and guardian, we accept the dedication of the late Robert Brock Carter, Eleanor de Carter and Geoffrey Raymond Carter as the heirs to the Carter line. Eleanor de Carter please arise, and take thy place beside thy father-in-law who stands in thy husband's place."

Eleanor and Sir Raymond rose as beckoned, and the Head Master reached down to lift Geoffrey off the floor.

"As Guardians, we now ask that you be joined in blood bond to seal your fates together as Guards of this treasure and the heir to the Carter line. I ask these knights here present to witness this bond and the vows that have been made this day."

Eleanor watched fascinated as another of the Guardians came forward with a small dagger in his hand. A third gripped the hands of her and Sir Raymond and raised them to allow the child to be held under the hands.

"By the power and protection of Archangels Michael, Gabriel, Raphael and Uriel, we, the Guardians of the Temple, witness and commit this blood oath of the Carter family heirs.

Eleanor felt startled to see the dagger descend to nick her wrist and then her sons. Geoffrey started to cry as the dagger made its mark.

"Let the mingling of this blood seal the bond between thee forever to uphold the ongoing service of these dedicated Guardians to the power and secrecy of our order. In the name of God, our Dear Lady Mary, and the Lord Jesus, let it be done."

*****

Kelly bolted awakened, hearing the echo of a baby's cries in her ears. Not again! Another nightmare! This was getting ridiculous. She could count on one hand the number of uninterrupted nights of sleep she had been getting. She had little recollection of most of the dreams that woke her, but a quick glance at the diary by her bed reminded her of how much she was able to write down. She quickly grabbed her pen and jotted down what she could remember of this one.

Finished writing, she settled back in bed to relax. It was almost time to get up so it didn't make sense to even try to fall back to sleep. It was now December twenty-seventh. Christmas had passed uneventfully. The day with her brother had been peaceful, if hectic, with the entire family and a few dogs running around. She had stayed for two days, but was now back at home and ready to concentrate on getting her book finished. She had a lot of work to do since she promised her editor that she would have a copy by the New Year. Kelly sighed. She was so unsettled by the stream of dreams and nightmares that she had been having. They were growing more intense. She needed to figure out what was going on. But she might as well get started on her day. The more writing she got done, the happier her editor would be.

*****

Kelly was busily writing away at her desk when she was startled by the ringing of the doorbell. She looked at the front door, wondering who could be here, since she wasn't expecting anyone. As she wandered toward the front of the house, she caught a glimpse outside of a limousine. Curious she opened the door to find Katrine Adams standing on her front step.

"Katrine? What are you doing here?"

"Kelly, I'm so glad you're here. My father is with me, may we come in?"

"Of course, but what are you doing in Canada?"

"Let me get Dad, he can explain better than I."

"Please, bring him in."

Katrine turned back to the limo and was only half way back to it, when the door opened and her father jumped out of the car and walked up the driveway to join them.

"Kelly, about time I saw you again. I was devastated when you left England and didn't come back to us. You and Neil are made for each other. I can't believe that my grandson let you leave and didn't come after you."

"Dad, really, must you start in so direct?"

"I'm too old, Katrine, to pussy foot around. It's time she and Neil got their collective acts together. I want to bounce my great grandchild on my knees before I die."

"Dad!"

"It's nice to see you again too, Gramps." Kelly laughed as she reached out to embrace the old man. "What brings you two to Canada? But where are my manners, please come in. I hope you don't mind dogs?"

"Not at all, I love dogs. And look at that beauty. What's her name?"

"She's Sandy. Here, Sandy, come meet Katrine and Gramps Robert."

Gramps reached down to pat Sandy. She gave him a good sniff, then licked his hand as if she had known him all her life.

"Please come and sit in the living room. Can I get you coffee or tea?"

"Tea would be nice. We just got to town a couple of hours ago."

"Okay, let me whip up something." Kelly left Katrine and her dad in the living room, entertaining Sandy. She was stunned to see the two of them here in Canada, especially so close to Christmas. What on earth had brought them here?

A few minutes later she returned with tea and some snacks for her guests.

"Here we are. The tea needs to steep a bit, but I brought a few snacks, in case you were hungry. I'm guessing it's five to you both, so you must be getting hungry."

"Thank you, Kelly. I imagine you're trying to figure out what brought us to Canada?"

"Well, yes, the thought did cross my mind."

Gramps and Katrine looked at each other. "You start, Katrine."

"All right Dad, we have two reasons. The first is obviously Neil. We are both absolutely concerned about him. Since you left in August, he's been going at a break-neck pace. He's pushing himself way too much. I've begged him to slow down, but he just won't. He didn't even come back to Derbyshire for Christmas. Chris and I talked and we feel Neil is working himself to death, trying to push all his feelings aside and just work. It's a pattern we see all too often in the men of the family when they don't have their soul mate around. It's for lack of a better word, a curse the Carter men deal with. They become restless and almost self-destructive when they are alone. I've watched my brother for years commit himself entirely to the business he built. He would never admit that the business is his lover and other half, but it is. And now I think Neil is going down the same path. All work, no pleasure, one hundred percent committed to other things than his own well-being. I suspect that you might have been doing the same thing? Trying to drown your sorrows in work?"

"I don't deny that I miss Neil more than I could imagine. But we live such different lives, from completely different worlds. I just don't see how we could sustain a relationship based on that. We're too different."

"Young lady, I don't believe that for a second. The two worlds you talk about are the illusion and the superficial world of our minds. At your core, you and Neil live in the same world. You're both just being stubborn, and scared as far as I can see. The love you two share is so rare. I can understand how it feels to be so in love it scares you. Abigail was that woman for me. But if I hadn't taken the risk, then none of the rest of them would be here. All of us in the Carter family know that feeling. You just have to trust that the risk is worth it."

"Gramps, I've loved and lost twice already. Once with my father, it nearly killed me too. And when Ken died, I just about gave up on life. I just can't take that risk again!"

"Kelly, my girl, please. Passion and love are always worth the risk. Life is worth the risk. Don't let the fear of the hurt stop you from living the moments that will make you happiest. Don't let the mind and ego stampede over the yearnings in your soul."

After a brief pause while they all looked at each other Katrine continued, "But we have another reason for being here. And this may sound a bit outlandish, but Dad and I have recently discovered that we are both having the same recurring dream about Eykel. I reached out to Jason to see if he could confirm any of the things I see. He startled me when he actually finished off my question. It seems he has been having the same dream."

Kelly looked at Gramps and Katrine in growing apprehension. "Dream? Of Eykel?"

"Yes, you look scared?"

"Well, I've been having recurring nightmares about Eykel, and others centered in London in the early 1700's. I've been doing some past life regression, and I'm beginning to believe it's all tied together. Certainly my hypnotist believes it is. She's read most of the notes I've jotted down after my nightmares, and my sessions. Her theory is that my visit to Eykel this summer, and all the 'memories' I had there, have been a trigger to reawaken a long-held soul compulsion."

Katrine looked at Kelly gently. "Would you mind if I read your journal? If your dreams are close to mine, I'll tell you. Otherwise we'll just leave this all alone."

Kelly hesitated, looking at Katrine and Gramps. She weighed the risk of showing them the journal and finding out whether or not her soul was actually tied to the Carter family. *It's a huge risk! I'll have to face my fears, and potentially completely dismantle all my long held beliefs and notions. But, I need resolution. The nightmares were only getting more frequent. If I can finally lay this all to rest maybe I'll find peace.* Or maybe as Gramps had said earlier, '*life is worth the risk.*'

She quietly stood up and shuffled her way to her bedroom, reluctance to share her writings warring with her new found desire to get to the bottom of everything. If she was connected to Gerard, Godfrey and the entire Carter clan then maybe this was her destiny. She looked at the book where she had left it this morning. She hesitated for a few seconds, her hand caressing the front of the diary. She had picked it up on a whim a few weeks ago. A flaming blue sword adorned the front. The hilt of the sword was engulfed in blue flames, lapping at the red jewels set into the cross piece. When she had first seen it she had been reminded of the legend of Excalibur, but looking at it now, she realized that it could easily be the Sword of Archangel Michael. She picked it up, held it to her chest, hesitated and then wandered back to the living room. In complete silence she offered it to Katrine, with a pleading look at Gramps.

"Thank you, Kelly. I know what a leap of faith this is."

Kelly turned away and walked back to the kitchen as she heard Gramps and Katrine settle in to read the book. Kelly sat down at the small table and put her head in her hands. Fear, despair, and longing all settled over her. She wasn't quite sure what she hoped for. Were the dreams just bits of nonsense pulled together by her subconscious from all the research work she had done? Or were they truly past memories of her soul, coming to the surface now because she went to Eykel and met Neil? She felt Sandy place her head on her lap. She looked at her. "Oh, Sandy, what have I gotten into?"

About fifteen minutes later, Kelly heard a gasp from the living room. Well, maybe she had her answer, for better or worse. That gasp could only mean that Katrine had found confirmation of her dreams. With great reluctance she pushed back her chair and got up from the kitchen table. She dragged her way back to the living room.

"Katrine?"

Katrine looked up at Kelly with shock in her eyes. Gramps too looked startled.

"Well, my girl, seems you have the same fascination with a certain ceremony in Eykel about seven hundred years ago that we all have. Your description matches almost verbatim with what Katrine has told me, and what I have encountered. I also read your account of the marriage at Temple Church. Was that from your memories when we were there in August or is that another dream?"

"The Temple Church was both a dream and came from a hypnotism session. Just this morning, I had another dream about a dedication ceremony for the son of Eleanor, Geoffrey Raymond Carter. His father was killed shortly after his son was born."

Kelly looked at Gramps with a thousand years of hurt shining through her eyes. She knew he was thinking about the haunting portraits in their gallery of Eleanor Carter, Robert Carter and their son Geoffrey. At that moment Kelly could feel the links she had with Gramps come through the years. She recognized in his eyes the same father-in-law who had stood by her side in that nightmare. This was the reincarnation of Sir Raymond Brock, then the father of Robert Brock Carter, her soul mate.

"It hurts so much, Gramps, to lose the other half of you. You know this better than anyone. You lost Abigail. How can I risk that yet again? I've lost him so many times through the eons. I can't risk that again."

"If you honor what has been fought for through the years, and the secrets that your soul has maintained, then you can take the risk. It is what your soul has yearned for all these years to be joined once again with your blood bond and your oath to maintain the secrets for all time. Let the time be now to break the cycle of the past, and open the vaults to the future."

V

Forty-eight hours later Kelly found herself once more on the Carter jet winging her way to Egypt. Gramps was laying down sleeping in the back, while she and Katrine were relaxing in the main cabin. Katrine had fallen asleep an hour ago, but Kelly couldn't relax enough to drop off. How quickly the last two days had passed. Gramps and Katrine had left her place shortly after reading the journal. They had agreed to think about the implications of the discoveries. Gramps had extracted a promise from her to think about what he had said, and to consider coming with them to Eykel. They had planned to leave the next day.

Kelly had slept poorly that night. Her mind wouldn't let go of the words that Gramps had said to her. At four in the morning, she had finally allowed herself to acknowledge that she truly loved Neil and wanted to be with him. Her soul yearned to be with him. And she knew that *passion and love are always worth the risk*. She had waited until seven to call Katrine.

"Katrine, it's Kelly. I want to come with you. But I need a day to sort some things out here. Can you delay until the twenty-ninth?"

"Yes, Kelly, we can. All the better. We can celebrate the New Year in Eykel. Would we be celebrating a New Year, and a new life?"

"I don't know yet, Katrine. But I do know that I need to understand more about what has happened to me. And it seems the Carters and Eykel are my link to the past."

"Fair enough, Kelly. I'll let Dad know that we'll be here for another day. We'll send a car to pick you up tomorrow. Is eight too early?"

"No, I'll be ready tomorrow morning."

And now here she was, on her way to Eykel- and her destiny? Or more heart break? She didn't know which she feared more. All she knew was that Neil and the Carter family were intimately tied to her future.

VI

Kelly sat at the front of the old church in Eykel, contemplating the last few days. Why had she agreed to come here again? She was now uncertain that she had made the right choice. Katrine had told her this morning that Gramps had managed to get hold of Neil, and Jason had left just a little while ago to go to the airport to pick him up. Kelly wrung her hands in nervous energy. What would Neil say when he saw her again? She had been so cruel to him in the fall, and how she remembered the anger in his voice when he had said he never wanted to see her again. From the description that Katrine had supplied, he had done a good job of putting her out of his life as quickly as he could. It didn't really matter that he was running from his pain. He was moving on with his life. How would he take her invading his territory yet again? She knew what it was to get on with life after heartache. The last thing he needed was one more reminder of her. And yet, how could she rest if she never got to the bottom of the nightmares she was having. These nightmares were disturbing Gramps, Katrine, Kendra, and Jason as well. What connection did the six of them have that was driving them all to congregate here in Eykel?

"Kelly, are you in here?"

"Yes, Katrine, I'm here."

"Good. Neil should be here before too long. Now in the meantime, why don't we all go to the Nave and see what our joint memories can discover that is familiar to us. I for one am very curious why we all are having such a similar dream."

"Kelly, from what Katrine has said about the scene in your diary, the dedication ceremony was done at the center of the altar. Can you pinpoint the area?"

"Let me see, Kendra. I'm not certain. This doesn't look quite right here. Something is wrong with the altar."

"Okay, what do you think is wrong? This is a reconstruction done by experts a few years ago. It may not be entirely accurate. Can you give me more to work from?"

"I'm sorry, Kendra, but it's just a feeling I have. It doesn't feel right to me and I don't know why. I wish I could be more helpful."

"My girl, will you trust an old friend here to help guide you to the answer? Will you let me guide you to meditate and see if we can find an answer that way?"

"Grampa Robert, I'd try anything right about now."

"All right, let's go sit in the front pew and see if we can find the truth between us."

Kelly and Gramps sat and turned to face the altar.

"Kelly, let me hold your hand. I want you to concentrate solely on my hand and how it feels in yours. Let the rest of the world fade away and feel just the connection point of my hand to yours. Let your mind be still and focus only on my words and my hand. I want to guide your thoughts and a memory of a dream you had of a time long ago. Free your mind to come back here to this same church as you see it in your mind's eye. Let your current vision recede and see only with your mind's eye. Do you see the altar before you?"

"Yes, I do."

"Can you describe what you see?"

"The altar is short and square, it's about four feet by four feet, centered in the Nave and no taller than three feet. It's a one-piece stone that was brought here to be the central altar for this specific church. It's a Templar stone, carved in intricate details." Kelly gasped.

"What is it my girl? What do you see?"

"The sigil of Archangel Michael is carved on the front of it. Not the image of him, but the circular seal that is unique to Michael. I know this seal, I've seen it before."

"Relax, Kelly; release the excitement of the sigil. We need you to concentrate solely on the altar. What else can you tell us about it? Allow your current knowledge of the altar to superimpose on the one you see. What adjustments need to be made?"

"The current one is too far forward and too long. The altar needs to be shorter by one foot."

"You've done great, Kelly. Now just sit in peace for a minute. Let yourself slowly return to today. Allow your mind to come back to the now."

"All right, Gramps, what is so critically important that you've dragged me half way around the world to get here. This is the last place on earth I ever want to see again."

"Neil, that's uncalled for."

"Mom, what are you doing here? Don't tell me Gramps has involved you in this lunacy too? I'm sick of this place; I don't ever want to come here again."

Kelly braced herself and with great reluctance rose and turned to Neil. "Hello, Neil."

"What the hell is she doing here? I told you I never ever wanted to see you again. I'm out of here. Gramps, how dare you bring her here and force me to see her again. I'm leaving right now."

"Neil, please."

"No, Mom, she had the chance twice to break my heart. I'll never give her that luxury again."

"Neil, please, this is important. We've all been having nightmares about this place. Dad isn't sleeping at night because of it. The nightmare is so vivid and needs to be explained before we all go crazy."

"Nightmares? Get real. Tell me you didn't drag me across the world for simple nightmares, Gramps."

"Not simple nightmares, Neil," Kelly interrupted him. "These are tied to the Templar treasure that was sent from here by Godfrey with William of Lothian." She paused for a brief moment, then added, "Sent by you, with Jason to safety."

Neil had made it back to the entrance to the church when Kelly's final comment registered with him. *Sent by him?* Had he heard right? He paused at the door. The Templar treasure from Eykel was something the family had been trying to find for generations. What was going on that these five people would be having nightmares about it? He turned to look at the four arranged at the front of the church, and then at Jason beside him. "Okay, you have my attention. What is this about?"

Kelly looked back at Neil at the front of the church with Jason beside him. His anger was making him stand tall and rigid, with his chin thrust out. His indignation was evident in every tense line of his body. But to her imagination he looked the image of a Knight Templar, with the strong military bearing. Her head started to reel. She felt dizzy and disoriented. Neil's mouth was moving, but the words she was hearing were not the ones that he was speaking. She was hearing the echo of long ago words.

"As you know we are sending the bulk of the treasure with William this morning to safety. Yet there is some that we simply cannot risk in transport, so they will be hidden here to remain safe until the time is come for them to be revealed. We wish to bind you and your soul to the protection of this as a Guardian of the Temple."

Kelly felt her grip on reality become tenuous. She could clearly see Godfrey de Cruce and William of Lothian standing where Neil and Jason should have been. She shook her head trying to clear her vision, but nothing cleared. She could see the inside of the church as it had been back in the 1300's not as it was today. It was too much, she felt like she was slipping into unconsciousness and wobbled. "Godfrey, Neil," she whispered, "Help me." And she started to slump and fall.

Neil had watched as Kelly first started to sway and she seemed to lose focus on what was in front of her; then he clearly heard her call to Godfrey. She collapsed at the front of the church before Kendra or his mom could catch her.

"Oh my God, Kelly! Jason, call Tom and get him out here!"

Neil instinctively ran to the front of the church where Kelly lay in a heap. He just prayed that she hadn't hit her head too hard when she fell. No one had been able to stop that tumble this time.

"Kelly, can you hear me? Kelly, tell me you're okay?"

"Easy, Neil, I think she fainted, but I don't think she hit her head. I was able to move just fast enough to stop her head from hitting the pew."

"Thank God, Kendra. I caught her the last time, but was too far away this time."

"What do you mean 'last time' Neil? Is this not the first time she's collapsed?"

"No, Gramps, this happened the last time she was here in Eykel. We had been in the abbey when the bells were rung back in August. She could only describe that she saw a dual vision of Godfrey and me standing in the same place in the abbey office. You were with us at Temple Church. She convinced me then that nothing was wrong, but I should've known. I think she had a vision then too. When Tom gets here, I want you to take her back to the hotel to make sure she's okay."

Kelly started to moan and her eyes fluttered open. "Where am I? What happened to me?"

"It's okay, Kelly, you're here in Eykel and you fainted," said Katrine. "I think I should take you back to the hotel to rest. We can resume this discussion tomorrow when you feel rested."

"Did I dream that Neil was here?"

"No, you didn't. I am here, but not entirely sure why, or that I'll stay," he said as the anger resurfaced within him. How dare this woman do this to him again? Here he was running to rescue her once again. He knew better than that. She didn't want or need his help. Better to get this farce over with and soon. "Gramps had better come up with some good explanations on

this one. I'll be at the offices when you're ready to talk, Gramps."
Neil got up then and stormed out of the church.

Kelly sighed. "Guess he isn't ready to forgive me for what I
did to him. I don't blame him at all. I was cruel. I'm sorry. I don't
know that I can continue on with this. Please, can you take me
back to my room, so I can rest and then arrange a plane home?"

"As you wish, Kelly, but hold off on the plane just yet. Let
me talk to that stubborn grandson of mine. I don't think he quite
gets the notion of joined souls just yet. I may have to beat it into
his stubborn brain."

VII

About thirty minutes later Gramps and Katrine made their way to Neil's office.

"All right, young man, let's have this out once and for all right now. You were incredibly rude to Kelly today. I'll not have it. You were raised with better manners than that."

"How dare you bring her here, Gramps? You know what she's done to me. She led me on a merry chase for two years. Showing up here, letting me believe she loves me. She doesn't know what love is. Then she runs away at the first sign of any trouble. No way. You had no right to bring her here, and to force me to see her again."

"Neil, we had every right. If you would simply listen to what Dad has to say about all of this. I think you'll understand in your core the stunning importance to our family, to the Templars, and frankly, to the world of what we have discovered, or more accurately are about to discover if you would just put aside your ego, and live in your soul."

"Mom, that's not fair."

"My boy, it's all that is fair. One of the things we Carter men are taught is never to judge until you have all the facts. So I'm going to tell you the facts. Then you'll understand why we brought Kelly here. She's the key that we've been looking for. You know how we always believed that some of the treasure of the Templars was left behind in hidden chapels all through the Holy Lands and pilgrimage routes. Well it seems some of it might be right here in Eykel, at least that is the strong indication we've been getting given the dreams that I've had."

"Dreams again, Gramps? You're basing this all on dreams."

"Not just his, Neil, but mine, Jason's, Kendra's, and Kelly's. We're all having a similar dream. I bet if you just acknowledged it, you've been woken many nights by the same nightmare."

Neil stared at his mom and Gramps in disbelief and resentment. How could they do this to him? They knew his feelings for Kelly, and how she had stomped all over his heart. He was just now coming to terms with the emptiness in his soul. How could they bring her back again with fanciful notions of these dreams? He exhaled in exasperation. These people of all in the world should know the impact of losing the other half of himself. He couldn't do this again. Couldn't risk it all again. Better to let the restlessness that seized him now take over and drive him to exhaustion. Then at least he could sleep in peace each night. He turned away to go to the window to stare out into the village. Sleep in peace? Who was he kidding?

"Okay, Mom, I'm listening. I won't promise anything, but I'm listening."

*****

At the same time, Kelly was opening the door to her hotel room. Jason had escorted her back after she was given the 'all clear' by Tom. Thanks to Kendra's quick action, she hadn't hit her head when she collapsed, but she knew that she would still have some bumps and bruises to nurse on her trip back home.

"All right, Kelly, let me get you a bottle of water and see you settled. I'm not going to leave here until you've gotten some rest. I want to make sure that you're truly okay."

"That's not necessary, Jason. I'm fine; just a simple case of fatigue and not enough to eat, plus the shock of seeing Neil again."

"Don't give me that line. Remember, I've been with you when you've had visions before. You had another one didn't you?"

Kelly let out a small groan. "Damn, I knew I wouldn't be able to hide that."

"Not from me and not from Neil. I know he's angry as hell right now, but don't think he didn't realize deep down what was going on. Tell me, what did you see?"

"It was an echo of a dream or rather nightmare I've been having. It started in late September. A young boy, Gerard by name, is initiated into a group called the "Guardians of the Temple". Godfrey and William of Lothian are his sponsors. I know you'll recognize all of those names."

Jason looked at her and let a breath escape from him in surprise. "Wow."

"Yeah, wow says it, doesn't it? I guess from what Katrine and your gramps said, it's pretty similar to what you've all been dreaming about."

"Yeah, you could say that. Mine is tied more to William's departure from Eykel. Mine starts when yours ends. My dreams haven't gotten all the way to Scotland, although we know the treasure made it. The camel train is attacked on the way to what is now Alexandria. We escape, but lose some men and a few of the camels. But the bulk of the treasure does get to the ships awaiting us, or so I assume."

"Why? Why are we having these dreams now? I don't understand it." Kelly sat down, and looked to Jason as if he might have the answers to the questions she was having. Was she reliving past life experiences? Why now? Or was she really just going insane?

"If I had a guess I would say, to quote from my dream, '*We will wall it and seal it now to be revealed again when the two who dedicate the seal through a blood bond are reunited and the time has come for all this to come to light again.*' I suspect we are living in momentous times when this all is to come to light."

Kelly stared at Jason in wide eyed astonishment. To hear her own dreams echoed back at her, word for word, was startling. Was this what it meant? Were she and Neil actually those blood bonded souls, and now was the time to reveal the location of the treasure? She slumped in her chair.

"I don't know, Jason, it seems so far-fetched to my mind, but yet what you say seems to echo in my soul, and I feel such an inner peace and joy at being back here and especially to be surrounded by your family. Gramps feels like a father to me." She blinked at Jason through the tears welling in her eyes. "It's like I'm home and finally able to relax and rest. Does that make any sense at all?"

"To me, yes, perfect sense. It's the way I feel here. And why I stay. And Neil does too, whether he'll admit it now or not. But this is home to our souls."

Kelly deliberated over Jason's observation. *Home? Is this really my home?* She thought long and hard about the implications staying. *I'll have to confront Neil. And that will be hard; it might even leave me scarred for life. But on the other hand, I might just get final closure on all the images that have been haunting me for well over a year.* Maybe what she heard at Halloween last year was true. Maybe she should 'trust her instincts'. After a few minutes weighing the risks and the rewards, Kelly turned back to Jason again.

"I think I better lie down and get some rest. If we're going to tap into this dream we're all having, I need to be refreshed. The way I treated him, I suspect Neil will fight us all the way, and I don't blame him."

"So, you'll stay?"

"Yes, I'll stay. For me, I need to get to the bottom of all this. I need to know the answers. Maybe then I can go back to Canada, and finally live in peace."

"Sure, Kelly, home, wherever that home will end up being."

On that cryptic note Jason got up and left her hotel room. Kelly watched the closed door for a few seconds, and then made her way to the bedroom to rest. Sleep was out of the question, but rest she would do.

VIII

Kelly had spent the next morning wandering through Eykel, and now found herself standing inside the banking hall. She had never spent much time in this area of the ruins and was fascinated by the inside of the hall. Its proportions reminded her so much of some of the buildings in London. How many buildings were truly built by the Templars but hidden away in history because of the so called "downfall" of them? How history was distorted because the Kings of France and the Pope decided the Templars were too powerful and a threat to them, and had to be exterminated. She was just examining the restoration work that was being done to the murals on the walls, when she heard her name called.

"Kelly, are you in here?"

"Yes, Kendra, I'm here. What's up?"

"Can you come with me to the church? We've had some work done to the altar; I think you need to see what we found after we rearranged it. I suspect that the original altar was exactly as you described, but it was changed many years ago to conceal something special."

"What do you mean, 'conceal'?"

"Just come with me and you'll see."

Intrigued, Kelly followed Kendra down the street and into the church. When she arrived, she could see that the altar had been moved back from its original position, more in line with her own description of it. She saw Jason and Gramps staring at the ground where the altar had sat. Kelly could feel the tingle of awareness come to life within her. Something important had been revealed here.

"Kelly, you have to see this." She could see the awe in Jason's eyes as he looked up to see her at the entrance. For a moment, yet again, the Templar Knight William of Lothian gazed back at her, then Jason moved, and the image was obscured again. Shaking, Kelly hesitated for a second and against her inclination, felt compelled to walk forward to see what was at the foot of the altar.

When she reached Jason's side, she gazed down at the stone work at her feet. Worn with age, she could just see the outline of a seal in the stone. The outside of the circle had faint writing in it that she could barely make out. But in the center was a clear capital S over an M. Kelly shivered in awareness; the seal of Saint Michael, just as she had seen it in her dreams. Slowly she reached into her pocket of her jeans and pulled out her silver medallion of Archangel Michael. She passed it over to Gramps, who whistled in appreciation.

"So, Archangel Michael, the Guardian of God's warriors. Who is more appropriate to be the Guardian and Patron of the Templars? Where did you get this, Kelly?"

"I've had it for many years. My dad invoked Saint Michael to protect his voyages. I've been wearing his old pendant for the past couple of years." Kelly reached inside her t-shirt to reveal the Saint Michael pendant that hung around her neck.

"This seal was in the house when we cleaned it up when Mom moved. I'd forgotten I had it but found it again this summer, when I started dreaming about this place. I don't suspect that was a coincidence."

"No, I suspect not. Archangel Michael is incredibly powerful. If he has been guiding you over the past while, then your presence here in Eykel is no coincidence. It's time to reveal the secrets held within here."

Kelly looked at Jason, and then they both looked at Gramps.

"You too, Gramps? You have that same feeling? The time is here?"

"Yes, Jason, I do. It's the New Year as of midnight tonight; a time of renewal and a time of revelation. My gut is telling me that we all need to be here again at midnight, as the New Year is revealed. I feel that so strongly right now. We all need to be here."

The four of them stared at each other. The past was echoing all around them. Kelly could feel a powerful presence reverberating in the stone, a presence that beckoned her soul to remember. How clearly she remembered the same pull when she had been at Temple Church. The effigies had spoken to her soul of long hidden truths that were hers to tap. Then she resisted the pull. She was fearful of the impact to her life and long held beliefs were she to acknowledge the power within. But now, here, she knew that she needed to tap this knowledge. She finally felt that she could open herself to the past and let the memories flow. She allowed her physical senses to recede and opened her soul to the energy near around her. She glanced at the four present. Gramps was overlaid by the image of a powerful Knight Templar, but more importantly as Sir Raymond Brock, her own father in law and the man who guarded her and her infant son those many years ago. Kendra and Jason were revealed as Knights Templar, Jason in particular in his power as William of Lothian. Kelly felt the warmth and approval of the three in front of her and the even more powerful blessing permeating her soul at her acceptance of the past.

"Yes, Gramps," she whispered, "tonight is the time of discovery."

*****

Midnight arrived and saw four of them gathered again in the church. Neil was carefully avoiding looking at or even acknowledging that Kelly was there. He was standing close to Kendra, a little apart from the rest of them. Kelly was trying her best to keep her distance, knowing that her presence was causing him pain, but also knowing they all needed to be there. Since the afternoon she had kept to herself at the hotel, going through the last few months carefully in her mind. She now recognized the fear that had led her to dismiss Neil from her life this fall. It was fear, pure and simple, fear of the unknown, and fear of being left behind. She knew deep down that a big part of that fear was from her past lives as Gerard and Eleanor. In both of those incarnations, Neil had left her to fend for herself, leaving her to die as a slave in the 1300's and to raise three children alone in the 1700's. How the remembered pain of those years had led her to shut herself off from him and not allow him to hurt her again in that way. What a mistake that had been. After much contemplation this afternoon, she was finally ready to admit that Neil really and truly was the other half of her, and that he was her one and true soul mate. Together they were greater than the sum of each other. Together they could find peace and contentment, like they never had before. The blood bonds that bound them as one were unbreakable; they were destined to be with each other.

Gramps was the last to arrive with Katrine.

"I'm glad everyone is here. I think we need to recreate that ceremony from years ago, as best we can. Kelly, you have the most vivid memories of it, can you direct us all where to stand?"

"Sure, Gramps, as best as I can. I'm not entirely sure what role Kendra and Katrine play, other than being at the ceremony. I think if you took east, Jason in the west, and Kendra and Katrine at north and south. Neil and I should stand in the middle of the circle you create."

They all moved to do as Kelly bid, settling into their designated positions. The flames of the candles they held flickered in the breeze blowing through the open doors, creating strange shadows.

"Okay, we are all placed. Now, Kelly my girl, I'm going to ask you to trust me like you did yesterday. I need you to go into a trance so that we can proceed."

"Gramps, is that necessary? She's always collapsed when she's had these visions," Neil asked.

"Trust me too, Neil, this is necessary."

"Please, Neil, I need to do this. I need to find the answers that are buried here. I'll be all right. I've done regressions in the past few months. I know what to expect."

Neil nodded his acceptance of the plan and stood slightly back from Kelly, so she could look directly at Gramps.

"Okay, Kelly, let's start. First allow yourself to relax and clear your mind of all thoughts. Focus your attention solely on the seal beneath your feet. Allow the power of Saint Michael to surround you and transport you to the time of your blood bond with the Guardians of the Temple."

. Kelly did as Gramps bid her, and once she was centered as she did for hypnosis, she could feel the seal beneath her feet begin to tingle. The power she could feel in the simple seal was immense and scary, but at the same time, a loving energy. She reached out with her senses around her to find the thread that would open the door to the past that she knew was within reach.

"I feel the presence of Archangel Michael, as he is invoked in the seal beneath my feet. He is here with us and providing us his protection as we carry through on our desire to understand the history we all share."

"Go deeper, Kelly, reach for your past. Delve deep into your soul, and find Gerard. He was here with us that night. Bring forth his memories of the ceremony and the moments after that will reveal what we need to know."

Kelly listened in abstract attention to Gramps words and felt her connection to the current world recede as she fell easily into a deep trance. The images in front of her now were thoroughly familiar. They had haunted her dreams for months.

"I'm standing on the seal with my brothers in arms. Godfrey and William are here with me. My hand is bound to Godfrey's, as William lowers a dagger to our wrists to seal the blood bond we are making."

"Go with it, Kelly, allow the memory to flow. Neil, take her hand in remembrance of that old ceremony. Jason, hold them both as she sees it."

Kelly felt her hand being lifted. The grip was so familiar, the touch electric. It was Godfrey, Robert, and Neil all in one.

She shuddered as her soul reached for the connection she felt to these men. Suddenly she was catapulted back in time, and could clearly see all that had happened that night.

She gasped in pain.

1301 Eykel

"By the power and protection of Archangels Michael, Gabriel, Raphael, and Uriel, we, the Guardians of the Temple witness and commit this blood oath between Godfrey de Cruce and Gerard né Laney de Cruce to seal this wall against intrusion and detection until such time as their souls are reunited in love and harmony, and in the presence of these four souls to lift the burden placed on these two. In the name of God, our Dear Lady Mary, and the Lord Jesus let it be done."

Gerard watched in detached fascination as the dagger was drawn across both his and Godfrey's wrists. One of the Knights held a basin under their arms where the blood gathered as it dripped from the wounds. After a few minutes, the Knights wrapped the two injuries to prevent infection. He knew that the scar would be with him for life.

The blood collected, the four protective knights moved to the entrance to the stairwell. They finished blocking it up with the stones that were gathered there. The last few rows were sealed with mortar that was mixed with their blood. The mysterious Sir Rai bin Hassan invoked an old blessing in a language that Gerard did not understand. He watched in awe as the doorway was sealed and seemed to magically disappear from view.

The chant finished, the old Knight, a master of tremendous power, turned to them, "Gerard and Godfrey, the door is now sealed. We ask that you both come here to seal in your soul the exact position of this doorway. We know in time that the treasure held within here will be revealed once again, and you two shall be instrumental in that act. But you need to know the precise placement of this door in order to find the stairs. Please commit to memory this precise location."

Gerard stepped forward as bid and carefully noted the exact position of the door in relation to the altar and the Archangel Michael seal in the floor.

The Knight seemed satisfied with the effort expended this night.

"Congratulations my brothers-in-arms. We have successfully protected the treasure of our order until such time as it should be revealed again to the world. Now it would be prudent for William of Lothian to leave in order to begin his journey home. The rest of us have our own tasks to do. With your leave Godfrey, I will also journey on this night to return in time to Eykel."

"My thanks, Sir Rai bin Hassan, for your assistance this night. I didn't expect your arrival in such a timely fashion. Your wisdom and knowledge have always been gratefully accepted. Please go in peace and safety."

Gerard watched as Sir Rai bin Hassan and William of Lothian departed the church to begin their journeys to far flung lands. His life was now tied with even tighter bonds to this land. He turned in some confusion to Godfrey.

"May I ask what treasures were hidden below that could not be risked on the journey to our homeland?"

"Information. You will discover in time that information and knowledge are a double-edged sword. They can lead to great power and wealth, but they can also lead to your downfall. Especially if your information contradicts what the rich and powerful wish you to believe. But the truth will always win, eventually. Until that time is here, the Knights Templar will protect this information with our blood, and the blood of our successors."

*****

"Kelly, listen to the sound of my voice. I want you to tell me what you see before you. Can you describe the location of the door?"

Kelly drifted along with Gramps voice, tinged now with the lilt and accent of Sir Rai bin Hassan. She tried to hold the threads of the knowledge she gained in her conscious mind.

"I walked three paces off the seal to the wall. Then I walked another three paces towards the back of the church. The door stands directly opposite the altar end. It's about four feet tall and two feet wide."

"Very good, Kelly. Now stay in trance for a few minutes more. Let the essence of the church in its day fill your soul. Can you see anything else of importance to us?"

"No, the knights are all gathering up their tools and departing the church. I'm directed to go back to my dorm. The evening's work is done."

"Rest easy, Kelly. Allow yourself to return to the present as comfortably as you need to."

Kelly blinked her eyes as she refocused on the people around her. She could see that Neil and Jason had moved to the portion of the wall that she had described.

"There must be a seam here of some sort. We've got to be able to find that door."

"Remember it's been hidden now for seven hundred years and covered in sand. It may well be here, but will take time to find it."

Kelly wandered to the altar and turned to face the wall. She could still see in her mind the position of the door as it was being bricked in. "Let me. I can still see the door. It's right here, directly in front of me now."

Neil looked at Kelly and realized she was still in a light trance. "Tell me what you see, Kelly. Describe the door to me."

"It's a wooden door, recessed into the stone wall. The new stones were laid in front and bring the wall into a smooth surface. Here, this is the edge of the door, and it runs two feet to the left."

Neil and Jason bent to examine the stones directly in front of where Kelly was pointing. "If there is a difference in these stones, I can't tell. But I trust you, Kelly."

Kelly stood gazing in fascination at the doorway before her. She could feel the power of Archangel Michael as he beckoned her to move forward to the wall. She reached out her hand almost involuntarily to place it on the stones just about chest high. Absently she realized it was the same arm that had been cut in the ceremony so many years ago. She could feel the vibration coming from them. She reached out with her other hand to Neil. "Godfrey, join your hand with mine. The seal is blood bonded by us. Now is the time to release the power and allow that which is hidden to be revealed."

"Do it, Neil," Gramps urged.

Neil reluctantly raised his hand to place it over Kelly's on the wall. He gazed into her eyes and realized she was still viewing the past.

"What do you see and feel, Kelly? Tell me."

"My brother Knight, I have kept the secrecy in faith and honor through the years. Is now the time to release the bond that has kept us in service to the Knights?"

Gramps rushed to Kelly and Neil's sides. "Neil, go deep in trance, follow her where she is going!"

"I will, Gramps." And Neil closed his eyes to allow the power in the church to take him back in time. He felt his mind gently put aside, as something deep in his soul stirred at the contact of his hand on Kelly's and with the stones on the wall. His eyes opened again, but he knew he was seeing something from the past. Before him he could see a young squire and knew instantly that it was Kelly from his past, his brother- in-arms Gerard.

"Gerard," he whispered in awe. "You've come back to me, as we promised we would."

"Godfrey, our souls were bound together here in this church to maintain the secrets of our order."

"I know, my brother." Neil could feel his true soul rise inside as he continued to look at Kelly/Gerard. As he connected to her soul he could see the eons of commitment they had both made, and knew the costs of years of separation and pain they had paid when they made this bargain. "I knew not the burden I was placing on both of our souls when I invoked the blood bond. I apologize."

"It is of no moment. The treasure we have hidden is worth all that we have endured. Now though the time has come to release that burden on our souls. We have both completed our duty to the Knights. We can now rest and allow our successors to reveal the information within. Let us release our blood bond."

"Yes, let us release the bond of secrecy."

The two of them turned to face the door and grasped their hands, then laid the opposite hand on the stones at chest high.

"Gerard né Laney de Cruce, many years ago we did commit a blood bond to hold in secrecy the location of this treasure of the Knights Templar. In faith and honor have you upheld your oath?"

"Godfrey de Cruce, you also committed that same blood bond and have maintained it in honor and faith. Through our many years have we honored the Knights who made us what we are?"

"We are together again, in love and faith, to release the blood bond we did swear."

They could feel a third person join them at the wall. They both looked over and saw Gramps, but also Sir Rai bin Hassan and Raymond Brock, place his hand on the wall over theirs.

"Your souls have endured much separation and hurt in the eons gone by. The swearing of the blood oath has kept you apart until such time as it was safe to reveal that which has been hidden. Your service is now at an end. By the power and protection of Archangels Michael, Gabriel, Raphael, and Uriel, we, the Guardians of the Temple, witness and release the blood oath between these two souls to seal this wall against intrusion and detection. Now is the time when we can lift the burden placed on these two. In the name of God, our Dear Lady Mary, and the Lord Jesus, let it be done."

Kelly could feel her soul rejoice at the lifting of the oath she had committed so many years ago. The world started to swirl around her. She could hear people around her talking but couldn't focus on anything except the wall in front of her, and her hand, joined to Neil's. She observed in fascination as her vision swirled around and her focus narrowed, gradually growing darker and darker. Soon her grasp on the now was lost, her eyes rolled up into her head, and she collapsed.

IX

Kelly was sitting one last time at the front of the church in Eykel. It was January 3rd, and she was getting ready to head back to Canada and her real life. The last few days had been so busy that she barely had time to gather her thoughts. She had not come to until late on January 1st. What she gathered from talking to Katrine was that she, Neil, and Gramps had all collapsed after they had joined hands at the wall. None of them had returned to consciousness for at least twelve hours. Neil had been the first to regain his senses and had flown out to London within a few hours of that. She had not seen him at all.

As yet, no changes had been made to the church. The Carters had decided to leave the door undisturbed for a few more weeks. They wanted to have the best Templar archaeologists they could find to proceed with the work. The extent of the treasure beyond the door was unknown, and Gramps had wanted the best in the business to work with them. She recalled the conversation yesterday amongst them.

"It'll take time, Gramps," Jason had complained. "This is going to be slow and painstaking work."

"I know, but we've got time now. We know it's here, and that's the important part. We still don't know what all is buried in the chamber beyond this. Who knows what impact this will have when it is revealed? I think we need to proceed very carefully as we unlock this. Many knights have died to protect this information. Let's not add any more to that list."

"Why did Neil leave so abruptly yesterday?"

"I wish I knew. Even Katrine can't explain it. But he jumped on the jet almost as soon as he was awake."

Kelly sighed. She figured he was glad to be released from the burden and no longer tied to her. He hadn't even waited for her to regain consciousness before tearing out of the area. It was pretty clear that he had no intention of allowing her back in his life. *Guess I'll just head back to Canada and forget that any of this has ever happened to me.* It was for the best. Now hopefully with the release of the blood oath, she could return to a normal life and put behind her all of the nightmares she had been experiencing.

She got up and meandered to the seal of Saint Michael embossed in the floor of the Nave. How much power she had felt coming from this seal before, but no longer. It seemed to be empty now. She let herself close her physical senses and open to her other senses. She could feel the slightest of tingles in the seal at her feet. Perhaps it wasn't so dormant after all. She closed her eyes and sought for the message within the seal. A feeling of love and accomplishment washed over her, as if someone was pleased with her. Suddenly she felt a higher energy in the seal, and knew deep within her that Neil had walked into the church. She opened her eyes and could see Neil, but also Godfrey de Cruce, and Robert Brock Carter enter the church. She could also sense many other personalities that Neil's soul had occupied over the years, all shining from his eyes. But most important of all, she could see his soul; that same soul that was the match to her own.

She shuddered in dawning recognition of the eons they had been together and separated, all in the service of the Knights Templar.

"Kelly, I'm glad you're still here. I feared you might run away again before I could get back."

"No, I'm still here, but planning on leaving tomorrow to go back to Canada. I have to be back in the classroom by January 6."

"I'm going to ask you to reconsider going back to Canada. I'm here one last time to ask you to marry me. Please, Kelly. I love you, mind, body and most importantly soul. You are the other half of me. Please, consider moving with me to England and become my wife. Haven't our souls gone through enough over the eons we've been apart holding to the secrets we were charged to keep? Let's honor what we've endured, by becoming one now."

Kelly looked at Neil as he approached her. She could feel the echo of the pain in his soul that occupied the center of her. Here was a man she had loved many times over the years; first as her step brother and then as Robert Brock Carter, and many other physical bodies she had not yet met. But every time they had been together, they were ripped apart by death. Could she risk her own heart again? To bear the loss of him again would kill her. But yet, how could she not take that risk? He was the other half of her. Was this the time now that they could be together without fearing the consequences? She looked down at the seal she stood on. She briefly closed her eyes to see if she could get any guidance. All she felt was a loving approval. She opened her eyes to find that Neil had approached closer.

"I went back to Derbyshire, to get this from the family vault. It has become the traditional engagement ring of the heirs of the Carters. It once belonged to Robert Brock Carter, and was given by him to his wife Eleanor when she bore him a son, Geoffrey. She gave it to Geoffrey when he became engaged many years later. Since then, it has passed down through the years to each heir. Gramps suggested it might be the most appropriate ring that I give to you to seal our souls together."

Kelly looked at the ring in his hand, and reached out to touch it, a beautiful sapphire and ruby ring. Sapphire, the stone of wisdom, its shining blue the symbol of hope and faith; Ruby, the fiery red of an inextinguishable flame, its bright red a symbol of passionate commitment. The combined stones a true joining of faith and commitment. She looked into his eyes and could feel the draw to the past of Eleanor Carter. With this man at her side, she would finally find the peace her soul had craved over the years.

"Yes," she barely whispered.

He looked at her with love shining in his eyes and slid the ring onto her third finger. He lightly held her hand, and rubbed his thumb over the ring, then raised his eyes to her. "I, Neil Carter Adams, do promise to God and our dear Lady Mary to contract honorable marriage with you, Kelly Taylor, if you will have me."

"I will, Neil. I will."

Neil looked into her eyes and then bent his head to claim her lips in a kiss filled with passion and promise; a promise to love for lifetimes, and a passion to heal their souls.

EPILOGUE

It was mid-April. Kelly stared outside the window to look at the beautiful grounds in Derbyshire, England. She was dressed in a beautiful pale pink and champagne colored gown. It was a mermaid style with a small train. The back plunged into a deep V and had ribbon-style straps to hold it all up. The gown was chiffon with a champagne lace overlay. In her hair, she had a small tiara and a veil that cascaded down her back almost to the floor. She was dressed for her wedding. She moved away from the window and went back to the full length mirror in her room.

"My dear, you look positively gorgeous in that gown. I'm so glad that you consented to be married here at the family grounds and could wear the veil from my own wedding."

"Katrine, I feel like Cinderella again. This can't be real."

"It is very much real, my dear. You're a truly lovely bride. And I know Neil will be stunned when he sees you shortly."

A sharp knock came at the door. "Kelly, are you ready? They are set downstairs," said Hannah as she entered the room. "You look stunning!"

"Thanks, Hannah. And yes, I'm ready for this. I can't wait to see Neil."

"Well, then come. Your brothers are waiting outside to escort you."

Kelly left the room, and followed Hannah and Katrine into the hallway.

She passed through the portrait gallery on her way to the main staircase. She paused for a minute at the portrait of Eleanor and Robert Carter. A portrait from just after their marriage had been found in the basement. It had been restored and was now here where it belonged. She looked at the two people in the picture. How happy they looked shortly after their marriage and still so much in love. She stared at the eyes as they had been captured by the artist. There was a depth there that captured her soul.

"Finally, my Robert," she whispered, "we have a chance at love to last a true lifetime."

Katrine stepped up beside her. "Our ancestors, together as you and Neil will be for lifetimes."

"Yes, a love to last lifetimes."

"Come, Kelly, its time," said Hannah and gently guided her to the stairs. Her brothers waited at the bottom to escort her to the family chapel. When Neil had suggested they have a quiet wedding with a justice of the peace, Kelly had argued for a wedding here at his family's property in England. She had done enough research on the mansion and knew the importance of it to the Templar legacy the family had. She felt it only fitting that given their unique Templar history, that they should be joined in marriage in a Templar chapel. Kelly had moved to England to be with Neil. After the adventure in Egypt she felt ready at last to commit her entire life to Neil, the Carter family, and the Templar legacy that they all shared, and committed to be a Guardian once again. She had sold the townhouse, packed up herself and Sandy, and been in England by the end of March.

The women, accompanied by Kelly's brothers left the house, and entered the Brougham carriages awaiting them in front. They set off for the short journey to the chapel. After reaching it and descending from the carriages, Kelly looked to her brothers.

"Kelly, you look so happy. I'm glad that you finally agreed to marry Neil. You deserve all the happiness in the world. I'm proud of you, little sis. You've done well."

"Yeah, sis. You've done well. Be happy!"

"Thanks, guys. I am happy, and most especially that all of you could come at such short notice. I'm glad my family is all here, and that Mom has agreed to stay for a few months. I think she will love England."

"Yes, I'm sure she will. And you know I'll be back in a couple of months. Neil's uncle wants me to come over and review some of the work they are doing here, to incorporate our ideas and plans into their work. You will see lots of me and Kathy- if I can convince her to come with me."

The doors to the chapel were opened by footmen. At that signal, the violinist and cellist started to play *Canon in D* by Pachelbel, one of Kelly's favorite classical pieces. Hannah started down the center aisle of the chapel. Once she was part down, Kelly with her brothers at her side, started to walk. She was halfway down when she finally saw Neil at the front. He was dressed in a black tuxedo, with a bowtie and vest in champagne that almost matched her gown. He had never looked as handsome to her as he did at that moment. She could see in his eyes the look that said all it needed to. His love was shining in his eyes and soul, as she was sure it was shining in hers. She approached him, and felt her brother take her hand from his arm, and lay it in Neil's.

"Neil, we give you our sister. May your love grow together."
Neil looked to her brothers, and then at her mother in the first row. "I will love Kelly for eternity."

Neil and Kelly moved to the front of the chapel to the altar, and turned to face each other. Kelly could see the promise of forever in Neil's eyes. Today she finally believed in all that Neil had told her. It was a love of lifetimes. Souls reunited, forever. She felt her soul rejoice as they exchanged the vows that linked them together for the rest of their lives.